"Just beautiful..."

Those two words, muttered so close to Amanda's ear, made her jump. She turned away from the car window to find that Ross had leaned over in order to better see the crystalline lake below them. Except right now he was looking at *her*.

Confused, she swallowed hard. Ross's eyes were glimmering like the lake down there, concealing deep mysteries beneath a mirrored-blue surface. His body heat radiated across the short gap between them and warmed her skin, a delicious contrast to the chill seeping in the open window. On his breath she could smell the coffee they'd stopped for back in Reno.

Amanda's gaze dropped to his mouth, and she shivered. In a couple of hours this man would be her *husband*. This man she'd never even...kissed.

Dear Reader,

Once again, Intimate Moments offers you top-notch romantic reading, with six more great books from six more great authors. First up is *Gage Butler's Reckoning,* the latest in Justine Davis's TRINITY STREET WEST miniseries. It seems Gage has a past, a past that includes a girl—now a woman—with reason to both hate him and love him. And his past is just about to become his present.

Maria Ferrarella's *A Husband Waiting To Happen* is a story of second chances that will make you smile, while Maura Seger's *Possession* is a tale of revenge and matrimony that will have you longing for a cooling breeze—even if it *is* only March! You'll notice our new Conveniently Wed flash on Kayla Daniels' *Her First Mother.* We'll be putting this flash on more marriage of convenience books in the future, but this is a wonderful and emotional way to begin. Another flash, The Loving Arms of the Law, has been chosen to signify novels featuring sheriffs, those perfect Western heroes. And Kay David's *Lone-Star Lawman* is an equally perfect introduction. Finally, enjoy *Montoya's Heart,* Bonnie Gardner's second novel, following her successful debut, *Stranger In Her Bed.*

And, of course, don't forget to come back next month, when we'll have six more Intimate Moments novels guaranteed to sweep you away into a world of excitement and passion.

Enjoy!

Leslie J. Wainger
Senior Editor and Editorial Coordinator

Please address questions and book requests to:
Silhouette Reader Service
U.S.: 3010 Walden Ave., P.O. Box 1325, Buffalo, NY 14269
Canadian: P.O. Box 609, Fort Erie, Ont. L2A 5X3

HER FIRST MOTHER

KAYLA DANIELS

Published by Silhouette Books

America's Publisher of Contemporary Romance

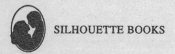

SILHOUETTE BOOKS

ISBN 0-373-07844-7

HER FIRST MOTHER

Copyright © 1998 by Karin Hofland

Printed in U.S.A.

KAYLA DANIELS

is a former computer programmer who enjoys travel, ballroom dancing and playing with her nieces and nephews. She grew up in southern California and has lived in Alaska, Norway, Minnesota, Alabama and Louisiana. Currently she makes her home in Grass Valley, California.

To my grandparents,
Carl and Joyce Hofland,
whose love of family and love of learning
have always inspired me.

Chapter 1

"I want you to marry me."

Amanda Prentiss blinked. This was hardly the answer she'd expected when she'd angrily demanded what the man on her doorstep wanted.

. Now, bewilderment joined forces with the shock and resentment that had erupted inside her the instant she'd recognized Ross Chandler.

More than three years since she'd last laid eyes on the man.

If only she could have gone another three hundred.

"Is this your twisted idea of a joke?" she asked in as cool a voice as she could summon.

The evening breeze off Nantucket Sound lifted a few strands of his expensive haircut. "I assure you, I'm perfectly serious."

He looked serious all right, towering above her in a dark hand-tailored suit that probably cost more than Amanda earned in a month. The porch light gilded his tanned features, spangled his blue eyes like sunshine on twin mountain lakes and circled his artfully tousled blond hair with a golden halo.

He looked like a well-dressed Greek god approaching Mount Olympus to request a small favor from Zeus.

"Please," he said, sounding as though the word didn't come out of his mouth very often, "could we, er, go inside and talk?"

Instinctively, Amanda narrowed the gap between the door and its frame, as if trying to shut out not only Ross Chandler, but also the anguished memories his unexpected appearance had aroused.

"There's nothing to talk about," she replied, her hand tightening its stranglehold on the doorknob. "I don't know what you expected to accomplish by coming here with such a ludicrous proposal, but—"

"Mrs. Weston—I mean, Ms. Prentiss—please. I know you don't owe me anything, but I'm asking you to hear me out." Then he played his trump card. "Please. For Jamie's sake."

Amanda flinched as if he'd struck her. A gully of pain opened up inside her, so dizzying, so deep, it snatched her breath away.

Jamie. Her little girl.

The child she'd loved and raised for four years.

The child Ross Chandler's family had stolen from her.

"Jamie's all right, isn't she?" Amanda asked as soon as she could breathe again.

"Yes, of course," he replied quickly. "I'm sorry, I didn't mean to alarm you."

She shouldn't let him in. Prolonging this absurd conversation would only prolong the grief that would follow if Amanda let him crack open the Pandora's box of pain and bitterness she'd tried to lock away forever.

"Come in," she said.

As Ross Chandler stepped across the threshold of her rented guest cottage, a thousand questions swirled out of Pandora's box and circled through Amanda's brain.

How is Jamie? Is she happy?

What does she look like now?

Does she still remember me?

And, most puzzling of all...

What in heaven's name could have prompted Jamie's uncle to come here and ask me to marry him?

Amanda ushered Ross into her cozy living room, where she'd been working on a brochure for the art gallery until interrupted by the knock at her door. She scooped up the clutter of papers strewn along the couch and motioned him to sit down.

She lowered herself into an armchair, casually sliding her hands beneath her thighs so he wouldn't see they were trembling. "How did you find me?" she asked. It was the least emotion-charged question she could come up with.

"After I discovered you were no longer living on Long Island, I, uh—" he adjusted his already plumb silk tie "—I hired a private detective."

Of course. People like the Chandlers always hired others to do their dirty work for them.

"Why?" she asked. "What do you want from me? And *don't*—" she shoved her palm forward like a traffic cop "—*don't* repeat that ridiculous proposal. Please."

He ran a finger beneath his immaculate, perfectly ironed collar. "Maybe I should back up a bit."

"Excellent idea." *Good, Amanda. Calm. Rational. For heaven's sake, don't let him see how rattled you really are.*

He dragged a hand over his square jaw. "First off, I want you to know I've always thought you got a raw deal. Where Jamie's concerned, I mean."

A spurt of anger forced its way through the lid Amanda

was struggling to clamp down on the chaos inside her. "A little late for that now, isn't it?" She dug her nails into the chair cushion. "You should have spoken up three years ago while you were up on that witness stand."

Something with an uncanny resemblance to guilt sailed across his eyes and slipped out of sight, like a glimpse of a distant yacht right before it dipped below the horizon.

"It wouldn't have made any difference," he said quietly.

"It would have been the decent thing to do," Amanda retorted.

Ross Chandler cleared his throat. "Yes, well, I certainly can't argue with that."

Amanda fought to contain herself. What good would it do now, pleading her case again? And to one of the high-and-mighty Chandlers, of all people.

"They were lies, you know." The words pried their way out through her teeth. "Paul and I never coerced your sister into giving Jamie up for adoption. We didn't trick her, or manipulate her, or do any of those things she claimed we did. She willingly involved us in her life while she was pregnant and couldn't wait to give us Jamie the minute she was born." Amanda's cheeks felt flushed, hot, as if her skin would sizzle to the touch. "Paige had no interest in having a baby. She didn't even bother asking what we'd named her! She was as delighted as we were the day we signed the adoption papers."

Ross forced himself to meet Amanda Prentiss's accusing gaze. Long ago, he'd chosen sides, and honor demanded he pay the price. He refused to take the coward's way out by dodging the pain and outrage that lashed him like a whipcord from the depths of her stormy dark eyes.

"I believe you," he said. "I believed you then."

"Then how could you...? Why didn't you...?" She

gripped the arms of her chair as if trying to restrain herself from leaping across the coffee table to strangle him.

Ross could hardly blame her. Nor did he intend to try to justify himself. Abstract concepts like family loyalty were bound to sound pretty feeble to a woman who'd lost her child.

Besides, whether Amanda knew it or not, nothing Ross had said or done during the year of custody hearings would have made any difference in the end. A fact Ross himself had only recently discovered.

The memory of that discovery stirred up the fear that had plagued him for the past ten days, reminding him of why he was here.

"The reason I wanted to find you," he said, "is because Jamie...well, Jamie's been asking questions about you lately."

Amanda swallowed. "She has?" Her hostile expression fled, replaced by a blend of hope, longing and desperation that was almost painful to see.

The guilt Ross had carried around for so long settled even more heavily on his shoulders. "Jamie's reached an age where she's curious about everything." He peered at Amanda uncertainly. "She's, er, seven now, you know."

"Seven and a half," Amanda said evenly. Her voice had an edge to it.

"Right." Tactless, Chandler. Of *course* she'd kept track of her own child's age! "Anyway, Jamie's full of questions," he continued. "Why people on the other side of the earth don't fall off. How caterpillars turn into butterflies." His mouth curved. "Why she can't eat chocolate cake for breakfast."

The fond smile on Ross's lips unleashed another flood of resentment inside Amanda. Jamie should have been asking *her* all those questions! She'd so looked forward to sharing with her daughter all the joys and mysteries of growing up…

Until the Chandlers had robbed her of the chance.

Agitation propelled Amanda to her feet. "What sort of questions has Jamie been asking about me?" She felt Ross's gaze tracking her as she paced the room, rubbing her hands briskly up and down the sleeves of her blouse as if the pressure cooker of her resentment required the physical outlet of motion.

"Jamie has some…hazy memories," he said cautiously. "About you and your ex-husband. Mostly about you."

A poignant mixture of gratitude and tenderness swept through Amanda. So the Chandlers hadn't been able to completely obliterate her from Jamie's life after all!

"I suppose that's not so surprising," she said, crossing her arms as she came to a halt in front of the fireplace. "Considering Jamie was over four years old when she was taken from me. Old enough to remember."

Once again, Amanda could have sworn she saw guilt cloud Ross Chandler's rugged features. "Yes." He coughed into his fist. "Anyway, Jamie's recently started asking questions that I don't know how to answer. Questions about her early childhood."

Amanda jerked up her chin. "Have you told her the truth?"

"About the adoption? The custody fight? Yes."

No need to wonder what the official Chandler version was. Heaven knows, Amanda had heard it repeated often enough from the witness stand.

Ross studied her from across the room. Her stance was both challenging and defensive, every line of her posture as tightly drawn as a bowstring. It wasn't hard to figure out why. His presence here was yanking Amanda in two different directions at once. Her barely concealed hunger for the smallest snippets of information about Jamie was playing tug-of-war with her determination to keep the past buried.

An image crashed through Ross's brain—the image that had haunted him ever since the day he'd been forced to watch while Amanda handed her child over to Paige.

Four-year-old Jamie, her fragile arms latched tightly around Amanda's neck, sobbing and kicking and screaming that she didn't want to go.

Amanda, grief and agony etched across her tear-streaked face as she struggled to tear her own child from her body, to give her back to the woman who'd once given her away.

Thunder crashing overhead, raindrops pelting the Westons' driveway with wet gray splotches, wind whipping Amanda's dark hair around her head to entwine with her daughter's pale blond strands.

Jamie's terrified wails. "Mommy, Mommy, please don't make me go! I wanna stay with you, Mo-ommeee...."

Ross shuddered. He shook his head to clear it.

Amanda stood waiting, her arms folded, every rigid line of her body proclaiming her resistance to whatever he might say.

"I thought if Jamie saw you again, if she could talk to you, it might help." Ross fumbled for convincing words. "Help her to make sense of—of what happened to her."

Amanda aimed a skeptical gaze in his direction. "I don't see how I could be of much help," she said, "since it's never made any sense to me, either."

Ross felt a dart of panic. If she was reluctant even to *see* Jamie, how was he ever going to persuade her to go along with the rest of it?

He came up off the couch. "When I found out from the private detective that you and your husband had divorced, that gave me another idea."

Impatience crimped the corners of Amanda's mouth.

She flipped a wing of dark hair back over her shoulder. "You're referring to this absurd marriage idea, I presume?"

Ross edged slowly around the coffee table like a hunter trying not to startle his prey. "I know it seems crazy on the surface," he said, giving her what he hoped was a disarming smile. "But if you think about it, you'll see that this marriage would benefit all three of us."

"All *three* of us?" Amanda narrowed her eyes at him, managing to convey both suspicion and confusion at once.

Ross held up his fingers one by one. "You, me and Jamie."

Amanda blew a scornful gust of air through her bangs. "Aren't you forgetting number four?"

"Number...?"

She drummed her fingers on the fireplace mantel. "How does Jamie's moth—" Her mouth twisted as if she'd bitten into something sour. "How does your sister, Paige, fit into this equation? Somehow I can't quite picture her happily throwing rice at our wedding. Unless it was cooked first."

With an unpleasant jolt, Ross remembered that Amanda didn't know about Paige. How dumb could he be? He'd meticulously lined up his arguments in favor of marriage, but he'd forgotten to inform his intended bride of one crucial fact.

He hauled in a long breath. "Paige is dead," he said gently.

His words struck Amanda like a blow, knocking the air right out of her lungs. She gripped the edge of the mantel to steady herself. "Dead?" she gasped.

"She died nearly two years ago. In Spain." Ross's mouth tightened into a grim seam. "The driver of the car she was riding in was drunk and swerved off the road. Two other passengers were killed, as well."

"My God." Amanda felt sick. Dizzy. Ice-cold. "What about Jamie? Was she with her? Was she hurt?"

"Jamie? With Paige?" A rueful look that seemed part sadness, part exasperation, crossed his chiseled features. "No. Jamie wasn't in Europe when the accident happened. She was home on the family estate in California."

Amanda welded her hands together to keep them from shaking. "Ross, I—I'm so very sorry," she said. And was amazed to discover she actually was.

During the long nightmare of the custody battle, she'd hated and feared Paige Chandler in equal overwhelming measure. Once it was all over and Amanda had had to rebuild her life from its shattered wreckage, she'd tried her best to put the past behind her. To accept her loss. To smother her hatred.

But sometimes, especially at first, it had felt like hatred was going to smother *her*.

Back then, she would have expected to rejoice at the news of Paige's death. Yet, oddly enough, all she felt now was a sympathetic twinge behind her breastbone, like the throb of a bruise.

Jamie must have been devastated.

"That's the most important reason for us to get married." Ross stepped closer. "I've done my best to help raise Jamie ever since she came to live with us, but the fact is, she still needs a mother."

She had *a mother,* Amanda thought with a jab of annoyance. *Until you and your scheming family stole her right out of my arms.*

Dear God. Was there actually a chance she could get Jamie back?

Amanda inspected her fingernails, pleased to notice her hands were steady. "And what exactly—just for the sake of argument—what would be some of the *other* reasons for us to get married?"

Ross's eyes glinted as if he sensed he'd just hooked her. "Well, there's *you*, for example." He spread his hands. "I realize there's no way to make up for all the unhappiness you've suffered…" He dangled the tempting bait in front of her. "But if you and I married, you could be a mother to Jamie again."

Amanda tapped her chin with one finger. "Are you saying that you and I would adopt Jamie after we got married?" She knew all too well that such a legal formality wouldn't make much difference where the Chandlers were concerned. But she wasn't about to enter into this arrangement without strengthening her own position as much as possible.

Good heavens, was she actually considering Ross's insane proposal?

"Well, the fact is…" A muscle flexed along his jaw as if the fishing line he was using to reel her in had caught on a snag. "Caleb, my grandfather, became Jamie's legal guardian when Paige died."

Amanda gritted her teeth at his mention of the elderly patriarch of the Chandler clan. She had some vague memory that Caleb had raised young Ross and Paige after their parents had died.

She also had an extremely *vivid* memory of Caleb Chandler's bullying personality and haughty demeanor. He'd been present at every single court hearing, shooting intimidating looks at Amanda, whispering in Paige's ear, haranguing their personal army of high-priced lawyers.

"So, what you're saying is that Caleb would have to approve of our adopting Jamie," Amanda said slowly.

"I don't foresee that as a problem." Obviously, Ross hadn't yet broached the subject with Caleb. Which also meant he hadn't informed Caleb of his plan to marry her.

Probably because the idea would have thrown the old tyrant into an apoplectic rage.

Hmm. What kind of power struggle was being waged behind the tightly knit facade of that impenetrable Chandler family unity? And what possible advantage could Ross hope to gain by marrying her?

"What about you?" Amanda arched her brows. "You've explained why a marriage between us would benefit Jamie and me. But what's in it for you?"

Ross took his time before replying. Amanda's decision could depend on how believable he sounded.

"It has to do with what I told you earlier," he said finally. "The truth is, I feel partly responsible for the terrible injustice you suffered because of my family." And that *was* the truth. Just not all of it. "I'd like to do whatever I can to make amends."

"By marrying a total *stranger?*" Amanda's voice matched her incredulous expression.

Ross thought of all the women he'd known during his thirty-four years who'd wanted to marry him. How eventually he'd come to realize that they were only after his wealth, his status, his prestigious family name.

That certainly wasn't the case with Amanda. She had every good reason for despising the Chandler name and family fortune.

Besides, Ross had seen for himself what a devoted mother she would be to Jamie. He would certainly never find a better one.

And, not that it was relevant to his purpose, but he found himself unexpectedly attracted to Amanda Prentiss. He'd forgotten how pretty she was, with her delicate facial bone structure and gleaming, coffee-colored hair that spilled to her shoulders.

Until this evening, Ross had still envisioned her as the pale, anxious woman he'd remembered from the custody hearings. Her sad, dark eyes had always been slightly puffy, as if she'd been crying. She'd been thin as a reed, almost to the point of gauntness, with hollow cheekbones and gray smudges beneath her eyes.

She was still slender, but her face was fuller, softer, the haunted shadows gone, so that she actually looked younger than she had at twenty-nine. Her skin had regained a healthy glow that spoke of sunshine and fresh ocean air. For the first time, Ross stood close enough to notice that her eyes were the same rich coffee shade as her hair.

All in all, he decided, marrying Amanda Prentiss could hardly be called a bad bargain. Even if he didn't take into account the *real* reason he was determined to make her his wife.

"Amanda." Ross looked deep into those dubious, dark brown eyes. "I knew from the beginning that you would be a better mother to Jamie than Paige could ever be. Yet I kept silent because she was my sister." After all this time, guilt still scraped at his conscience. "Now I have a chance to make up for it," he said. "To give back to Jamie the mother she should have had all along."

Amanda probed her cheek with her tongue. "Let me get this straight." She drew herself up to her full five-feet-seven-inch height. "What this comes down to is that you're willing to marry someone you barely know because you feel *guilty?* To correct some past miscarriage of *justice?*"

"I want to do the right thing." Ross shrugged. "Is that so difficult to believe?"

Amanda didn't know what to believe. Standing here in her living room was a man who, until half an hour ago, she'd considered her enemy. Who might still *be* her enemy. Asking her to be his wife.

She drifted to the coffee table and picked up the mug of tea she'd been brewing when Ross had come knocking at her door. "Hypothetically," she said, dunking the cold, soggy tea bag up and down, "what exactly did you have in mind in terms of our, um, living arrangements?"

"Living arrangements?" Ross came up behind her, close enough for Amanda to catch a hint of his aftershave. It smelled expensive. Subtle. Masculine. "We'd have our own private wing of the house," he explained. "My grandfather is bedridden now, so he—"

"That's not what I meant." Amanda felt heat rise up through her cheeks.

"Then…? Oh." There was an awkward pause as if this was one detail of their marriage he didn't have all worked out yet. "I guess…under the circumstances…since this would hardly be what you'd call a conventional marriage…"

Amanda's face grew hotter.

Ross grasped her shoulders and turned her around to face him. Amanda stared straight ahead into his tasteful silk tie. "We wouldn't have to share the same bed," he said quietly. His fingers tightened briefly. "Not until…I mean, unless, of course, you…"

She watched his broad chest rise and fall in a muffled sigh of…of what?

"Presumably your mansion has plenty of bedrooms." Her lips twisted as she shrugged off his hands and turned away, reluctant to meet his eyes just now.

"Amanda, I know I've caught you off guard, that you need time to think about this."

A wry laugh hurtled from her throat. "You can say that again." She could still feel the imprint of his hands on her shoulders.

He drew a cream-colored business card from inside his suit jacket. His fingers briefly touched Amanda's when he handed it to her. The elegant, embossed letters read Chandler Winery.

"I've written the name and phone number of the hotel where I'm staying on the back."

Amanda flipped over the card and read his bold scribble. The fanciest place on the island. It figured.

If I married him, then I'd *be staying at the most expensive places, too.*

The prospect hardly pleased her. She knew from bitter experience what kind of trouble the Chandlers' unlimited wealth could buy.

"I'll be here on Nantucket for two more days." Ross hesitated, then gently grasped her wrist. "Please." The business card quivered slightly between her fingers. "Think over what I've said. It would mean a lot to Jamie. To me." He squeezed Amanda's wrist. "To all of us."

She was surprised to feel his hand was hard and callused, as if he regularly labored in his own vineyards. Glancing down, she noticed his nails were clean and close-cropped, but a bit ragged around the edges.

Not at all the kind of hands she would have expected to belong to the chairman of the board, or whatever exalted position it was he held in the family company.

Heat circled her wrist where he touched her. All at once, his hold felt as heavy and oppressive as an iron manacle. Amanda detached herself from his grip, pretending an immediate need to tuck the business card into her address book next to the phone.

"I can't make any promises," she warned him.

But her heart gave a little leap as she showed him to the door. *Jamie, Jamie! I could have you back and be your mother again!*

Ross paused on the front step. "All I ask is that you think about it."

No, Amanda reflected. He was asking a lot more than that.

She watched through her front curtains as he followed the flagstone path that led past the main house and out to the street. Even in the darkness, she could make out his confident stride, the aristocratic set of his shoulders.

A man used to getting what he wanted.

Amanda let the curtain drop. Ross Chandler, crown prince of the Chandler family. Asking her—no, more like *pleading* with her to marry him.

Incredible.

She rubbed her wrist where his fingers had touched her. What could be the *real* reason he was so determined to marry her? Or was resentment over the past blinding her to the sincerity of his motives?

Did it even matter?

Because one all-important fact was certain no matter how Amanda weighted all the factors.

If she married Ross Chandler, she would get Jamie back.

A flutter of excitement stirred inside her. This was the chance she'd once prayed for so desperately. The chance she'd given up any hope of long ago.

She dug her nails into her palms. "Jamie," she whispered. "Dear God, how I've missed you...."

A lump rose to her throat. Then the pressure building inside that Pandora's box of grief and love finally flung the lid wide open and spilled out the glaring truth.

"Oh, Jamie." Amanda pressed her fists to her mouth. "I'd do absolutely *anything* to get you back."

Through the agitated pounding in her ears, she heard the muffled sound of a car starting up in the distance. Without conscious decision, she flung open the door and rushed out to the street.

Halfway down the block, red taillights glowed in the dark. Amanda reached the luxury rental car just as it started to glide away from the curb. Panting, she rapped her knuckles frantically on the passenger-side window.

Seconds later, the glass lowered with a discreet whir. Ross leaned over from behind the steering wheel. The dashboard lights illuminated his puzzled frown. "What is it?"

Amanda flattened her palm over her chest, trying to calm the rapid thudding of her heart. Become Ross's wife? Join the hated Chandler family? Live under the same roof with her former enemies? Might as well stroll unarmed into a den full of lions.

"I'll marry you," she said as soon as she could catch her breath.

Tie loosened, sleeves rolled up, Ross stared into the darkness outside his hotel-room window. He couldn't see the Atlantic Ocean, but the breeze carried its briny scent to his nose and the thunder of crashing waves to his ears.

He tilted back his head and downed another hefty swallow of wine. He'd ordered a bottle of Chandler Cabernet from room service but drank it without his usual critical appraisal. Almost without tasting it at all.

He hoisted his glass in a mock toast to his reflection in the open window. This was, after all, sort of his own one-man bachelor party. Because tomorrow he intended to marry Amanda Prentiss.

She'd only accepted his proposal a couple of hours ago. But, having accomplished that miracle of persuasion, Ross figured it wouldn't be too difficult to convince her to have the ceremony right away.

Was he making a terrible mistake? Would this marriage be unfair to Amanda, unfair to him?

Ross grimaced at his reflection. Too late for cold feet now. He had no other choice. Not if he didn't want to risk losing Jamie.

He had to marry Amanda, and he had to do it quick. Before she stumbled onto the fact Ross himself had accidentally discovered ten days ago.

Before she found out that Caleb Chandler had bribed the judge who'd given Jamie back to Paige.

Chapter 2

This must be the wildest wedding day in history, Amanda decided.

She'd only agreed to marry Ross last night, but at his urging she'd already given notice to her landlord and quit her job as manager of the Nantucket art gallery where she'd worked for the past two years.

All this before noon.

Her boss hadn't been exactly pleased with her for quitting on such short notice. But the expensive seascape Ross had purchased had smoothed his ruffled feathers considerably.

Magically, shortly after lunch, movers had arrived to pack up the few possessions Amanda wanted to take with her to California.

Amazing what miracles money could buy.

She supposed she ought to be flattered that Ross was in such a hurry to marry her. But she was a realist, not a romantic. His apparent haste was simply a typical example of the Chandler style, which was to plow straight ahead and bulldoze any obstacles aside once a course of action had been decided upon.

Before Amanda had even had a chance to absorb the incredible turn her life had suddenly taken, she'd found herself on a plane headed for Reno, Nevada.

"We'll rent a car there and drive up to Lake Tahoe," Ross had informed her. "We can get married right away on the Nevada side, and the setting is a little more... uplifting than Reno."

Amanda, already envisioning a drive-through wedding chapel with an Elvis impersonator performing the ceremony, had quickly agreed to his plan. Under ordinary circumstances, she would have chafed at the way Ross had hustled her along and completely taken charge of everything. Then again, no one in her right mind would call these ordinary circumstances.

"Pretty, isn't it?" Ross shifted his glance from the road long enough to give Amanda a brief smile. Evidently, he'd taken her prolonged silence for fascination with the scenery.

"Hmm? Oh, yes. Magnificent." In truth, she'd barely noticed the spectacular landscape they were driving through. Her brain had been spinning like an overloaded washing machine, whirling with all the astonishing events that had taken place during the past twenty-four hours of her life.

She hadn't reset her watch yet for the three-hour time difference between here and the East Coast. Back home it was approaching 11:00 p.m., but here it was still light enough to see the towering pines, the breathtaking canyons, the majestic Sierra Nevada peaks.

"There's still snow on the mountains," Amanda observed with surprise.

Ross nodded. "It's only mid-May," he said. "At these

higher elevations, it's not unusual for the snow to stick around till the Fourth of July. Even later, some years.''

"Funny. I always thought of California as being hot.''

"We have it all,'' Ross said cheerfully. "Mountains, deserts, snow, earthquakes...''

And Jamie, Amanda thought. *You also have my child.* Her stomach performed another flip-flop of anticipation. Tomorrow she would see her little girl again.

As the car came around a curve in the road, the terrain dropped away to give Amanda her first glimpse of Lake Tahoe. It gleamed like a flat expanse of pewter, enclosed by craggy, pine-studded slopes that seemed to rise straight up from the water's edge.

"Oh!'' Her eyes widened.

"Fantastic, isn't it?'' Ross steered the car onto a turnout. "No matter how often I come to Tahoe, it always startles me how impressive it is.''

He braced his arm over the steering wheel and together they admired the view. The sinking sun had outlined the distant peaks with burgundy and gold, setting streaks of cloud on fire. A hawk wheeled slowly overhead, gliding in lazy circles down into the trees. The silvery lake reflected it all.

Amanda pushed a button to lower her window and filled her lungs with the bracing tonic of crisp, cool, pine-scented air. So different from the moist, salty smell of the sea she'd lived near most of her life.

Now, a new chapter of her life was about to begin.

"Just beautiful.'' Those two words, muttered so close to Amanda's ear, made her jump. She turned from the window to find Ross had leaned over in order to see the view better. Except, right now, he was looking at her.

Confused, Amanda swallowed hard. Ross's eyes glimmered like that lake down there, concealing deep mysteries beneath a blue, mirrored surface. His body heat radiated across the short gap between them and warmed her skin, a delicious contrast to the chill seeping in the open window. On his breath she could smell the coffee they'd stopped for back in Reno.

Amanda shivered. In a couple of hours, this man would be her husband. This man she'd never even...kissed.

Her gaze dropped to his mouth. Funny, but she'd never before appreciated how sensual a man's lips could be. Ross's lips were full, with a hint of asymmetry that gave them a rakish quirk at odds with the rest of his sober, self-contained appearance. They looked like strong, capable lips. Amanda swayed toward him slightly, before she even realized what she was doing.

Maybe it was just coincidence, but Ross chose that exact moment to straighten up and reposition himself behind the wheel. "Guess we'd better get moving," he said, shifting the car into gear, "if we're going to find a justice of the peace still open for business."

Amanda flushed. Somehow she almost felt...rejected. Then Ross's words sank in, sending a thrill of nervousness to chase away her embarrassment. "Won't it be too late already?" She raised her window as the car glided back onto the road. "Maybe we'll have to wait until tomorrow."

"Not chickening out, are you?" Beneath the teasing challenge in his voice, Amanda detected a trace of concern. Not for the first time, she wondered why Ross was so dead set on marrying *her*, when he could have any woman he wanted.

"Don't worry," she assured him. "I haven't changed my mind." Part of her was as anxious as he was to make their marriage official. Now that she'd grown used to the idea of reuniting with Jamie, the possibility that something could go wrong filled her with dread.

It would be like losing Jamie all over again.

"I realize this has all happened incredibly fast," Ross said. "And I don't mean to rush you. But I thought it would be better if we were already married when I bring you home to the estate. Less…confusing, perhaps, for Jamie."

And less chance, Amanda speculated, of Caleb throwing a monkey wrench into Ross's carefully laid plans.

"Does your grandfather know you're bringing me with you?" she asked boldly.

A muscle flickered along his jaw. "No."

Amanda expelled a bitter laugh. "You didn't warn me to pack for World War III."

The line of his profile shifted to convey grim determination. "Caleb won't cause you any trouble. I'll see to that."

Amanda held her tongue. She wasn't about to contradict Ross, but she wasn't about to underestimate his stubborn, controlling grandfather, either.

And if Ross was truly as confident as he claimed about handling Caleb, Amanda doubted he'd be in such a hurry to make their marriage a fait accompli.

Their marriage. *My God, what kind of pact have I made with the devil?* she wondered.

A twinkling necklace of lights glittered around the shoreline as darkness settled over the lake. The first star appeared in the purple velvet sky.

Amanda's heart gave a little hitch inside her chest. Apprehension dampened her palms.

This gorgeous spring evening was soon to become her wedding night.

"Do you, Ross, take this woman…"

He gazed down into Amanda's pale, pretty face. The voice of the justice of the peace seemed to fade and grow distant. Ross squeezed Amanda's hand, both in reassurance and apology.

Last chance to back out, Chandler, warned the voice inside his skull. *You can still tell her the truth, call this whole thing off....*

On the movie screen of his memory, he replayed that fateful scene from his business trip to New York a week and a half ago. He watched himself sitting down to breakfast in his room at the Plaza Hotel, unfolding the *New York Times...*

And nearly choking on his croissant when he spotted a small back-page article and read with mounting dismay that the judge in Jamie's custody case was currently being investigated for bribery.

Then, his urgent flight home to confront his grandfather. The angry accusations. The indignant denials. Finally, Caleb's grudging, ill-tempered confession.

Ross had been desperate to track down Jamie's former adoptive parents before they, too, learned about the corrupt judge and decided to reopen the custody case. He wasn't sure what he intended to do when he found them. Try to bribe them himself, probably.

Then he found out about the divorce and realized only Jamie's first mother would pose problems. So he came up with his plan to make sure Jamie would continue to live at the Chandler estate. A drastic measure, to be sure. But Ross couldn't risk losing the child he'd come to love like his own.

All at once, he realized both Amanda and the justice of the peace were watching him expectantly.

"I do," Ross said hastily. And meant it.

Amanda couldn't shake the sensation that she was trapped in a dream. Not a particularly pleasant dream, either. Her stomach was on a roller-coaster ride, and her wobbly legs threatened to buckle any second. She was about to become Ross Chandler's wife. And she was petrified.

"Rings?" The justice of the peace arched his thick gray brows at them.

Amanda gulped down a groan. Good heavens, she hadn't even *thought* about needing...

Ross plucked one out of the pocket of his sport coat.

Amanda stared at it, then at him. When had he...? How...?

This wasn't the first surprise he'd produced this evening. On their arrival at the lake, he'd stopped at a pay phone to call around and locate someone who could marry them right away. Afterward, he'd ducked into the nearby supermarket.

When he came out, he handed Amanda an armful of purple-and-yellow irises wrapped in green paper. "I managed to find an all-night justice of the peace," he said. "But I thought I might be pushing my luck to count on finding a florist open this late."

Amanda didn't know quite what to make of the flowers at first. "For me?"

Ross shrugged sheepishly. "I know it's not much of a wedding bouquet—"

"No, no—they're beautiful. Thank you." Amanda had been surprised and touched by his gesture.

Now, another unexpected act of thoughtfulness. Amanda's flowers trembled as Ross lifted her other hand and slipped the gold band on her finger. The intimacy and significance of the moment was oddly moving, considering that this ceremony was really nothing more than a legal transaction.

"By the power vested in me by the state of Nevada, I now pronounce you husband and wife." The justice of the peace beamed at them, folded his hands over his slight paunch and rocked back and forth, waiting.

Amanda felt her cheeks go crimson when she caught Ross's eye. The next words hovered in the air before the justice of the peace even spoke them.

He winked at Ross. "You may kiss your bride, sir," he prompted in a loud stage whisper.

Amanda had assumed nothing could feel more awkward than having a near stranger slip a wedding ring on her finger, but she'd been wrong.

Ross cleared his throat. His mouth quirked and his broad shoulders lifted a fraction of an inch as if to say, "In for a penny, in for a pound."

He lowered his mouth to Amanda's.

The kiss was over before she knew it. She'd closed her eyes instinctively but barely had time to blink before the brief, impersonal pressure of his lips was gone. She felt a strange, empty kind of letdown. No doubt it was simply relief that the awkward moment had passed.

"Whew! I'm glad that's over," Ross said as they stepped outside. The cool mountain air was like the brisk slap of aftershave in the morning. Then he saw Amanda's spine stiffen and heard the echo of his own words. "I didn't mean that the way it sounded," he said quickly, loosening his tie. "Not like it was some terrible ordeal."

Amanda's rigid posture relaxed a bit. "I guess most people wouldn't actually describe their wedding ceremony as *fun*. Even when they're getting married for, um, more traditional reasons than we are." She stepped aside to let Ross open the car door for her. "I know I was *way* too nervous to enjoy my wedding." She flung him an uncomfortable glance as she slipped into her seat. "My *first* wedding, I mean."

A small stab of jealousy caught Ross off guard. Good grief, her marriage to Paul Weston had ended a long time ago! Besides, it wasn't as if he himself had any emotional claim on her. Purely a practical one.

Husband and wife.

Amazing how a few words spoken by the proper official could turn a man possessive.

He started the car. "I hope you like the hotel I've picked out. It's my favorite place to stay when I come up here to go skiing."

Amanda tilted her face into the bouquet of irises. "I'm sure it'll be fine," she said faintly. The stems quivered. A moment later, she said, "I want you to know how much I appreciate your thoughtfulness. These flowers. The ring."

"It's nothing." Those tokens were the least she deserved after the way Ross had tricked her. "I wish I could promise you'll never regret marrying me, Amanda. But all I can promise is that I intend to do everything in my power to make sure you don't."

When he glanced over, she was watching him with huge dark eyes that glittered…with tears? No. Probably just a reflection from the streetlights they were passing. Still, for a moment, she appeared so wistful, so vulnerable, Ross had to fight the urge to pull the car over to the curb and put his arms around her.

Protective as well as possessive, he thought ruefully. *Guess I'm already getting the hang of this husband stuff.*

They drove past a strip of glitzy hotels and casinos. The dazzle of neon glinted off the ring on Amanda's finger. She held up her hand, examining the ring in the flashing lights from outside.

"It's beautiful," she said. "Such delicate tracery around the edges…"

"It's meant to represent grapevines," Ross told her. "The ring was my grandmother's, and her mother's before that."

The startled expression on Amanda's face warned him he might have made an error in judgment. It should have occurred to him that she might not be exactly delighted about wearing such a conspicuous symbol of the Chandler heritage on her finger.

"We can buy a new ring," Ross said quickly. "It's just that there wasn't much time, and I figured it would do for the ceremony, so I brought it with me."

Bands of light and shadow slipped across Amanda's face like passing signposts, giving no clue, however, to the direction of her thoughts.

"You must have been pretty confident I'd marry you," she said finally.

"Confident?" Ross recalled the seasick churning in his gut, the panicked hammering of his heart against his ribs when he'd gone to propose. "Not exactly. But I wanted to be prepared." He steered into the circular driveway of the hotel. "On the way home tomorrow, we can stop at a jewelry store and—"

"No, no, that won't be necessary." She swept her hand through the air so that gold glints danced off the ring. "After all, I'm a Chandler now, aren't I?" Bitterness stung her voice. "Might as well learn to act the part."

Ross swallowed his defensive pride. She had every good reason to despise his family. He couldn't expect her to adjust right away to the overwhelming irony of suddenly becoming a member of it.

Inside the hotel, the desk clerk's eyebrows jumped upward when he glanced at the register Ross had just signed. "Congratulations, Mr. Chandler," he said, offering a genial smile and a handshake.

Amanda saw him surreptitiously peer past Ross and across the lobby to the spot where she was perched uneasily on the edge of a plush sofa. Obviously, Ross was well-known here. No doubt the sudden existence of a new wife would provoke plenty of gossip among the staff.

As if she didn't feel self-conscious enough as it was, sitting here in the same wrinkled dress she'd been traveling in all day, a bunch of wilting flowers clutched in her lap. And the sacred Chandler wedding ring prominently displayed on her finger.

She supposed she should be honored Ross had given it to her. She held up her hand to study the ring in decent light for the first time. It *was* beautiful, she had to admit. The detailed etching of the grapevines was a marvel of craftsmanship.

But somehow, rather than a symbol of two lives joined together, the ring felt more like a link in the chain that would shackle Amanda to the ruthless Chandler clan from this day forward. She would wear those shackles gladly, though. As the price she was willing to pay for the chance to be Jamie's mother again.

Ross strode toward her across the lobby's deep-piled carpet. "We're all checked in."

Amanda rose unsteadily to her feet. Exhaustion and apprehension made her light-headed. The whirlwind of today's events had distracted her from dwelling on too many unsettling speculations about tonight's conclusion. The time had arrived, however, for her to face some of the consequences of marrying a man she barely knew.

"Would you like to have a drink first, before we go upstairs?" Ross indicated the bar and dining room adjoining the lobby. "Maybe a bite to eat? That airplane meal wasn't exactly filling."

His offer was certainly tempting. Not because Amanda thought she could possibly choke down any food or drink. But because it would postpone the inevitable.

"I'm awfully tired," she admitted. "I think I'd rather just go upstairs." *And get this over with.*

"Sounds good to me."

But Amanda had already learned enough about her new husband to realize he would have made the same polite response whether she'd chosen to have a drink or suggested a nighttime waterskiing expedition on the lake. Ross was certainly a pro at hiding his true feelings.

While they waited for the elevator, Amanda sneaked a peek at his hand, anxious for the answer to the question that had plucked at her nerves ever since they'd entered the hotel.

One key, or two?

Unfortunately, Ross must have slipped the key, singular or plural, into his pocket.

They were the only two passengers in the elevator that carried them upstairs. But to Amanda, it felt more claustrophobic than it would have if they'd been jammed elbow to elbow with a crowd of other people.

The elevator door slid open. Amanda's heart rate picked up its tempo.

"This way." Ross ushered her down a long hallway. What lay at the end of it? The honeymoon suite? A heart-shaped bed and king-size bathtub?

This visual imagery was *not* helping calm her nerves.

The door stood open, their luggage already inside. Ross tipped the bellhop. "Anything else I can get for you, Mr. Chandler? Mrs. Chandler?"

Mrs. Chandler. The first time anyone had ever called her that. She felt a funny little tug inside her chest.

"Amanda? Can you think of anything you need?"

My head examined, she thought wildly. *Why on earth did I agree to go through with this?* The reason, with her pale blond hair and angelic blue eyes, popped into Amanda's mind. She managed to control her panic.

"I can't think of anything else I need, thank you." She mustered a smile for the departing bellhop. With a muted click, the door shut behind him, leaving Amanda and Ross alone.

Shifting the flowers from one hand to the other, Amanda discreetly wiped her clammy palms on her dress and made a rapid survey of the room.

Elegantly decorated in soothing grays and blues, with two armchairs and a couch arranged in front of a large curtained window. Wet bar, small refrigerator and a teak cabinet holding a television, VCR and stereo system.

All the comforts of home. In fact, it looked a good deal more comfortable than Amanda's own home. *Former* home, that is.

But the room's furnishings didn't interest her nearly as much as the doors. *Two* doors. One on each side of the living room.

"I thought we might be more comfortable in a suite," Ross said. He shrugged off his sport coat and hung it over the back of a chair.

Score one point in the husband competition. He didn't dump his clothes on the floor.

"Would you like some champagne?" he asked.

Amanda hadn't even noticed the silver ice bucket on the bar during her hasty scan of her surroundings. Maybe some liquid courage would ease her jitters.

"Sure," she said. "I'd love some."

Ross unbuttoned his cuffs and rolled up his sleeves. Amanda laid her flowers on the bar and watched as he draped a towel over the neck of the champagne bottle. His mouth compressed in concentration as he wiggled the cork upward. Muscles tensed along his forearms, which were sprinkled with curly golden hairs.

Amanda's mouth went dry. Of course, that's what flying did to you, made you dehydrated. All of a sudden, she could hardly wait for the champagne.

With a hollow sound like a hiccup, the cork popped out

of the bottle. Ross removed the towel and poured them each a glass, never spilling a drop.

"You've had lots of practice at this, I can tell."

He grinned at Amanda's comment, the first spontaneous, heartfelt smile she'd ever seen from him. "Learned at my daddy's knee," he said.

Creases gathered at the corners of his twinkling blue eyes. Amanda was intrigued by how his attractive grin transformed his features, making him seem far less reserved, less…unreachable than he usually appeared.

She accepted a glass from his hand. "Speaking of your parents…" she began.

"They drowned in a boating accident when I was eleven and Paige was three." His smile dimmed.

"I'm sorry." Amanda bit her lip. "I shouldn't have brought it up. It's just that there's so much you and I don't know about each other."

"Strange, isn't it? Yet here we are, about to toast our marriage." Ross lifted his glass. "Here's to a long and happy life together."

Amanda chimed her glass against his. Once again she had to shake off a disorienting sense of unreality. Yesterday, she'd been a poorly paid art gallery manager, pretty much alone in the world, struggling to overcome the tragedy life had dealt her.

Tonight, she was Ross Chandler's wife.

Tomorrow, she would be Jamie's mother again.

Ross studied her while he sipped. "What about *your* family?" he asked.

The champagne bubbles tickled Amanda's nose. "I don't remember my mother," she replied. "She died when I was a baby. I was an only child. My father passed away during my last year at college." She swirled the champagne around her glass. "In retrospect, that's probably why I was so eager to marry Paul. He was nine years older than me—one of my college professors."

"A substitute father figure to replace the one you'd just lost?"

"Yes." She took another sip of champagne. "He wasn't all that interested in having children. I was the one who pressed for adoption as soon as we found out we couldn't have any."

Ross settled himself on the bar stool next to her. "Was he a good father to Jamie?"

Amanda eased off one shoe and let it dangle from her toe. "He went through the proper motions. Paid the bills. Changed the occasional diaper. But he was always a lot more wrapped up in his career than he was with our child. Or with me." She shrugged and took another swallow.

Ross reached for the bottle and refilled her glass. "You were divorced within a year after the custody fight ended."

Amanda raised her eyebrows. "You've been doing your homework." She hoisted her glass in a mock salute. "Let's just say the pressures of the court battle and the stress of losing our child proved too much for a marriage that was built on a rather shaky foundation to begin with."

"Mmm." Ross thoughtfully rubbed his jaw, his whiskers rasping beneath his hand. He hadn't been out of Amanda's sight for more than a minute all day, so she knew he hadn't shaved since early this morning. With his tie loosened and his shirtsleeves rolled up, it was the first time she'd ever seen him looking the least bit disheveled.

Goodness, but this champagne was sure a lot tastier than the inexpensive stuff she was used to being served at New Year's Eve parties! Like an entirely different drink.

She scrutinized her new husband over the rim of her glass. Really, even in his rumpled state, he was undeniably attractive. Downright handsome, in fact. Why did some people have all the luck? Money, power, incredible good looks…

And now he was all hers. Amanda pressed her fingertips to her mouth and giggled.

Ross's eyes gleamed with amusement. Did he get the joke, too? Such sexy blue eyes…

He swung off the bar stool and stretched his arms toward the ceiling. "I don't know about you, but I'm dead tired," he said with a yawn.

Amanda dragged her attention from the buttons straining across his wide chest. "Um, me, too." Tired. Dazed. A little bit dizzy.

"I'll carry your suitcase to your room for you."

Amanda finally succeeded in slipping her shoe back on. *Just like Cinderella,* she thought. *Only Prince Charming is apparently sleeping in the other bedroom tonight.*

She teetered along in his wake. Must be more tired than she'd thought. By the time she'd trailed Ross into her room, he'd already set her suitcase on the luggage rack and was drawing the curtains shut. The bedroom was spacious, yet homey. The bed itself was enormous.

"It's only a four- or five-hour drive home tomorrow," Ross told her. His mouth twitched as if he was trying to stifle a yawn. Or maybe a smile. "No need to get an early start, so feel free to sleep in as late as you want."

"Okay." Part of her wanted to dive into bed, yank the covers up over her head and sleep for about a year. Yet another part of her felt oddly restless, as if the fizz in the champagne were floating around in her bloodstream.

Ross brought his hand to the side of her face. "Good night, Amanda."

She leaned her head against his palm, her eyelids as heavy as if they had weights attached to them. "G'night," she echoed dreamily.

His face loomed above hers. Such a nice face, she

mused. Why had she thought he was such a rotten creep all these years?

He's going to kiss me after all, she realized as he lowered his head to hers. Confused anticipation made her heart beat faster. Her eyes drifted closed.

She felt the warm imprint of his lips against her forehead. Smelled champagne on his breath and the ghost of laundry soap rising from his collar. Inhaled the pleasant, masculine scent she was already coming to recognize as uniquely his own.

Before Amanda could draw another breath, Ross was gone. Her eyes struggled open just in time to see the door closing quietly behind him.

She collapsed onto the edge of the bed, drained and relieved and deflated all at once. "Well, what did you expect him to do?" she mumbled. "Assert his husbandly rights?"

They had an agreement after all. A purely practical arrangement that didn't involve sharing anything besides the roof over their heads.

Amanda drooped to one side, feeling her bones start to melt like a snowman left out in the sun too long. She barely managed to kick off her shoes and peel off her dress before her head hit the pillow.

Instead of the room spinning around her, it felt as if *she* were spinning. As if the bed were a raft trapped in a slow-moving whirlpool.

She was exhausted. Jet-lagged. Perhaps a teeny bit looped.

And all alone.

"What a way to spend a wedding night," she murmured groggily. Then she promptly fell asleep.

Chapter 3

The Napa Valley.

Amanda could hardly have felt more alienated from her surroundings if they'd been driving through one of the valleys on the moon. The scenery was pretty enough—gently rolling hills, brown-and-white cows grazing beneath majestic oaks, fields of grapevines stitched into neat rows as far as the eye could see.

But she couldn't forget for a second that she was an impostor who didn't belong here. Though she was going to live in this picturesque valley from now on, it would never be her home.

And though she'd been married to Ross for…oh, going on sixteen hours now, she would never, ever be a Chandler. Not after the entire ruthless clan had banded together to take away the most precious part of Amanda's life.

Soon, very soon, those terrible years of separation would be over. Every mile, every minute that passed brought her closer and closer to her long-lost child.

Amanda's heart began to hammer.

"Tell me about Jamie," she said, suddenly apprehensive about what changes she might find in her little girl.

Ross's dark sunglasses made the glance he threw Amanda even more unreadable than usual. But there was no mistaking the affection that quirked his lips in a half smile as he turned his attention back to the road.

"Jamie? Well, she's a terrific kid. Outgoing, inquisitive, loves animals…" He flicked a comma of platinum hair from his eyes. He had his sleeves rolled up and his window rolled down, so that the rush of warm air was playing havoc with his high-priced haircut. "She's just finishing second grade now. Top student in her class."

Despite her resentment at having to grill him about her own child, Amanda was amused by the note of pride in his voice. Somehow she doubted they were ranking seven-year-olds by grade point average these days.

Ross, however, appeared fully confident of Jamie's academic superiority. "She can read at a fifth-grade level. And she's already got her times tables memorized up through the sixes. Spelling tests?" He gave a dismissive flip of his hand. "Never misses a word."

"You sound like you're pretty involved with her schooling." Amanda fought to keep the jealousy from her voice. If there had been any justice in the world, *she* would have been the person entitled to sing Jamie's praises!

Ross must have sensed the two-edged nature of her question. He rubbed his jaw before replying, and his answer was far more restrained than his enthusiastic description of Jamie's scholastic achievements.

"I guess I've turned out to be more like a father to Jamie than an uncle," he said. "My grandfather…well, he dotes on Jamie, but he's not about to show up at PTA meetings or chauffeur Jamie and her friends to a movie matinee. As for Paige…"

A troubled look drifted over his face, like the shadow of a hawk circling overhead. Obviously, he was thinking of the parental void in Jamie's life that he'd stepped in to fill after Paige's death.

"I understand," Amanda said quickly. She hadn't meant to stir up his grief over the loss of his sister. "Jamie's... been very lucky to have you." Though the words stuck in her throat like splinters, once she forced them out, she was surprised to discover she meant them. Maybe this whole crazy arrangement was going to work out after all.

Ross turned the car off the main highway onto a narrower road that climbed gradually through gentle hills blanketed with more fields of grapevines. "Those are Cabernet grapes," he said, pointing. "They grow best up here at the north end of the Napa Valley, where it's warmer. Chardonnay grapes prefer the cooler weather in the south end of the valley."

"I see." Amanda's first viticulture lesson was largely wasted on her. As she sensed the end of their journey drawing near, her nerves began to twang like overstretched guitar strings.

Soon, Jamie. Very soon.

She blinked back a mist of tears.

Ross watched Amanda struggle for control out of the corner of his eye. He couldn't begin to imagine what she must be feeling right now. Anticipation...eagerness...and no doubt an element of sheer panic over her approaching reunion with the child she'd thought she would never see again.

Ross himself was feeling a measure of dread about the immediate future. Caleb Chandler was going to hit the roof when his grandson brought Amanda Prentiss home as his bride.

His bride.

That disorienting sensation of unreality gripped Ross again. From behind his sunglasses, he admired his new wife. Her dark hair was pulled back today, revealing the classic beauty of her profile and tiny gold loops adorning her dainty earlobes.

Strain was evident in the pale, nearly translucent skin stretched taut across her high cheekbones, and in the white ridge of her knuckles as she clutched her hands together in her lap. Beneath the thin silk of her plum-colored blouse, her breasts rose and fell at a tempo suggesting she was a long way from calm.

Heat stirred in his loins, catching Ross off guard. He forced himself to stop speculating what it might feel like to take her in his arms, to whisper soothing words into her sweet-smelling hair, to kiss away the worries trembling on her soft, full lips.

He might be Amanda's husband, but he was also a man of honor. He wasn't about to violate the terms of their marriage agreement just because he found himself unexpectedly attracted to her.

"Butterflies in your stomach?" On impulse, he reached over to cover the hands knotted tensely in her lap.

She jumped at his touch. Her gorgeous eyes were as dark and wide as a moonless night when she swiveled her head in his direction. An ironic smile touched her mouth. "More like seagulls."

Ross squeezed her hand. "Don't worry. You and Jamie will hit it off just fine."

Her skin was as cold as ice. "Do you..." She swallowed. "How well do you think she remembers me?"

Ross heard the echoes of Jamie's long-ago sobs when she'd first come to live with them. *Mommy! Mommy! I want my mo-ommeee...*

He saw her tear-swollen, four-year-old face and relived the anguish that had twisted in his gut like a knife whenever he'd taken his turn trying to comfort the heartbroken child after Paige had thrown up her hands in despair.

Gradually, inevitably, Jamie had grown used to her new home. The bouts of inconsolable crying had come farther and farther apart until they stopped altogether. But Ross had never deceived himself that such a traumatic upheaval hadn't left a cloud somewhere beneath the surface of his niece's sunny disposition.

"She hasn't forgotten you," he said quietly. "On some level, you've always stayed a part of her."

Amanda's lips opened on a sound that was half sob, half sigh. She wove her fingers through his and gripped tightly. "Thank you," she whispered.

The car slowed, and Ross made a move to restore his hand to the steering wheel. Amanda let go as if his touch had suddenly scorched her. For heaven's sake, what was she doing holding hands with him, thanking him for…for what? Stealing her daughter?

She couldn't afford to forget for a second that he was a Chandler. And that no Chandler could be trusted. No matter how charming and sympathetic he seemed.

No matter what kind of foolish yearnings the mere touch of his hand could arouse inside her.

Ross flicked on the turn indicator and braked. Amanda dug her nails into the buttery leather upholstery when she glimpsed the ornate arch of wrought-iron letters spanning the roadway they'd just turned onto.

Chandler Winery.

This was it, then. The place where Jamie had come to live after she'd been wrenched from Amanda's arms.

The setting for so many of Amanda's nightmares.

Massive oak gates that looked as if they could withstand a medieval battering ram stood wide open. Not what Amanda would have expected to find at the entrance to the Chandler fortress.

Then she saw a discreet sign announcing that the tasting room was open and recalled that this was a place of business as well as a home.

They cruised slowly past a visitors' parking lot and several winery buildings whose functions Ross explained and which Amanda promptly forgot. Adrenaline was racing through her blood, and any rational thoughts she attempted to hold on to seemed to leak right out of her skull.

Jamie, I'm coming...I'm almost there.... She dragged her damp palms along her slacks. Excitement and apprehension percolated through her stomach like acid. *So close now...so close, after all these years....*

They came to a locked iron gate with a sign reading Private—No Visitors. Ross reached out his open window and punched a code into a keypad. Watching the wrought-iron bars lurch into slow motion and automatically slide past each other, Amanda couldn't help but think of the doors of a prison. She felt rather than heard the gates clang shut behind them as the car continued up the gradually sloping road.

Shadows dappled her sleeve as they passed beneath a leafy arcade of oaks. Then they emerged into full sunlight again, and the Chandler mansion came into view.

Amanda's heart began to throb even more wildly. Mansion? More like a palace. An architectural masterpiece. A sprawling, multileveled extravaganza of wood and glass and stone that emerged from the gentle hillside as naturally as if it had grown here. Surrounded by magnificent landscaping that surely kept an army of gardeners busy twenty-four hours a day. Italian cypresses, palm trees, a profusion of rosebushes and tropical flowers, an emerald swatch of perfectly manicured lawn.

Good heavens. This is where she was supposed to *live* from now on? In this California version of Versailles?

She could only imagine how overwhelming this place must have seemed to a frightened four-year-old.

Ross eased the car around the circular driveway and coasted to a stop at the base of the front steps. When he tugged off his sunglasses, Amanda saw commiseration in his eyes. "How are those seagulls doing?"

She drew in a deep, shuddering breath. The cloying perfume of roses made her queasy. "They're doing loop the loops," she replied unsteadily.

His mouth tightened in understanding. Except that Ross couldn't *possibly* understand what she was going through right now.

He consulted his watch. "The bus won't be dropping Jamie home from school for a half hour or so. That should give you a chance to get settled in first."

Bus? she thought half-hysterically as Ross came around to open her car door. *What* is *this? The chauffeur's day off?*

She stood there gaping up at the imposing facade of her new home while Ross hoisted her suitcases out of the trunk. She hadn't been this terrified since the day she lost Jamie.

Ross slammed the trunk lid, then grimaced when he noted Amanda's expression. "Takes a bit of getting used to, doesn't it?"

"Not if you were born here, I imagine." Her tone was dry. Her mouth was dry. Her entire *throat* was dry, in fact. Not her palms, though. Her palms were slick with sweat.

"When I was growing up, I used to be kind of embarrassed to bring friends over for the first time." Ross ushered her up the broad slate steps.

"Ah, the curse of wealth," Amanda muttered under her breath.

They crossed a wide veranda to the front door. Teak, she thought. Elaborately carved with the kind of craftsmanship you probably couldn't even find nowadays, even if you were rich enough to afford it.

Her heart thumped frantically against her ribs while Ross set down her luggage and pulled out a key to unlock the door.

Last chance to back out, Amanda! You could catch the next plane back east, have the marriage annulled…

Ross swung open the door and stood aside for her to enter.

Jamie, she thought. *Mommy's here.*

Her legs felt as teetery as toothpicks. She licked her lips and flattened a shaky hand over her stomach. Then she stepped into the Chandler mansion and found herself in a vast, sunlit entrance hall floored with earth-toned terra-cotta tiles.

Ross closed the door. The sound echoed like a gunshot through the museumlike silence. "Here we are," he said. "Would you like to see your room first, or have—"

Just then, rapid footsteps pounded a tattoo like artillery fire. Amanda's jangled nerves were definitely starting to feel under siege.

A calico cat streaked across the entrance hall.

"Crackerjack, you come back here, you bad kitty! You know you're not s'posed to…"

Amanda's hand flew to her mouth. She caught her breath. And at that moment, she couldn't have let it go if her life depended on it.

A child burst through one of the archways leading out of the hall, arms pinwheeling as she braked to a halt and skidded on one of the throw rugs.

A little girl with unruly blond curls that tumbled to her waist. With big blue eyes that grew even wider when she focused them on Amanda and Ross. A little girl with a milk mustache, a dusting of flour on her striped T-shirt and a smear of what looked like chocolate on her cheek.

Amanda's heart swelled till she thought it would burst from her chest.

Jamie.

Ross bit back a moan of dismay. This wasn't at all the carefully choreographed reunion he'd mentally orchestrated during the long drive from Tahoe.

He hadn't had time yet to break the news to Jamie that he'd gotten married, to prepare her for the major change that was going to take place in their lives. He hadn't had a chance to explain to her exactly who this new member of the household really was.

"Uncle Ross! You're back from your business trip!" She skipped across the tiles and flung her arms around his waist. Ross hugged her warm little body against him and bent over to growl playfully into her neck. She giggled and twisted away from him. "Grampa didn't tell me you were coming home today."

"Grampa didn't know." He tweaked her nose. "How come you're home so early from school?"

She bounced from one sandaled foot to the other, her glance sliding curiously toward Amanda. "No school today. All the teachers had to go to this bi-i-i-g meeting." She stretched her arms way out to demonstrate.

"I see." Instinctively, Ross moved closer to Amanda and laid a reassuring hand against the small of her back. Through her silk blouse, he could feel her muscles had gone rigid as stone. Her heart felt like a jackhammer drilling against concrete. "Been helping Nora out in the kitchen, have you?"

"We're making chocolate cake. Only Crackerjack knocked the eggs off the counter so Nora got mad and said he has to go outside." She twirled a ribbon of pale gold hair around her finger, her gaze darting back and forth between the two adults. "Nora said Crackerjack's in the doghouse. Only how can he be in the doghouse if he's a cat?''

Ross felt a quiver go up Amanda's spine. With relief, he saw her mouth twitch with a hint of a smile. He chuckled. ''Being in the doghouse means being in trouble. Even if you're a cat.''

''Oh.'' Now Jamie was staring openly at Amanda, and for the first time, Ross saw a spark of uncertainty in her eyes. A glimmer of recognition, perhaps?

He took a deep breath. No more postponing this awkward introduction. After giving Amanda's shoulder an encouraging squeeze, he crouched onto his heels so he and Jamie were eye-to-eye.

He took one of her hands between his. ''I guess maybe I belong in the doghouse, too, Jamie. 'Cause I told a little fib to you and Grampa when I said I was going away for a few days on a business trip.''

''You *did?*'' She blinked her long, adorable lashes in disbelief. ''But, Uncle Ross, you *never* tell fibs.''

Ouch. He controlled his features so neither Jamie nor Amanda would wonder why he'd winced. The truth was, he was tangled up in the biggest fib of his life right now—a fly caught in a spider's web of deception. All he could do was move cautiously and hope that those tangled, sticky strands would eventually unsnarl themselves.

''I told you I was going away on a business trip,'' he confessed, ''because the real reason was kind of complicated, and I didn't know how it would turn out.''

Jamie might be only seven and a half, but she was amazingly perceptive for a kid her age. Once more, she shifted an uncertain look toward Amanda. Puzzled crinkles gathered between her eyebrows. Obviously, she sensed that the woman her uncle had brought home with him had something to do with the astonishing fact that he'd told a lie.

Nervous sweat filmed Ross's forehead. He forced himself to smile as he met Jamie's eyes. "You see, the real reason I went on this trip was to get married."

Jamie blinked again. "Married?" As she absorbed this incomprehensible news, a finger crept into the corner of her mouth.

That small, achingly familiar gesture hooked Amanda's memory with a jolt. It was the same instinctive movement a much younger Jamie had responded with in times of confusion or fear.

For the first time, it fully dawned on Amanda what a rash action she and Ross had taken. Why had they been in such a hurry to get married? Why hadn't they waited a while, given Jamie a chance to get used to the idea?

But deep down inside, Amanda knew the answer to that. At least, what her *own* motives had been. She'd been frantic to seal a permanent connection to Jamie before Ross changed his mind.

As for Ross's motives...

Well, she would have plenty of time now to figure them out, wouldn't she? At the moment, however, her main concern was for Jamie.

Ross pushed himself to his feet and reached for Amanda's hand. After a second's hesitation, she took it. "Jamie, this is my wife, Amanda," he said. "She's going to be living here with us from now on."

My wife, Amanda.

She told herself that the odd, wistful pluck at her heart-strings was all part of her reaction to seeing Jamie again.

The warm pressure of Ross's hand increased. "You might not remember, Jamie, but you and Amanda used to know each other when you were little."

Amanda's pulse drummed faster, louder, in her ears.

Jamie took her finger out of her mouth and wound a corkscrew of hair around it. She studied Amanda with somber blue eyes. "You're the mommy that adopted me," she said shyly.

Tears sprang to Amanda's eyes, and for a split second her knees threatened to give way. Then her long unused but still reliable maternal instincts kicked in, not the least bit rusty. It was Jamie's emotions that mattered now, not Amanda's.

She withdrew her hand from Ross's and knelt in front of her daughter. "That's right," she said in a voice that surprised her with its steady cheerfulness. "You lived with me until you were four years old, before you came to live here with your other mommy and Uncle Ross." Though the words tasted like poison on her lips, she didn't let Jamie see it.

"And Grampa," Jamie corrected.

Amanda's facial muscles obediently formed a smile. "And your grandpa, too, of course."

Jamie tugged on the curl wound around her finger. "My other mommy died," she said softly.

Sorrow snagged in Amanda's throat. "I know, sweetheart." As naturally as breathing, she reached out to caress Jamie's hair. "I was awfully sad to hear about that. I know she loved you very much."

"I was five years old when she died. But I still have Uncle Ross and Grampa and Nora to take care of me." She beamed a smile of pure worship at her uncle. Amanda marveled over the silky texture of her hair. How long it was now! How beautiful the blond curls were, soft and pale as an angel's wings....

Ross chucked his niece's chin. "Now you have Amanda to take care of you, too," he said.

Amanda held her breath. Children weren't like chess pieces you could arrange to suit your idea of a happy ending. They had their own ideas. Who could blame Jamie for being jealous or resentful about the prospect of sharing her beloved uncle with an intruder? If only Jamie could understand that Amanda had absolutely no intention of competing for her uncle's affections…

Jamie tilted her head to one side. Amanda could have sworn a sly gleam shimmered for a second in her daughter's eyes before they turned all big and blue with innocence. "Can I stay up till ten o'clock from now on?" she asked Amanda. "Uncle Ross makes me go to bed when it's nine o'clock, but all my friends get to stay up *lots* later than that." She rolled her eyes disdainfully.

Laughter welled up inside Amanda like a warm, healing balm. She looked up to exchange an amused glance with Ross. He was making an effort to keep a straight face, and just for a second Amanda felt the strangest sense of…connection to him. For once, his twinkling blue eyes seemed as easy to read as a billboard.

Rather disconcerting, this unexpected feeling of being allies instead of adversaries.

Ross folded his arms with mock sternness. "Sorry, young lady. I'm afraid that strategy isn't going to work."

Jamie shrugged one shoulder as if she'd already lost interest in the subject of her bedtime. "I have a pet goldfish," she told Amanda. "Do you wanna see him?"

Amanda touched her daughter's cheek. "I'd love to see him, sweetheart." Her body fairly ached with the urge to bundle her little girl into her arms and smother her with kisses. But the last thing she wanted was to come on too strong, to frighten Jamie with the depths of her own fierce need. She rose to her feet. "First, though, I think I'd better—"

"Jamie? *¿Dónde estás?* Where are you?" Footsteps thudded in the distance, growing closer. "Did you put that no-good cat outside like I told you? I thought you were helping me to bake a ca—*ay!*" A stout woman with dark hair pulled into a loose bun clapped a hand to her substantial bosom and braked to a halt on the tiles. "Why, Mr. Ross, you are back!" She began to fuss with her silver-threaded hair, tucking wayward strands behind her ears.

"Hello, Nora." Ross stepped close to Amanda in that protective way she had to admit she was coming to appreciate. "Amanda, I'd like you to meet Nora Escobar. She runs the house and does the cooking and in general makes herself indispensable around here."

"Oh, *stop*." Nora reddened and twisted her apron in her plump hands. But it was obvious she was pleased.

"I have some news I'm sure will come as a big surprise, Nora...." Ross's hand tightened on Amanda's elbow, and she wondered if he was bracing her or himself. "This is my wife, Amanda."

Surprise was hardly an adequate word for it. Nora's chin dropped to her chest. "Your—" she knotted her apron like a rope "—wife?" she squeaked.

"She's the lady that adopted me," Jamie piped up.

Nora gaped even more closely at Amanda. She began to fan her face with her apron and mutter under her breath. It sounded almost like praying.

"Pleased to meet you," Amanda said with a feeble smile.

Ross cleared his throat. "Nora, would you mind keeping Jamie occupied a while longer? I'm going to show Amanda upstairs and then look in on my grandfather."

Nora pulled herself together, though she couldn't take her eyes off Amanda. "Come, Jamie. You were helping me to bake a cake, remember?" She took Jamie by the hand and muttered, "I cannot believe Mr. Caleb did not say a word about this to me."

"Er, Mr. Caleb doesn't know yet." Ross massaged the back of his neck.

"He does not *know?*" Nora's dark eyes went wide with astonishment again.

"I'm just on my way up to tell him." Ross lifted Amanda's suitcases.

Nora's glance shifted rapidly between the two of them. Amanda could have sworn she intercepted a gleam of pity within the confused depths of the woman's bewilderment.

Then, tugging Jamie along in her wake like a barge towing a dinghy, she headed toward the kitchen, shaking her head and mumbling under her breath again. The only two words Amanda could make out were "good luck."

This time it sounded like a warning instead of a prayer.

Ross crossed the entrance hall to the foot of the wide, curving staircase. Amanda followed reluctantly, like Anne Boleyn on her way to the executioner.

As Ross stood aside for her to precede him, Amanda read the look of rueful irony carved on his features. "Welcome home," he said.

Chapter 4

"You married *who?*"

The soup bowl sailed past Ross's head and crashed into the wall. Fortunately, it was almost empty.

"I see those exercises the physical therapist gave you are doing some good," he said.

"Exercises be damned," the old man in the bed snarled. "Have you gone insane? What the hell possessed you to go and marry that woman?"

"What other choice did I have once I realized there was a chance we could lose Jamie?" Ross hastily removed the lunch tray from the bedside table in case his grandfather decided to hurl more dishes around the room. "If Amanda ever found out that Judge Franklin was under investigation, how long do you think it would have taken her to accuse you of paying him off?"

Caleb Chandler's mouth puckered as if he'd tasted something foul. "Accusations are one thing. Proof is another."

"What if the judge himself confessed to it?" Ross took the linen napkin from the lunch tray and calmly used it to wipe up the soup spatters. "Once it came out that Paige was awarded custody because you bribed him, another judge could just as easily have given Jamie back to Amanda."

"Bah!" Caleb made a swipe at the air with one clawed, arthritic hand. "So your damnfool solution was to *marry* that woman, even after all the trouble it took to get her out of our lives?"

Ross dropped the napkin back onto the tray. More than twenty years of living under his grandfather's roof had taught him that an endless supply of patience was the most useful weapon for dealing with his cantankerousness.

"Amanda deserves this chance to be part of Jamie's life again," he said, gathering up the newspapers Caleb had strewn all over his bed. "You know as well as I do that she got a raw deal three years ago."

"A raw deal?" Amazing what a roar an eighty-six-year-old man with a weak heart could still produce when he got riled up. "That woman has no one to blame but herself! Jamie belonged to *us!* If that woman hadn't tricked poor Paige into giving our Jamie up for adoption, none of it would have happened."

"That's not how it was, and you know it."

"I know that woman caused us nothing but trouble. And here you go, bringing her here to stir up some more!"

"Jamie needs a mother."

"That woman was never her mother and never *will* be her mother!" Caleb made a grab for the bedside phone and shook the receiver at Ross. "You call that fancy law firm I'm bankrolling and get this so-called marriage annulled!"

"That's not going to happen." Caleb's parchment-pale skin flushed an apoplectic red. Ross quickly snatched the phone out of his grasp before his grandfather could send it flying through the French doors on the far side of the room. "For Pete's sake, don't get so worked up," he said. "It won't change anything, and besides, it's bad for your heart."

"You should have thought of that before you went sneaking behind my back and betrayed us all." Caleb's wizened fingers plucked at the bedcover as if trying to tear it to pieces.

"I haven't betrayed anybody." *Except Amanda,* whispered Ross's conscience. *Not to mention lied to her. Deceived her. Tricked her into marrying you.*

Caleb lurched up from his pillow. "What about Paige?" he demanded. "What about your loyalty to your own sister?"

Ross dragged a hand over his face. "I was loyal to Paige all her life," he said wearily. "But there's a difference between being loyal and doing what's right."

"Not in this family!"

"I guess not." Ross gazed steadily into his grandfather's furious eyes. "Not until now anyway."

The two men glared at each other like a pair of stubborn bulls locked by the horns in combat.

"Grampa, look what I found outside!" Jamie skipped into the room, then pulled up short as if she'd physically bumped into the tension in the air.

Ross made a conscious effort to relax his neck and shoulder muscles. "What've you got there, James?" He pointed to her clenched fist.

Jamie tiptoed closer to the bed, her glance darting warily between her uncle and great-grandfather. She uncurled her fingers to reveal a rock about an inch in diameter resting on her flattened palm. "Do you think it might be gold?" she asked breathlessly, her blue eyes shimmering with excitement.

Caleb took the rock and made a pretense of examining it carefully, studying it from all angles. It never failed to amaze Ross what a soft spot his crusty old grandfather had for Jamie. If Ross or Paige had discovered that same rock while growing up, Caleb would have scoffed at the notion of gold, flung the discovery aside and delivered a lecture about spending more time on schoolwork and less time grubbing around in the dirt.

Jamie scrambled up to sit on the edge of his bed. "If it's gold, does that mean I'm rich?"

"We're already rich," Caleb reminded her. He popped the stone back into her hand, curled her fingers around it and patted her fist. "Sorry, princess. That's a chunk of what they call fool's gold."

She unclenched her fingers to examine the rock dubiously. "What's that?"

"A nickname for a mineral called iron pyrite."

"They call it fool's gold because it fools a lot of people into thinking it's real gold," Ross added.

"Oh." Jamie tucked the rock into the pocket of her shorts and shrugged off her disappointment. "Grampa, did you know Uncle Ross got married?"

Caleb fired off a scowl in Ross's direction. "Your uncle just informed me of that fact."

Jamie swung her legs back and forth. "And the lady he married used to be my mommy a long time ago."

The prominent cords in Caleb's withered neck strained with the effort of swallowing his anger. "Paige Chandler was always your mother, princess." He patted Jamie's knee. "Don't you ever forget that."

"Granddad..." Ross warned.

Jamie cocked her head to one side. "Then how come she used to not like it if I called her Mommy? How come I was s'posed to call her Paige?"

"Er..." Caleb harrumphed loudly, overcome by a rare attack of speechlessness.

Ross fought to keep his lips from twitching. "I think it made your mother feel younger to be called Paige," he told Jamie. That was Paige in a nutshell, he thought. Always anxious to remain the perpetual teenager. Carefree, no responsibilities, no one to look after but herself.

It was difficult to fit the existence of a child into that self-defined image. Easier for Paige to pretend she was still as fun-loving and footloose as ever, without a little girl tagging along calling her Mommy all the time.

It had never been *Paige's* idea to sue for Jamie's custody. But Ross had no intention of explaining all that to Jamie. Ever. "Did you show Amanda your goldfish yet?" he asked.

Caleb stiffened at the mention of Amanda's name.

"Uh-uh. I was helping Nora bake our cake."

Ross sniffed the air appreciatively. "Mmm. Smells good." From the corner of his eye, he could see his grandfather building up steam like an ancient boiler about to explode. "Why don't you go find Amanda and show her your room?" he suggested to Jamie. "I bet she'd like to see it."

"'Kay." Jamie bounced off the bed and made a beeline for the door. Then she skidded to a stop, pivoted, and raced back to the bed. "Bye, Grampa." She planted a kiss on Caleb's cheek, oblivious to the simmering anger he was struggling to clamp a lid on for her sake. She flew out of the room, her long hair trailing behind her like gold streamers.

Caleb's overheated temper finally blew up. "How could you bring that woman here and take the chance of her stealing Jamie away from us?" he demanded.

Ross bit back a sigh. "She's not going to do that. Besides, if anyone around here has had her child stolen, it's Amanda."

"You make it sound like we committed some sort of crime!"

"Hmm." Ross tapped his chin. "I believe bribery *is* considered a crime."

"*Pah!*" Caleb jabbed a finger in the air. "All we did was take back what was ours by rights."

"And what about Amanda's rights?" Ross knew it was useless to plow this ground up. Caleb's blind, pigheaded stubbornness made the subject of Jamie's custody barren soil for any rational discussion.

During the hearings, Ross had held his tongue for the sake of family loyalty. And he'd despised himself for it ever since.

"Paige gave Jamie up for adoption," he pointed out. "Amanda and her former husband were her parents in every legal, moral, emotional sense of the word."

"They coerced Paige into giving her up!"

"Don't be absurd. No one could coerce Paige into doing anything she didn't want to do, and you know it."

Caleb spluttered in rage and frustration. Ross felt his own blood pressure creeping upward. He'd always believed that Caleb thrived on conflict and confrontation, but surely this level of antagonism couldn't do *anyone's* heart any good.

Despite their frequent clashes, Ross loved and respected his grandfather. And owed him a lot. He would never forgive himself if anything happened to the old man because of him.

"I'm going to see how Amanda's settling in," he said. "Can I get you anything before I leave? A glass of water? Something more to eat?"

"Whiskey," Caleb spat out. "Make it a double."

"Sorry." Ross reached for the control box that raised

or lowered the level of Caleb's high-tech hospital bed. "Against doctor's orders."

"Give me that thing." Caleb swiped the box from Ross's hand. "I'm perfectly capable of adjusting my own damn bed. I'm not some drooling, helpless old bag of bones who can't even push a button, thank God. Not yet anyway."

"You're a long way from that, for sure."

"Hold your horses, boy. Don't you slink out of here so fast!"

"Granddad, I think we've said everything there is to say."

"You send that Weston woman back to where she came from! You hear me? And then call the lawyers. Come back here! Ross! Do you hear me?"

Ross heard him loud and clear. All the way down the hall and into the opposite wing of the house.

Obviously, this wasn't a good time to mention to his grandfather that he and his new wife planned to adopt Jamie all over again.

"Dinner was delicious, Nora." Amanda smiled as Nora removed her plate. She had to force herself to remain seated instead of helping clear the dishes. Earlier, when she'd offered to help put dinner on the table, Nora had stared at her as if Amanda had suggested serving the cat as the main course.

Chandlers, it seemed, were to be waited on. And Amanda was a Chandler now. At least in name.

After stumbling across the formal dining room during her earlier explorations of the house, Amanda had envisioned dinner as an awkward affair. Ross at the head of the table, separated from Amanda at the other end by a football field of polished mahogany, with Jamie lost somewhere in the middle. They would have to use megaphones to make dinner conversation, for heaven's sake!

Instead, they'd eaten in a pleasant sunroom, with a normal-size table, lots of hanging plants and broad panes of glass so they could watch the sun set while they ate.

Amanda even forgot to worry about which fork to use.

"More wine?" Ross held the bottle over her glass.

"No, thank you." She'd barely touched what he'd already poured earlier. For months after losing Jamie, Amanda hadn't even been able to push her shopping cart past the wine display in the supermarket without bursting into tears. The sight of the Chandler label still made her insides recoil.

Jamie set down her empty milk glass. "Uncle Ross, how come you never ask if I want any wine?"

"I'll give you three guesses."

"Mmm..." She squinted thoughtfully at the oak-beamed ceiling. "'Cause I'm too *little*."

"Got it in one." Ross winked at her.

It had required every fragment of Amanda's self-control to keep from staring at her daughter all through dinner. She couldn't get over the differences three years had made.

Although Jamie was only seven, she somehow seemed so grown-up! All traces of baby fat had melted away so that the chubby cheeks Amanda had kissed every night had disappeared. She was much taller, with thin, sturdy limbs that were constantly in motion. Even her speech seemed very advanced for a child her age. Amanda couldn't believe the clever words and perceptive observations that came out of her mouth.

Still, this was unquestionably her same darling girl. Was it any wonder that Amanda kept losing track of what she was eating, that her fork would hover halfway to her mouth while she stared in awe across the table at the child she'd thought she'd lost forever?

Nora returned with coffee and chocolate cake.

"Has my grandfather finished his dinner yet?" Ross asked.

"Humph." Nora poured coffee for Amanda. It smelled heavenly. "I guess you could call it finished." She filled Ross's cup. "He told me the chicken was overcooked, the vegetables were not cooked enough, and the potatoes were lumpy. Then he shoved the tray at me and ordered me to take it away." She sniffed indignantly. "So, yes. He is finished."

Ross offered her a crooked smile. "Sometimes his medication puts him off food a little."

Nora shook her head and scooped up a handful of silverware. "It is not his medicine," she grumbled. "It is his *meanness.*"

"Well, thank you for putting up with it. You know that deep down inside he appreciates everything you do for him. For all of us."

She snorted. "Over thirty years I work for that impossible man. You would think by now he would have learned how to say thank-you." She left the room with a sniff.

Amanda took a sip of coffee. "I guess Caleb didn't take the joyful news of our nuptials too well," she murmured to Ross.

"Let's just say he didn't offer to pay for a honeymoon." Ross's mouth curved wryly. He looked tired. Exhausted, really. The tiny crinkles at the corners of his eyes were etched more deeply than usual.

Amanda could almost feel sorry for him. She actually had to squash an impulse to reach over and brush a drooping lock of hair from his furrowed brow. The past two days had been a frenzy of activity and change for both of them, and on top of that, Ross now had to assume the role of referee between the various members of the household. She suspected it was a role he was accustomed to playing.

"May I please be excused from the table?" Jamie dropped her cake fork with a *clink* and pushed back her chair. "I'm gonna go up and read with Grampa now."

"Um..." Amanda's alarm antenna went up. Surely this was no time for Jamie to intrude on Caleb's bad temper.

"Sure, James." Ross curved the back of his hand to his mouth and whispered behind it. "Why don't you stop by the kitchen on the way and see if Nora will whip up a chicken sandwich for you to take up to him?"

"Okay." She dashed off on her mission of mercy.

Amanda held her tongue. For about two seconds. After all, from now on Jamie was going to be *her* child, too. Not that she hadn't always been.

"Do you think it's wise to let her go up to his room, considering the circumstances?"

Above the rim of his cup, Ross's eyes were guarded. "*What* circumstances?"

Amanda emitted a sound of exasperation. "The fact that Caleb's temper sounds out of control right now! Good heavens, you could hear him hollering all over the house this afternoon. How do you know he won't decide to vent his spleen on Jamie by throwing that chicken sandwich at her or something?"

"Amanda." Ross covered her hand with his. "I don't expect you and Granddad to become best friends, but there's something you should understand."

Amanda injected a chill into her gaze. There was just the faintest whiff of that arrogant Chandler superiority in his attitude. He was patronizing her, treating her like a lower species of human who needed to have it carefully explained what life was like here on the exalted Chandler plane. Next thing she knew, he'd be patting her hand. Amanda pointedly withdrew it before he had the chance.

Ross sighed. "Look, I'm the first to admit that Granddad can be pretty difficult at times. But he would never, *ever* do anything to harm Jamie or hurt her feelings. He's crazy about her.''

Amanda tapped a spoon against her coffee cup. Past Ross's shoulder, she could look out through the glass and see acres and acres of carefully tended grapevines in the fields below the house. In the gathering dusk, their gnarled silhouettes looked as tangled and forbidding as barbed wire.

She'd agreed to marry Ross to get Jamie back. But she hadn't agreed to live like a prisoner or some kind of second-class citizen. She was going to be Jamie's mother again, and both Ross and Caleb were going to have to get used to the idea.

"How do you know he isn't up there right now, poisoning her mind against me?" she asked.

To her surprise, Ross chuckled. The tired lines around his eyes dissolved for a moment, and even in her irritation Amanda couldn't help thinking how handsome he was.

"Funny," he replied. "That's exactly what Granddad worries *you'll* do."

"What?" Amanda frowned in confusion.

"He's afraid you're going to turn Jamie against us. That you've come here to steal her away."

"That's ridiculous." Amanda shoved back her chair and went to stand by the windows. Lights flickered here and there across the shadowed landscape.

Was Caleb's accusation so ridiculous? a tiny voice chided inside her head. Maybe at some subconscious level, the idea was buried that she might eventually win Jamie over and have her child all to herself someday.

Amanda took a deep breath and let her shoulders fall. No. Not that the idea wasn't appealing. But she would never uproot Jamie again, or force her to repeat the traumatic upheaval she'd already had to suffer once before in her young life. Whether Amanda liked it or not, this was Jamie's home now. The place where she belonged.

If only Amanda could ever hope to belong here, too.

Ross came and stood beside her. She was acutely aware of his tall, solid presence, the warmth of his body, the aura of masculinity that seemed to crowd out the air molecules that surrounded him and make it hard for her to breathe.

He brought a hand to her shoulder so that he was almost standing with his arm around her. "I know my grandfather's fears are groundless," he said. "I know you don't intend to steal Jamie away. But maybe you and he can call a truce if you can just understand each other's point of view."

For a fraction of an instant, Amanda was strongly tempted to turn into him, to slide her arms around his waist and tuck her head beneath his square jaw and believe him when he promised that everything would turn out all right. What could be more natural than seeking comfort from the man who was her lawfully wedded husband?

But she couldn't forget that he was also a Chandler. She couldn't let herself trust him, no matter how much she wanted to. Intuition warned her that this elegant mansion was filled with secret conflicts and hidden agendas.

Maybe the tension she sensed was nothing more than a power struggle between Ross and Caleb over who was going to run the winery now that Caleb was bedridden. But Amanda wasn't going to allow herself to become a pawn in whatever kind of real-life chess game the two men were playing.

She stepped away from Ross. "What did Jamie mean when she said she was going to read with Caleb?"

Ross dropped his hand. "Every evening after dinner, she goes up to his room for a while. Sometimes she reads to him, sometimes he reads to her."

"Reads what?"

"Storybooks, mostly. I think they're working on *Little House on the Prairie* right now."

"I see." The cozy scene his words brought to mind was hardly what Amanda had imagined. She'd pictured Caleb drilling Jamie on her homework or quizzing her about articles in the financial pages.

"After they finish reading and Jamie's brushed her teeth and fed her goldfish," Ross continued, "I generally tuck her into bed. If I'm not out of town on business, that is." His voice sounded deliberately casual when he said, "I assume you'd like to join me in saying good-night to her?"

All those lonely, tear-filled nights she'd only been able to say good night to her lost child by gazing up at the moon…

"Oh, yes," Amanda replied. *Just try to stop me.*

Ross had expected it to feel awkward, this first time he and Amanda put Jamie to bed together.

After all, it was a ritual he was used to performing solo. Even when Paige was alive and Caleb was still mobile, Ross was usually the one who made sure she'd brushed her teeth and brought her a glass of water if she asked for one and kissed her forehead before turning off the light. It was a ritual he'd also come to cherish. And he wasn't sure how he was going to feel about sharing it from now on.

To his surprise, it felt completely natural. He sat on one side of Jamie's canopy bed, Amanda on the other. He asked Jamie if she'd brushed her teeth, and Amanda fetched her a drink of water. He and Amanda didn't even bump foreheads in a race to kiss Jamie good-night first.

"G'night, Uncle Ross." Jamie gave an enormous, jaw-cracking yawn. "I still wish I could stay up till it's ten o'clock, though."

"In your dreams," he replied, hoping hers would be sweet.

She twisted the pink ribbon at the neck of her pajamas. ''G'night, Amanda,'' she murmured shyly.

Ross admired the way Amanda disguised what had to be incredibly poignant, bittersweet emotions. This was, after all, the first time in three years she'd tucked her child into bed.

A child who'd forgotten how to call her Mommy.

Ross noticed her eyes were artificially bright as she smiled and lowered her head to kiss Jamie's cheek. ''Good night, sweetheart.'' In her voice he heard only love.

He was startled to find himself wondering what it would be like to hear that same loving current in Amanda's voice when she spoke to *him*.

Ridiculous to speculate. Amanda had married him for one reason only, and that was to get Jamie back. Ross had only to watch the way she looked at her daughter for proof of that. Better get this crazy attraction to his wife under control, or he was in for some serious heartache.

They left Jamie's room together. ''You probably wish you could sit up with her all night, just watching her sleep,'' Ross said quietly as they slowly moved down the hall.

Amanda glanced up in surprise. ''You're right,'' she admitted. ''But I don't imagine it would exactly reassure Jamie to wake up in the middle of the night to find a strange woman staring at her.''

''You're hardly a stranger,'' Ross said. They arrived at the door of Amanda's room.

Pain flickered over her face like a flash of heat lightning in summer. ''She barely remembers me. I doubt she would have recognized me at all if you hadn't prompted her.''

The anguish in her voice touched him, stirred up the guilt that was never far from the surface. He brought his hand to her face. ''Give her time, Amanda. The memories will come back, I'm sure.''

"I just..." Her skin was cool and soft, her eyes turbulent, as she sought words to express the emotional storm inside her. "I know I should be grateful to have her back under any kind of terms, and I am, but..." A sob caught in her throat. "I just can't help thinking about all the time with her I've lost, about all the growing up she's done since the last time I saw her. About how I'll never, ever be able to get those three years back...."

Her pale, pretty features crumpled. Without hesitation, Ross drew her into his arms. "I'm sorry, Amanda...I'm so sorry," he whispered.

He bent his head close to hers, stroking her hair, holding her close. Beneath his hands, her slender body felt rigid—not in protest of his embrace, but in the obvious strain of trying to keep from weeping.

As he kept holding her, rubbing her back, Ross felt her muscles gradually relax. Her hair smelled like wildflowers as he murmured helpless words of comfort against the silky strands. Amazingly, he felt her arms slide tentatively around his torso till her hands eventually linked behind him.

Gladness poured through him, along with a sudden hot rush of desire. He couldn't believe how perfectly they fitted together, how incredible she felt in his arms....

But he couldn't let this embrace evolve into something he hadn't intended. Amanda was vulnerable and alone. It was only natural that she should cling to him, maybe even respond to him in a physical way. But any sparks between them now could lead no further than some hasty, meaningless encounter that would only embarrass them both afterward. And Ross had already had his fill of empty encounters. By now he'd lived enough years so that he refused to settle for less than the real thing.

At the moment, though, he was sorely tempted.

He grasped Amanda's arms and gently eased her back

so at least there was some breathing space between them. Her hands rested lightly on his waist, like doves that might spook and take flight any second. Her cheeks were flushed and her chin quivered slightly. Her dark brown eyes met his, glittering with a confused mixture of tears and surprise and what Ross could have sworn was a trace of desire.

God help him, but she was beautiful.

"Amanda." He savored the taste of her name on his tongue. Then, before rational thought could stop him, he lowered his head and brought his lips to hers.

Her response was restrained at first. Not that she pulled away or stiffened in shock or kept her mouth clamped tight. More as if she was analyzing the kiss and her own reaction to it before committing herself any further.

Inch by inch, her hands crept around his waist again. Her lips grew warmer, more pliant. Her soft breasts nudged against him as she pressed closer.

An urgent craving swept through Ross that made his earlier desire feel like a casual whim. His lustful imagination tiptoed down the hallway to his own bedroom. They'd agreed to sleep in separate rooms, separate beds, but he was man enough not to protest if Amanda changed her mind....

She didn't. A tiny sigh lodged in her throat as she disengaged herself from their embrace.

Ross let her go reluctantly. His body was throbbing in places it had never throbbed before.

Amanda, too, was breathing hard. "Ross, I—I think we'd better say good-night now." Her mouth gleamed with the moisture of his kiss.

He didn't want to say good-night. He wanted to say good-morning. Tomorrow. With Amanda next to him in bed. Naked.

But they had a bargain.

"Amanda, I'm...sorry about this. The kiss." This time,

he lied. He wasn't the least bit sorry. Just frustrated as hell.

She tucked a loose strand of hair behind her ear. Her gold earring winked at him in the subdued light. "It was as much my fault as yours. I—I just don't think this is a good idea. Not our marriage, I mean. Or adopting Jamie. But—" she made a vague rolling motion with her hand as if to encompass all that had just passed between them in the hallway "—this. This...attraction to each other." She rubbed her forehead. "Things are complicated enough already, without adding any more, er...uh, complications."

How could Ross argue with her? It was bad enough he'd married Amanda under false pretenses. How could he make love to her as long as he continued to lie to her?

Well, okay. If his body's current eager state was any indication, he *could* technically make love to her. He just couldn't live with himself afterward.

"You're right, of course." It was probably just his male ego deceiving him that he saw a glint of disappointment in her eyes. "Do you have everything you need? I mean towels, blankets, that sort of thing." Obviously, she didn't need *him*.

"Oh, yes, Nora's shown me where everything is." Relief was plain on her face that escape was imminent.

"I'll say good-night, then." Once more, he had the impulse to kiss her.

This time, he resisted it.

"Good night." She ducked quickly into her room.

Before Ross had proceeded two steps down the hall, he heard the door click shut behind him.

Moments later, he was in his own room. Normally, this would have been way too early to go to bed. Alone anyway. But today had been an exhausting day. Ross was worn out from arguing with his grandfather, from working to catch up on winery business, from fighting his own desires.

He shucked off his clothes in the dark and crawled between the sheets of his large four-poster. Until tonight, in fact, he'd never really noticed just how large his bed actually was.

He'd expected to doze off shortly after his head hit the pillow. But he tossed. He turned. After twenty minutes of this, he flung back the covers and leaped out of bed.

"I've got two words for you, Chandler," he growled as he stomped toward the adjoining bathroom. "Cold. Shower."

Chapter 5

Amanda overslept the next morning. Was it any wonder, when she'd been awake half the night, her mind endlessly replaying images like an out-of-control videocassette recorder?

Images of her reunion with Jamie. Of this strange new place she was supposed to call home.

Images of Ross. Compassion mellowing his rugged features. Amusement tilting his mouth into that lopsided grin that made her knees go weak. Desire flaring in his eyes when he'd lowered his head to kiss her.

With a groan of dismay, Amanda rolled over and buried her face in the pillow. Dear God, but she'd wanted him last night!

She thumped her pillow for emphasis. She *had* to *remember*…he was a *Chandler*. That he was *not*…to be *trusted*.

Sure. Now, if she could only get that message through to her infatuated hormones.

She flung herself onto her back and opened one bleary eye to peer at the bedside clock. "Yikes!" The bedcovers went flying. Eight-thirty already! She might be a woman of wealth now, but she wasn't about to turn into some kind of lazy slugabed.

Plush carpeting caressed her bare feet as she stumbled toward her own private bathroom. The bedroom itself was big enough to hold a high school prom in, furnished with an assortment of tasteful antiques that were, no doubt, family heirlooms. She couldn't picture a Chandler poking around some musty antique store looking for bargains.

The bathroom itself...well, Amanda had to admit, it was her idea of heaven. Actually, you could hold a prom in here, too—if it was a very small high school. Shiny brass fixtures, sparkling porcelain, gleaming white tile everywhere...

The tub was big enough for that same small high school to hold a swim meet. When Amanda looked closer, she saw whirlpool jets in the sides. Hmm. Maybe she could get used to living in the lap of luxury after all.

Delicious smells were emanating from the kitchen when she finally arrived downstairs. She ducked her head into the sunroom where they'd eaten dinner last night, but no sign of Ross or Jamie. Only the cat, curled up on a chair. So she let the mouthwatering aromas draw her toward their source like invisible beckoning fingers.

"Good morning, Nora."

The cook-cum-housekeeper immediately straightened up from loading the big, industrial-size dishwasher. "Good morning, Mrs. Chandler."

"Please, call me Amanda."

Nora pinched her lips as if to demonstrate that she would never allow such presumption to pass them.

"Goodness, that's quite a control panel on that dishwasher. It looks like you'd need a license to operate it."

A twitch that looked suspiciously like a smile made a brief appearance on Nora's mouth. "It is not so hard once you learn how. See? I will show you." She pressed switches and turned knobs, and the dishwasher came to life with the muffled roar of rushing water.

"It's certainly huge for a house with only a few people in it."

Nora moved over to a stainless-steel oven that also looked big enough to serve a restaurant. "Mr. Caleb used to do a lot of entertaining. For business, of course." She grabbed a pot holder. "He is too mean to have many friends, that one." She threw Amanda a hooded look, as if trying to assess her reaction to this treasonous comment.

Amanda smiled noncommittally. She wanted to be friends with Nora, but after all, the woman had been a faithful Chandler retainer for thirty years. Amanda hadn't yet had time to sort out all the shifting alliances and conflicting loyalties in this house. For all she knew, Nora could be Caleb's spy.

Nora pulled a tray of lightly browned cinnamon rolls out of the oven. Amanda's stomach grumbled. "But now Mr. Caleb, he has a bad heart, and so Mr. Ross is in charge of business. At least, when Mr. Caleb *lets* him be in charge." She winked at Amanda. "Mr. Ross, though, he does not like entertaining very much."

"Doesn't he?" Curiosity about her new husband warred with curiosity about what one of those yummy rolls would taste like.

"He says business people are boring. That most of them are…what is the word? Phonies."

"Really?" Amanda forgot about her grumbling stomach for a moment, so surprised was she to hear such sentiments attributed to a Chandler.

"Mr. Ross, I think he is happiest when it is just the family here. Sometimes he invites workers from the winery to come for a party, or brings a pretty young lady home for dinner...."

By the look on her face, Nora had just recalled whom she was talking to. She began banging pots and pans around with what seemed unnecessary vigor.

"Now, Miss Paige, *she* was another story! Oh, how she loved to give parties, to have all her friends here. She had her faults, that girl, but she was so pretty, so full of life...."

Amanda only half heard Nora's litany of Paige's virtues. The rest of her attention was busy picturing all the attractive women Ross had apparently been accustomed to bringing here. Had he kissed all of them good-night with the same seductive passion that had sent Amanda's senses reeling? She was willing to bet that at least some of them had made it all the way down the hall to Ross's bedroom.

Jealous? Good grief, what right did she have to be jealous? After all, until two days ago, Ross had been an eligible bachelor, a grown man with adult needs and desires. It was completely unreasonable for Amanda to begrudge him any women in his past.

Besides, it wasn't as if she had any emotional claim on him herself. Purely a legal one. What did she care if Ross had made love to a thousand women before? What did it matter, as long as she had no intention of becoming number one thousand and one?

"Where *is* Mr., uh, Ross?" she asked Nora. "Have he and Jamie had breakfast already?"

"Oh, yes, a long time ago. Mr. Ross walks Jamie down the road to the school-bus stop every morning before he goes to work." Suddenly, it must have occurred to Nora that she was being derelict in her duties. "What can I make you for breakfast? A nice omelette? Pancakes? French toast?"

Oddly enough, Amanda's appetite seemed to have fizzled. Maybe she was just disappointed at missing Jamie before she left for school. But the thought of feasting on a magnificent breakfast all by herself held no appeal.

She wondered what the attractive women Ross brought home with him had preferred for breakfast. Probably half a grapefruit and a sliver of dry toast. Accompanied by a glass of champagne.

"I'll just have coffee," she told Nora. "And maybe one of those delicious-looking cinnamon rolls."

Nora poured coffee into a delicate china cup. "Those rolls are Mr. Caleb's favorite," she said with pride. "I make them special just for him."

Amanda ate one anyway.

The rest of the morning passed at a glacierlike crawl. Amanda was having a hard time adjusting to her new role as lady of leisure. Yet she couldn't come up with any potential alternatives.

The role of mother? With a pang, she admitted that becoming Jamie's mother again was going to require more time and effort than simply moving back under the same roof as her child. Jamie hadn't exactly flung herself into Amanda's arms with a glad cry of "Mommy!"

The role of wife? Hah! Although she was never going to be a real wife to Ross, Amanda had at least envisioned herself standing next to him at parties, playing the gracious hostess. Only now she'd learned that Ross didn't even *like* parties.

So she wasn't to be either his helpmate or his bedmate. Which certainly left her with a lot of free time on her hands.

By this time she'd explored most of the Chandler mansion and part of the grounds. The one place where she hadn't ventured was the upstairs wing where Caleb's bedroom was located.

His unseen presence had loomed like an ominous thundercloud ever since Amanda's arrival. Maybe it was time to sneak a peek at him, to reassure herself that Caleb was old and feeble now, that he no longer posed a threat to her. Besides, she had quick reflexes. She could always duck if necessary.

She tiptoed toward his room, feeling vaguely ridiculous. What if Nora or Ross spotted her skulking down the hall like a burglar? Problem was, she wasn't sure which room was Caleb's. She listened first, then peered cautiously around each doorway she came to.

Bingo! With a muffled gasp, Amanda dodged back out of sight the instant she glimpsed the shiny metal framework of a hospital bed. A tantalizing whiff of cinnamon drifted out of the room. Her heart was stuttering so loudly she couldn't make out a sound from inside. No hum of heart monitors, no labored breathing.

Unfortunately, Caleb's hearing was a lot sharper than hers.

"Don't just stand out there cowering in the hall, for God's sake. Come in here where I can get a look at you."

Panic lashed through her, followed by a wave of self-disgust. He was just a sick old man now. An object of pity. He and his family had already succeeded in dealing her the most devastating blow of her life. He couldn't hurt her anymore.

Amanda straightened her spine and squared her shoulders. Then she stepped into the lion's den.

In her instantaneous whirl of impressions, he was smaller than she remembered. Shrunken. His skin was nearly as pale as the sheets, and the scanty remnants of white hair barely covered his mottled scalp.

But those ruthless eyes were the same. Beneath bristly white brows, they burned bright as coals—quick, piercing and merciless as a bird of prey's.

"Well, well, well," he said in a knife-edged voice that

made her skin crawl. "If it isn't my new granddaughter-in-law. Come to take a look at the decrepit old man, have you?"

She forced herself not to wince at his uncanny bull's-eye. "I was simply passing by—"

"You were sneaking is what you were doing. Humph. Not that I'm surprised."

"I beg your pardon?" Amanda dug her nails into her palms.

"I beg your pardon?" he mimicked in a prissy voice. "You heard me, young woman. You must be pretty pleased with yourself right now."

"What are you talking about?" Amanda tried to will the muscles in her body to relax. Despite his frail physical condition, Caleb still radiated the same force field of power and determination that had terrified her three years ago.

"Don't play coy with me, missy." He wagged a skeletal finger. "I know what you're up to, and don't think I'm going to let you get away with it. You may have my grandson bamboozled—"

"I haven't bamboozled anyone." Anger ignited inside her. "Ross came to *me*, in case he didn't make that clear to you."

"Ross is an idealistic young fool," his grandfather spat out. "No doubt he only came up with this brainless idea to marry you after you batted your pretty little eyelashes and wiggled your hips at him."

Amanda exploded with a sound that was half laughter, half outrage. "You don't know what you're talking about."

"Calling me senile now, are you?"

"Hardly. But—"

"I know everything that goes on around here, and don't you forget for a minute that I'm still running the show!" His sunken cheeks had turned lobster red. "Jamie is a

Chandler. She belongs *here,* being raised by her own family."

"Yes, well, I'm a Chandler now, too." Amanda had never thought she would hear herself say *those* words. They left a sour taste in her mouth.

"Bah! Just because it says so on a piece of paper doesn't mean anything. I'm Jamie's legal guardian, and what I say goes!"

He grabbed the push-button device that apparently controlled his bed. Amanda wondered if it was time to duck.

"I may look like I've got one foot in the grave," he rasped as he fumbled with the device, "but let me tell you, my ticker's still got plenty of mileage left on it." He thrust the gadget in the air for emphasis. "As long as there's a breath left in my body, I'll see to it that Jamie never, *ever* belongs to you!"

Once again, panic sent adrenaline rushing through Amanda's bloodstream. Ross had promised they would adopt Jamie, but without Caleb's shaky signature on the legal papers, that would never happen. He'd also claimed he could persuade his grandfather. But to Amanda, that seemed about as likely as persuading the Mississippi River to run backward.

The head of Caleb's bed rose slowly, lifting him to a more upright position. His crafty eyes narrowed as if he sensed his verbal missiles had reached their target. He looked like a wolf closing in on a wounded deer.

"And don't think you'll be getting your sticky little hands on even one penny of the Chandler fortune," he growled. "I've already called my lawyers, and by the time I'm done revising my will, you'll be lucky if you're still entitled to buy a bottle of Chandler wine at the grocery store!"

Amanda rallied to produce a bitter smile. "Believe me,

the Chandler fortune is the *last* thing I'm interested in getting my hands on.''

"You won't be getting your hands on my great-granddaughter, either, no matter what some damnfool judge—"

A fit of coughing interrupted Caleb's tirade. Amanda took a step backward, hoping to make her escape before he stopped spluttering. Except that he didn't. The veins in his neck bulged alarmingly as the coughing continued.

Quickly, she moved to the bedside table and grabbed the pitcher of water on it. Caleb's wheezing grew more intense as he clawed the air. Amanda whisked the glass to his lips, slopping a little water down the front of his pajamas.

Dear God, don't let him die! she thought wildly. *I'll be the prime suspect for sure.*

Gingerly, she placed a hand against his back to brace him. Even in her panic she was amazed by how thin and brittle his sharp bones felt. As if the spasms racking his body might snap them like twigs.

After he got down a sip or two, the coughing subsided. Amanda drew her hand away and retreated a step. "Are you all right?" she asked cautiously.

He nodded once, seeming irritated. Between the diminishing coughs, he managed to choke out, "Thanks."

So Nora was wrong. He *did* know how to say thank-you.

"Granddad? You okay?" Amanda spun around to find Ross hurrying across the room, his forehead creased with concern. "I heard you while I was coming up the stairs."

"I'm fine," Caleb snapped. "Here." He shoved the glass at Amanda.

Ross's features smoothed with relief, then immediately shifted to convey surprise at finding Amanda at his grandfather's bedside. "Thanks for coming to the rescue," he said, touching her arm.

Warmth spread across her skin. Ross smiled at her, giving her an abrupt, vivid reminder of what his lips had felt like against hers last night. Amanda smiled back as a ribbon of sweet, secret longing unfurled inside her.

Caleb brought them both back to the present with a loud snort. "Quit making goo-goo eyes at each other and get out," he said. "Both of you."

Ross's blue eyes flickered with apology and amusement before he glanced back at his grandfather. "You sure you're all right? You don't want me to call the doctor?"

"For God's sake, I just had a little tickle in my throat. Quit making a federal case out of it." He snatched a pair of glasses from the tray that also held a plate speckled with cinnamon-roll crumbs. "Now beat it," he said, stabbing on the glasses. He picked up a section of newspaper and rattled it impatiently in front of his face like a screen.

Ross rolled his eyes at Amanda, who had to repress a giggle. Not that the argument preceding Caleb's coughing spell was anything to laugh about.

"I'll check in on you later, Granddad," Ross called from the doorway.

"Don't bother," came the ill-tempered reply from behind the newspaper.

"Don't mind him," Ross told Amanda as they walked down the hall. "Granddad's always humiliated by any sign of weakness. He's just trying to cover his embarrassment that you witnessed him out of control like that." They paused at the top of the staircase. "Deep down inside, he really is grateful for your assistance."

"I doubt it," Amanda said. "He probably blames me for the whole thing."

"Why would he do that?" He tented his sandy brows

in uncertainty—not a look frequently associated with Ross Chandler.

He was dressed casually for work today, in tan chino slacks and a short-sleeved polo shirt the color of blueberries. His muscular arms were tanned, sprinkled with crinkly golden hairs. Beneath his shirt, the sculpted contours of his chest stood out in bold relief.

But Amanda wasn't about to let her husband's fabulous physique distract her from the disturbing problem her altercation with Caleb had raised.

"Ross, I wasn't just passing by Caleb's room when I heard him coughing. He and I were in the midst of a…discussion when it happened."

"Oh?" His eyebrows journeyed farther toward his hairline.

"He as much as told me that he'll never consent to my adopting Jamie."

"I see." Amazing how quickly that neutral expression dropped like a curtain to hide what Ross was really thinking.

Amanda gripped the carved walnut newel at the top of the stairs. "Ross, you assured me that Caleb's objections wouldn't stand in the way of our adopting Jamie. But you haven't even brought up the subject, have you?" It was an accusation, not a question.

Ross sighed. He dragged a hand through his hair so that all the carefully trimmed strands fell every which way, like a field of wheat after a tornado. "Amanda, you've seen how stubborn my grandfather can be." He took hold of her hand and quirked his mouth in that rueful, disarming way of his. "If I don't give him a little time to adjust to our marriage first, he'll dig in his heels like a mule when I hit him with our plan to adopt Jamie."

"Plan?" Amanda wriggled her hand free and gave him a cold stare. "This is more than just a *plan*, Ross. You

gave me your word that we were going to adopt Jamie, even if Caleb was against it.''

"Look, we can't just spring this idea on Jamie, either." Ross held out his palms. "We could *all* use some time to get used to this marriage before we make any more drastic changes.''

"Drastic changes?" Amanda's voice rose along with her temper. "*You* were the one so determined to rush into marriage. We could have waited a while instead of just showing up here and dropping this bombshell. Wouldn't it have made more sense to give people a chance to adjust to our marriage *before* it took place?"

Perhaps she just imagined it, but there seemed almost a furtive, guilty quality to Ross's expression when he glanced down the stairs. Maybe he was worried that Nora might overhear this little ripple in the smooth sea of Chandler domestic life.

Well, this little ripple was going to turn into a big tidal wave if Ross tried to change the terms of their bargain. "I only agreed to marry you to get Jamie back," Amanda said, digging her nails into the newel.

Now why would Ross's mouth tighten over a simple reiteration of a fact he already knew?

Never mind. "We had a deal, and I'm not going to let you weasel out of it just because you don't have the guts to stand up to your grandfather."

Amanda regretted her words even as anger propelled them out of her mouth. She knew Ross was no coward. And she couldn't blame him for not wanting to upset an old man whose health was obviously precarious.

But damn it, they *owed* her Jamie!

Ross's expression had turned as stony as one of those hideous Beaux Arts statues presiding over the fountains in the garden.

"I gave you my word," he said, moving only the muscles required for speech. "Don't worry. I intend to keep it."

Although they both stood as rigid and motionless as those statues outside, it seemed to Amanda that the distance between them had increased. Ross somehow seemed farther away. She wanted to reach out, to draw him closer to her again. *Come back,* pleaded a tiny voice inside her head.

Yet she was the one who had pushed him away. "I'll give you a week to talk to Caleb," she said stiffly. "That way, Jamie can get used to having me around before we bring up the subject of adoption."

And what if Jamie doesn't want *you to adopt her again?* asked that same fearful voice.

Mentally, Amanda covered her ears.

"Agreed." Ross motioned downstairs as if she was one of those pesky houseguests he found it bothersome to entertain. "Nora's fixed lunch for us. Care to join me?"

Amanda preceded him down the staircase. But for the second time that day, her appetite had fled.

Chapter 6

"Those artificial caves maintain a constant fifty-eight-degree temperature. Just think what we could save on air-conditioning bills! We'd recoup our investment in no time. Ross? Ross!"

"What? Oh, sorry, Ted." Ross turned away from his office window. He was supposed to be listening to Ted Cardoza, the winery operations manager, give his latest pitch for constructing underground caves to store the wine while it aged in French oak barrels. Instead, he'd been staring out at the vineyards while he tried to figure out how to patch things up with Amanda.

"You and the new missus have a fight?"

Ross picked up one of the computer-generated graphs Ted had brought with him, trying to conceal his discomfort at the man's uncannily accurate guess. "What makes you say that?"

Ted rasped a huge beefy hand over his iron gray crew cut. "It's not like you to let your attention get sidetracked during a business meeting.'' He lowered himself onto the edge of Ross's desk. ''Only big change around here lately that might distract you is your going off and getting married. So either you were daydreaming about taking your pretty new wife to bed, or...'' He shrugged. ''Judging by the scowl on your face, you were chewing over something considerably less pleasant.''

Word spread quickly around the winery. This morning, Ross had come prepared to announce his sudden marriage only to find his employees had already heard all about it.

Apparently, word *hadn't* gotten around yet that the Chandler newlyweds occupied separate bedrooms. Or perhaps that was merely considered one of the eccentric habits of the rich.

Ross liked and respected Ted, who'd been an enormous help as Ross had gradually taken over his grandfather's role as head of Chandler Winery. Before that, Ted had been Caleb's right-hand man for years. If anyone could sympathize with Ross's dilemma, it would be Ted. But he couldn't ask for advice without revealing the real reason he'd married Amanda.

Ted clearly sensed Ross's desire to avoid delving into personal topics. ''So, what do you think?'' he asked, slapping the thick pile of documents he'd brought to support his position. ''Digging the caves will require a lot of money up front, but did I also mention we'd only have to top off the wine every four to six weeks? No air-conditioning means higher humidity means less evaporation.''

''I believe you did mention that, yes.'' Ross sat down behind his desk and stacked his hands behind his head. ''Unfortunately, it's not me you have to convince. I'm sold on the idea already, remember?''

''Caleb.'' Ted's hopeful expression turned morose. ''You think he still won't go for it, huh?''

Ross sighed. "You know what he's like any time some new idea comes along."

"But the money we'd save in the long run—"

"I know, I know." Ross picked up a pencil and tapped it on his desk. "He's suspicious of change. He's convinced the old ways are best. Tradition, he calls it. And in some instances, he's right."

"Like spending money on genuine French oak barrels instead of buying cheaper American ones."

"Exactly."

Ted gathered up his charts and figures, a hint of defeat dragging down his shoulders. "Caleb was a fine businessman in his day. But isn't it about time for him to officially retire and let you start making all the decisions?"

Ross probed his cheek with his tongue. "I'm not going to pressure my grandfather to give up control," he said finally. "The winery is what keeps him going. Being put out to pasture, as he would look at it, might very well kill him."

"Yeah, you're probably right." Ted paused on his way out the door. "But promise me you'll talk to him about the caves again, will you? Hey, I could leave these figures here for you to show him—"

Ross held up his palm. "Thanks, but no thanks." He rubbed the bridge of his nose, where a knot of tension might be signaling the start of a headache. "Look, I'll talk to him about the caves, okay? Just don't get your hopes up."

"Good luck." Ted gave him a thumbs-up gesture as he left.

Ross let out an exasperated groan and keeled forward to bang his forehead against his desk a few times like ominous clangs of a bell tolling his doom. Everyone in the world, it seemed, was urging him to change Caleb's mind about *something*.

Unfortunately, years of aggravating experience had taught Ross what a frustrating, futile struggle it generally was to drag his grandfather around to a different way of thinking.

Ross was far more concerned about persuading Caleb to allow Jamie's adoption than he was about pushing Ted's campaign for the caves. What if his grandfather refused to consent to the adoption? Ross had assured Amanda that he could handle Caleb. But deep down inside, he didn't feel nearly the confidence he'd claimed during his desperate attempt to woo her into marriage.

Caleb had made it all too clear in the past that he would stop at nothing to keep Jamie firmly within the Chandler domain. It would require ironclad logic on Ross's part, not to mention skilled diplomacy and maybe a threat or two, to convince Caleb to loosen the legal ties that bound Jamie to him.

And if Caleb didn't allow the adoption…if Amanda ever discovered how he'd bribed the judge…if she decided that reopening the custody case was her only chance to become Jamie's legal mother again…

Ross shuddered. He sprang to his feet and returned to the window. From this position, all he could see of the house was a portion of its slate roof.

What if they couldn't adopt Jamie, but Amanda never learned about the bribery? Would she settle for living under the same roof as Jamie if that was the only way she could be part of her daughter's life?

Ross figured she probably would. Especially after he'd seen the magnitude of love and devotion that glowed on Amanda's face whenever she looked at Jamie. If worse came to worst, he couldn't imagine Amanda would call off their marriage, pack her bags and walk out of the Chandler mansion without her child.

But Ross had made her a promise. He'd gotten her

hopes up. If he couldn't fix it so they adopted Jamie, Amanda would be devastated. She would never forgive Ross for not living up to his half of their agreement.

And that was what bothered him most about this whole wretched mess.

A whoosh of exhaust from a passing truck whipped Amanda's hair. She and Nora were standing next to the road at the entrance to the winery, waiting for Jamie's school bus to appear.

Amanda had invited herself along once she learned this was Nora's daily errand. "If you meet Jamie here to walk her home every afternoon," she asked when the noise of the truck had receded, "doesn't that mean leaving Caleb all alone in the house for a while?"

"Oh, Mr. Caleb is the one who insists that someone be here to meet Jamie," Nora replied. "He is very protective of his little *princesa*."

Humph. Well, Amanda could hardly fault him for *that*. "But what if…something happens while you're not there? His heart, or—or…" She thought of this morning's coughing fit.

Nora gave her a measured glance as if trying to figure out why Amanda was so concerned about Caleb's health. But all Amanda was concerned with was learning more about the inner workings of the Chandler household.

"He is not so helpless as he seems," Nora said finally. "Mostly he needs me there so he has someone to complain to. Someone to wait on him hand and foot." Her lips pinched as if she was trying to conquer a smile. Plainly, she was a lot fonder of Caleb than she let on. "Besides, Mr. Ross gave him some kind of fancy gadget so that all he has to do is press a button, and the paramedics, they will be there like that." She snapped her fingers.

"I see."

Nora wore a sweater even though the day was pleasant and springlike. It seemed the definition of cold weather was different here in California than it had been back east.

The warmth of the sun felt good on Amanda's face. A breeze lifted her hair, carrying the scents of rich, dark earth and lots of growing things. It was a beautiful day, and she was waiting for her daughter to come home. For the first time in years, a seedling of pure, uncomplicated happiness took root inside her.

"Here comes the bus," Nora said, pointing.

Anticipation began to build inside Amanda. She still hadn't adjusted to the incredible fact that Jamie was with her again. Though she could hardly begrudge the hours Jamie spent in school, she could hardly wait for her to come home. There was so much she wanted to share with her little girl, to learn about her. So much catching up to do.

Amanda hugged herself as the bus lumbered to a stop. She started rehearsing all the questions she'd once thought she would never be able to ask her child. How was school today? What did you learn? Whom did you eat lunch with and play with at recess?

The bus door folded open with a metallic thud. Jamie jumped out. Amanda's heart soared with joy.

Then she saw Jamie's face.

As the bus pulled away, Jamie just stood there, her backpack drooping off one shoulder, her chin trembling. Her eyes were pink and puffy. She sniffled once, then burst into tears.

Amanda was already moving toward her when Jamie broke into a run. "Nora," she sobbed, "Nora, Mr. Peepers died!"

Her backpack slid from her arm. It landed near Amanda's feet as Jamie flew past, long blond hair streaming behind her. She hurled herself into Nora's waiting arms.

"When we got to school today, he was *dead!*" Jamie's voice broke on the last word, sending her headlong into another cascade of sobs.

Nora clasped her to the comforting shelter of her bosom. "Ah, you poor little one...I am so sorry, *cariña*...."

Amanda covered her mouth and stood numb with shock. *Dead?* Dear heavens. "Who...?" She lowered her hand. "Was Mr. Peepers her teacher?" she whispered to Nora.

Nora shook her head as she tenderly stroked Jamie's hair. "He was a hamster," she said. "At school. He belonged to their class." Muffled wails emerged from within the folds of her sweater. "There, there, don't cry, *angelita*. Nora is here...."

Relief took the edge off Amanda's shock. Her heart went out to Jamie for the loss of her class pet, but at least she hadn't lost another person she loved.

Now that the numbness had worn off, pain seeped into the corners of Amanda's heart. She could hardly miss the significance of the fact that Jamie had instinctively run to Nora for comfort instead of to her.

Her arms fairly ached to console her child. But she knew any overture would be rejected. Jamie had made it plain the person she considered a member of her family and the one who was still a stranger.

"Come, Jamie." Nora tucked the little girl under her arm and began to walk back to the house. "When we get home, I will bake you a *big* batch of your favorite peanut butter cookies!"

Jamie pushed a tangle of hair from her eyes, smearing her cheek with tears. "With chocolate chips in them?" she asked in a tiny voice.

"Of course! That is how you like them, *¿no es verdad?*"

Jamie nodded, sniffing.

"Maybe you would like to take some to school tomorrow to share with your class. I bet everyone there is feeling sad about Mr. Peepers, yes?"

"My teacher, Mrs. Morrison, says we can have a funeral for him."

"What a good idea! You can bring cookies, and maybe someone else will bring some punch, and..."

Amanda felt close to tears herself. She was struggling so hard not to feel jealous or resentful or hurt. But it was no use. Ignored and forgotten, she trailed behind Nora and Jamie, clutching the straps of Jamie's abandoned backpack.

"There you are." Ross found Amanda standing alone on the veranda, gazing through the darkness at the silvery outline of low hills across the valley. "You disappeared so quickly after we put Jamie to bed, I couldn't figure out where you'd gone." It had crossed his mind that perhaps she was deliberately avoiding him in order to escape a repeat of last night's kiss outside her bedroom door.

She rubbed her hands up and down her bare arms and gave him a halfhearted smile. "This place is so big, it's no wonder people have trouble finding each other." The distant glow from a lamp in the garden touched her face with gold, made her seem as if she were illuminated from within.

Ross braced his elbows behind him on the balustrade and leaned back to study her. The way he would study a fine work of art—a magnificent statue, a beautiful painting.

"You've been awfully quiet all evening," he said. "Is something wrong?"

Light flickered in her dark eyes like a reflection of the evening star just before she looked away from him again. "Nothing's wrong. I'm just...overwhelmed, I guess.

About all the sudden changes in my life. All the adjustments I have to make.''

Ross sensed she was dancing around the real reason, occasionally brushing up against the truth. Funny. He'd only actually known her a few days, yet it felt much longer.

''Gee, I don't know why you'd feel overwhelmed,'' he said, hoping to cajole her out of her somber mood. ''Just because in the past few days you've married a man you barely know, quit your job, moved clear across country to live with a bunch of strangers and been reunited with a child you haven't seen in over three years.''

She turned those alluring eyes on him again, and this time he saw a glint of humor. '''What I Did on My Summer Vacation,''' she said. Then she went back to gazing across the valley.

Ross felt an impulse to take the tip of his finger and trace it slowly down her exquisite profile. Looking at her somehow wasn't enough. He wanted to feel her heart beating beneath his hands, to bury his face in her hair and smell her sweet scent, to crush his lips to hers and taste—

Whoa there.

And what would you do afterward? he asked himself. *Cuddle up next to her in bed and tell her some more lies?*

''Is it what we talked about this morning?'' he asked. ''Are you worried that Granddad won't agree to the adoption?'' Ross hadn't meant to bring the subject up again until he had to. But darn it, Amanda looked so unhappy...he had to find out what was bothering her.

She hugged her arms against her ribs. ''You gave me your word,'' she said mildly. ''I've no reason to think you'll go back on it.''

''Well...good.'' Amanda's trust in him should have been a sign of progress. Unfortunately, it was also misplaced. She wouldn't trust him to take out the garbage if she ever learned the reason he'd married her. "You're cold," he said. "Would you like me to bring you a sweater?"

"Hmm? Oh, no. No, thank you." Even as she spoke, Ross could see goose bumps break out on her skin. She shivered.

So he moved behind her to rub his hands briskly up and down her arms. She stiffened at first, opened her mouth to protest. But gradually, she relaxed enough to lean back against him a little. The resulting heat that flowed through Ross's body wasn't due to friction.

He smelled her hair. Roses? Lilacs? Violets, maybe? An intoxicating bouquet, whatever it was.

Her skin was as soft and smooth as satin. Beneath his hands, her bones felt as delicate and fragile as a bird's. Once more, that overpowering urge to protect her came over Ross. He wished he could soothe away all her troubles as easily as he could banish the chill from her body.

If only he could make her smile, it would be a start. "*I* know why you were so quiet during dinner," he teased, almost but not quite nuzzling her ear. "I'll bet you were thinking about poor Mr. Peepers."

To his surprise, Amanda went rigid.

Ross hesitated, then continued rubbing her arms. "That's not really it, is it? I mean, I know Jamie was upset, but I think she's already getting over it, and..." He stopped. Her shoulders were shaking. "Amanda...?" Ross wheeled her around. "You're not crying, are you?"

She ducked her head and brought a hand to her mouth.

"Holy cow, you *are* crying! Amanda, honey, he was only a hamster! A very *old* hamster! I saw him myself a few weeks ago at the school open house, and believe me, that hamster had a good, long life. He was like the Methuselah of hamsterdom."

Ross coaxed her into his arms, helplessly patting her

back until the sobs subsided. "Come here and sit down," he said gently, leading her over to a cushioned bench. He kept an arm wrapped around her shoulders as he tilted up her chin with the crook of his finger. "Come on now, honey. What's this really all about?"

"Oh, Ross." Her face crumpled as if she was about to cry again, but she regained control of herself. Her eyes still glittered with tears. "This afternoon—I went with Nora to meet Jamie at the bus stop."

"Uh-huh…" he said encouragingly, smoothing her hair back from her face.

"And when Jamie got off the bus, she was so upset about Mr. Peepers she started to cry, and I wanted to comfort her and hug her, but she—she ran to Nora instead!" Amanda's lovely face dissolved in another flood of tears.

"Oh, Amanda. Sweetheart…" Ross drew her into the shelter of his embrace once more. He rocked her gently back and forth, trying to give her the comfort she'd so wanted to offer Jamie earlier that day.

Compassion stabbed his heart in a painful thrust. He loved Jamie like his own child. He could imagine what it would feel like if she rejected him for someone else.

"Amanda, it's going to take time," he murmured. "Jamie hasn't seen you since she was four years old. But Nora has been part of her life every single day."

"I know, I know," Amanda said into the front of his shirt. "It just gave me such a jolt." She lifted her head and wiped tears from her cheeks. "Jamie used to run to *me* when she was little, whenever she got scared or her feelings were hurt or she fell and scraped her knee. It was so automatic this afternoon for me to reach out and want to comfort her." She inhaled a deep, quivering breath. "It was an awful blow to discover that it wasn't still automatic for *her*."

Ross hugged her shoulders. "It will be again someday. Don't worry."

"It's just…I carried this picture of her in my head all these years, and even though I expected her to have changed *physically,* I wasn't prepared for all the *emotional* changes." The edge of her mouth hitched in a crooked smile. "I guess I thought it would be easy to step right back into the role I used to play. I forgot that Jamie herself might have something to say about it."

"Jamie's going to be thrilled to have you for her mother again. Just wait and see."

"I hope you're right."

Without even thinking about it, Ross pressed a kiss to her temple. "Of course I'm right."

Then, because it felt so natural, he kissed her cheek.

From there, it was only a short journey to her lips.

He took it slowly at first. He knew he shouldn't be kissing her at all, but Amanda didn't seem to mind. Her lips were soft and fluttery as butterfly wings. He caressed her hair with his fingertips, brushed his mouth against hers again…again…and again.

"Mmm," he whispered between their lips. "You're so beautiful, Amanda…."

He touched her tongue with his. A needle of incandescent heat quivered inside him like an electric filament. Savoring every exquisite sensation, he joined his mouth more firmly to hers, exploring, tasting, craving more and more of her. The electricity inside him burned hotter, brighter.

She was so soft, so warm, so sweet! Ross plunged his hands through her hair and let the gossamer strands sift through his fingers.

A tiny moan caught in Amanda's throat, and that faint sound was enough to make him dizzy. He was drunk with her, that's what he was. Why else would he be behaving so recklessly?

He brought his hand to her breast. Her flesh molded warmly against his palm so that her racing heartbeat was transmitted through his fingertips.

Oh, how he wanted her! Like no other woman he'd ever known before. Were his feelings for her real? Or was the desire that clawed frantically at his belly simply due to the fact that she was forbidden to him?

With Amanda's mouth moving eagerly beneath his, her body arching against him and the swell of her breast filling his hand, it took some effort for Ross to recall the reason she was off-limits.

Then, from the murky, passion-muddled depths of his brain, he dredged up the reason. It was called honor.

He'd been forced to deceive Amanda in order to keep his family intact. But that was no excuse to take advantage of her.

Reluctantly, Ross removed his hand from her breast.

Amanda felt a momentary pull inside her, perhaps the ebb of disappointment or the tug of loss. Desire clamored inside her like an impatient child, begging to be satisfied. Tonight when Ross had kissed her, she hadn't hesitated, hadn't stopped to assess the nature of her own reaction. She'd responded entirely by instinct. And instinct had led her straight into his arms, toward that thrilling promise of secret delights shared between a man and a woman.

Between husband and wife.

After all, that's what they were, weren't they? So how could it be wrong to submit to the seductive curve of his mouth, the heavenly touch of his hands? To be swept away by the trembling excitement that bubbled and boiled inside her till the heat of it practically scalded her...?

She'd never known desire could feel like this. With Paul, she'd felt safe. Pleasantly content. But with Ross, she felt wild and out of control. She tasted the spice of danger. And she would never be content until the churning hunger within her was sated by the one man who'd stirred such unsuspected passion within her, the man who'd plucked and played her till she was humming at a fever pitch of excitement. The man who even now was breaking off their kiss and pulling away from her.

Amanda gazed up at him in confusion, feeling heavy lidded, drugged.

"Darling." Ross brought his forehead to rest against hers. "Perhaps this isn't wise...."

What? Necking on the porch like a couple of teenagers? Or did he mean...?

"You said it yourself. We already have so many... complications to deal with." Ross slid his hand to the side of her face and absently stroked her jaw with his thumb. "So many new situations to get used to and sort out." He peered into her eyes. "Don't you think it's best that we not add another one right away?"

So that's what this was. A *situation*. A *complication*.

For a few crazy moments there, she'd thought it might be a marriage.

Well, she certainly wasn't going to beg Ross to make love to her. Not after extracting his solemn vow that he never would.

"You're absolutely right," Amanda said. She forced herself to laugh as she edged away from him, trying to restore some order to her hair by combing it with her fingers. "Amazing what a little wine and moonlight can lead to, isn't it?"

Ross shifted his weight and frowned, looking as if he was about to disagree.

"Well, I'm going up to bed." Amanda winced internally. In the cooling aftermath of the heated embrace they'd just shared, even the most innocent statement came out sounding suggestive. "I'll see you in the morning," she clarified, just in case it needed spelling out.

As she backed away, his voice drifted out of the shadows, his face unseen. "Good night, Amanda."

She hurried upstairs, shut the door to her room and braced herself back against it. As if she feared Ross might be hot on her heels, ready to claim his husbandly rights after all.

She needn't have worried. That was her pulse she heard pounding, not pursuing footsteps.

No use trying to pretend that that little aching hollow behind her breastbone wasn't disappointment. But something else nudged up against her heart, too.

Hope.

Darling. Ross had called her *darling*. Hadn't there even been a *honey* or two thrown in there this evening?

Amanda was hardly the voice of experience, but she suspected such words didn't tumble so easily from the lips of a man like Ross. Didn't that indicate at least *some* deep emotion behind those endearments?

She raised her left hand and thoughtfully studied her wedding ring. Maybe, by some miracle, there was actually a chance they could have a real marriage someday.

Chapter 7

The next morning, Amanda rose bright and early and actually made it to breakfast on time. The rich, dark fragrance of gourmet coffee filled the sunroom.

"Good morning," Ross said. As he poured her a cup, he greeted her with a smile that warmed her insides quicker than the coffee could have.

"Hi, Amanda," Jamie said brightly. Amanda felt her heart swell with that potent blend of love, amazement and gratitude that swept over her each time she laid eyes on her little girl.

"Morning, sweetie." She pulled out a chair and sat next to Jamie.

"Nora made pancakes this morning, 'specially for me, 'cause she said I needed cheering up about Mr. Peepers."

"Well, wasn't that nice of her?" Amanda felt Ross's gaze on her as she attempted to banish any lingering jealousy from her tone. She ought to be glad, not resentful, that Nora had such a close, caring relationship with Jamie.

"You can have some, too," Jamie said generously, pushing the platter of pancakes in Amanda's direction.

"Why, thank you! I believe I will." She speared a pancake onto her plate.

"Butter?" Ross set the butter knife back onto the dish and slid it across the table.

"Just syrup, thanks." She helped herself to the contents of a small ceramic pitcher. No plastic bottles in *this* house. She had to admit, though, all these luxurious little touches were rather nice.

Jamie popped a bite of pancake into her mouth. "Only ten more days of school!" she crowed happily.

"That still doesn't mean you can talk with your mouth full," Ross told her with a wink that took any sting out of his words.

"Oops! Sorry." She covered her mouth and rolled her eyes sheepishly.

"What are you going to do all summer?" Amanda asked.

Jamie swallowed before replying. "I'm going to take swimming lessons and go horseback riding and play soccer. Oh, yeah, and go to art class."

"My goodness!" Amanda raised her eyebrows even as her heart sank. "Such a busy schedule." One that certainly wouldn't allow much quality mother-daughter time for the two of them to get reacquainted.

Ross cleared his throat and dabbed his mouth with a napkin. "It sounds like a lot, but it's only weekday mornings," he explained. "Our problem is that we don't have anyone to look after Jamie full-time when she's not in school. I'm at work, Granddad is bedridden, and it's not fair to ask Nora to watch Jamie all day on top of doing the rest of her work."

Jamie lowered her glass, leaving a milk mustache outlining her upper lip. "I can watch myself," she announced helpfully.

"So…" Ross sent her a look of mock sternness. "Jamie and I sat down and worked out this plan together. This way she can be with her friends in the morning, and Nora can keep an eye on her in the afternoons." His voice took on a teasing tone. "And who knows, by the end of the summer, Jamie may actually learn how to swim."

"I already *know* how to swim!"

Ross grinned at the indignation in her voice. "I meant something besides the dog paddle."

"Oh."

Amanda had wadded the napkin in her lap into a crumpled ball. What about *her?* She was supposed to be Jamie's *mother,* for heaven's sake. Wasn't she considered competent to look after her own child?

In all fairness, of course, these plans must have been made before Ross came up with the idea of asking her to marry him. Still, she couldn't quite keep the injury out of her voice. "*I* could watch Jamie in the afternoons," she pointed out.

"Of course you can," Ross said swiftly. "But I didn't know—that is, we made these arrangements before—"

"I understand." No point in making him spell out the abrupt, unconventional circumstances of their marriage in front of Jamie.

Hmm. Maybe this child-care dilemma was the real reason Ross had asked her to marry him. But then…oh, never mind. What did it matter anyway? For better or worse, she was going to be Ross's wife from now on. Jamie's mother. Now that Amanda had made the commitment, there didn't seem much point in speculating about any hidden motives Ross might have originally had.

She hadn't foreseen the intimacy, the…attraction that had unexpectedly developed between them. In light of where it might lead, the future course of their marriage seemed far more significant than digging into the past to examine its roots.

"I've got an idea." Ross reached over to refill Amanda's coffee cup. "How about if the three of us take a trip to San Francisco this Saturday? Sort of a family outing."

"Yay!" Jamie bounced up and down in her chair.

Amanda's response was more subdued but no less enthusiastic. "That sounds marvelous." She held Ross's inquiring gaze for a few seconds longer than necessary, to let him know she appreciated his effort to help both her and Jamie adjust to their new status as a family.

His return smile etched crinkles at the corners of his eyes. So radiantly blue, those eyes. So warm. So sexy.

He made a ledge of his hand and propped his chin on it. "Have you ever been to San Francisco?"

"Hmm? Oh, no. No, I haven't." She sipped her coffee. From what she'd heard, though, it was one of the most romantic cities in the world.

"*I* want to go to Alcatraz," Jamie said, eyes sparkling in ghoulish anticipation. "And see where they locked up all those bad guys."

Her daughter's perspective on San Francisco's appeal was so different from her own, Amanda had to laugh.

Ross chuckled as they shared an amused glance. The mellow sound sent little ripples of pleasure along her nerve endings. "We'll have to get an early start if we're going to fit in a boat trip out to Alcatraz," he said.

"Can we see the sea lions? And drive down that crookedy street? And ride the cable cars?"

"Sure!" Ross winked at Amanda. "Jamie herself has been to San Francisco a time or two as you can perhaps tell."

"You'll have to show me all the sights, then." Amanda

impulsively squeezed her daughter's hand. So much bigger than the chubby little hand that used to snuggle so easily into hers...

Instinctively, she let go before Jamie began to fidget. At least she hadn't rejected the small display of affection, though.

Hope took another step forward inside Amanda's heart. She would have to take it slow, but she was daring to have confidence that eventually she could win Jamie over. That someday she would truly have her child back in every sense of the word.

She sneaked a peek at her handsome husband. Who knows? Maybe she would even wind up with more than she'd bargained for.

Puzzled, Ross followed the sound of pounding down the hall. Had the house sprung a leak since breakfast, or developed some other problem requiring repair?

He traced the noise to the closed door of the room he used for his home office. He frowned, not too happy about the idea of some workman alone in there with all those confidential business files.

He opened the door, displeasure creasing his brow. Then he pulled up short. "Amanda!"

Caught in midswing, she froze with the hammer drawn back over her shoulder, her pretty mouth forming an O of surprise. "Ross! What are you doing here?" She lowered the hammer, clearly flustered. "I mean, I didn't expect you till—you usually eat lunch at work."

"I thought it would be nice to have lunch together. Just the two of us." He walked slowly into the room, still trying to figure out what she'd been up to. He knew she probably resented the mansion, but still, taking a hammer to it seemed a bit extreme. Then he noticed the painting propped against his desk. "The seascape I bought in Nantucket!"

Amanda nudged a strand of hair off her forehead with her wrist. "They delivered it this morning. You'd mentioned you thought it would look good in your office, so I thought I'd surprise you by hanging it before you got home, but..." Her shoulders sagged, along with the edges of her mouth. "I'm sorry. I should have asked you first, before I started pounding nails into the walls."

"No, no—don't be silly." Ross was touched by her thoughtfulness. "This is your house, too, now. You don't need to ask permission to hang a picture, for Pete's sake." He took the hammer dangling from her hand. "But you could have called a handyman to do it for you. Nora has the phone number of a good, reliable one."

Amusement replaced the doubt in Amanda's dark eyes. "I was an art gallery manager for two years, remember?" She took back the hammer. "Believe me, I've hung a picture or two in my day. No need to call in the marines." With a couple of expert whacks, she finished the job to her satisfaction. "There! Want to help me hang the painting?"

Ross realized this was yet another quality he admired about his wife—her self-sufficiency. Her practical attitude. The no-nonsense way she rolled up her sleeves and plunged into the project at hand, whether it was hanging a picture or marrying a man she had every reason to despise.

Though hopefully she didn't despise him anymore.

He grasped one side of the frame, and together they lifted the seascape into place. Amanda stepped back to study it with a critical eye, leaning forward several times to make minute adjustments to its position, which already looked perfectly straight to Ross.

Finally, she folded her arms and stood beside him, contemplating the painting itself. "It's truly exceptional, isn't it?" she said after a moment.

"Magnificent," Ross replied, letting himself become part of the painting. He could almost smell the fresh, salty air, taste the spray on his face, feel the up-and-down swell of the waves as he stood on the deck of the nineteenth-century sailing vessel.

"Look at how the artist directs your eye toward the horizon," Amanda said, pointing, "so that there's a sense of motion, of excitement."

"Makes you eager to find out what lies just beyond it."

"Yes, exactly!" Amanda beamed at him. "This was always one of my favorites at the gallery."

"It appears we have similar tastes in art, then."

Her eyebrows hoisted a fraction of an inch, revealing mild surprise at this discovery. "I guess so."

As much as Ross enjoyed the painting, it couldn't hold a candle to the pleasure of looking at Amanda's face. "When I was a kid, I always dreamed of going to sea," he told her. Then he wondered why on earth *that* particular revelation had popped out of his mouth.

"Did you?" Amanda had a way of giving a person her complete attention so that you felt like you were the most fascinating, special person on earth. "What was it about the sea that appealed to you?"

Ross thought back. "The freedom, I suppose. The sense of never being tied down anywhere." He chuckled. "Maybe it was a reaction to growing up in a family with such deep roots in solid ground."

Amanda pursed her lips. "You did have an awfully heavy heritage for a kid to carry around."

"One summer, I even built a raft, just like Huck Finn, and tried to sail it down the Napa River."

"How far did you get?"

"The damn thing sank before I could even hop onto it."

A peal of laughter chimed from Amanda's slender throat. "Maybe you were destined to be a landlubber after all."

Ross grinned. "Maybe." He drew her hand through his arm. "Come on. I'll buy you lunch. I know a great place where the food's delicious and the price is right."

He savored the gentle pressure when Amanda squeezed his arm playfully. "I'll bet it's close by, too."

"Lucky for us I was able to get a reservation." Ross escorted his wife to the sunroom, where Nora had soup and sandwiches waiting for them.

He couldn't believe how soon it was time for him to go back to work.

Jamie's eyes grew round as saucers as she stared in awe at the display model in the museum gift shop. "Look! That's the same boat *we* were on!"

Earlier that afternoon, the three of them had toured the *Balclutha,* a three-masted sailing ship berthed near San Francisco's Maritime Museum. Amanda didn't know whether Jamie or Ross had had the most fun, exploring the historic vessel's wooden interior and examining all the old ship's relics on display.

Now Jamie's eyes shone with hopeful pleading as she tore her gaze from a box containing a *Balclutha* model kit. "Can I buy it, Uncle Ross? Please?"

Ross took his hand from the pocket of his suede bomber jacket and thoughtfully stroked his jaw. "I don't know, James. That depends on how much of your allowance money you've got left."

Her face fell. She rubbed one sneaker-clad foot against the other. "I thought…maybe…you could buy it for me."

"Hmm." He winked at Amanda over the top of Jamie's drooping blond head. "Well, Christmas is still a long way off. Maybe for your birthday."

"But my birthday's not till October!" she wailed.

Ross tugged playfully on her long ponytail. "Sorry, James. Guess you'll just have to wait a while."

"Oh, okay," she mumbled. Her lower lip pushed out as she trailed Ross and Amanda out of the gift shop, dragging her feet as if she were hauling an anchor behind her. But when they reached the foot of the Hyde Street Pier, right next to Fisherman's Wharf, her gloomy mood lifted miraculously. "Look! A clown!" A street performer surrounded by a crowd of children was juggling colorful balls while he regaled them with a story. "Can I go see him?" Jamie begged.

"Sure!" Ross pointed to a vacant bench. "We'll be waiting right over there."

Jamie's ponytail danced behind her as she raced over to the clown. Amanda followed Ross to the bench next to the railing overlooking the water.

The morning's fog and low clouds had lifted from the majestic towers of the Golden Gate Bridge, giving them a picture-postcard view of the bay. Popcorn clouds scudded across the blue skies, propelled by a no-nonsense breeze that made it jacket weather even in the sun.

Amanda nearly groaned with pleasure as she collapsed next to Ross. "I don't know about you, but my feet are killing me," she said, thankful that she'd had the foresight to follow Jamie's example and wear sneakers.

Ross draped his arm along the back of the bench, barely grazing Amanda's shoulders. "Where do kids get all their energy anyhow?" he asked. "I feel like I've spent the day working on a chain gang, but Jamie acts as if she could run up to the top of Coit Tower three or four times without even breathing hard."

Amanda smiled. She was worn out, it was true, but she couldn't remember the last time she'd had so much fun. Spending the day with Ross and Jamie had been everything she could have hoped for. She hunched her shoulders in a surge of pure happiness, remembering how Jamie had nonchalantly slipped her hand into Amanda's when they'd crossed a busy street.

"Cold?" Ross misinterpreted her gesture and rubbed his hand briskly up and down the arm of her sweater. Amanda didn't bother to correct him. "Is that better?" he asked.

"Oh, yes," she murmured. "Much better." She scooted a little closer to him. Bold, she thought. Very bold.

She drew in a deep breath, inhaling the tangy scent of fish and brine. The delicious aroma of garlic and basil wafted by, making her mouth water. Somewhere nearby, an Italian restaurant must be starting its dinner preparations.

A seagull landed on the railing behind them, clung briefly, then took off again with a plaintive squawk. Amanda found the entire scene enchanting. Exotic.

Through the parade of people strolling along the waterfront, she glimpsed Jamie watching the clown with fascination. Something the clown said or did prompted her to smile and clap her hands.

A shaft of love speared through Amanda, as sharp and dazzling as the sun's rays. No doubt about it. She and Ross had the most beautiful little girl in the world.

On impulse, she turned her head and kissed him.

His arm tightened around her, pulling her close against him. His mouth was warm and welcoming. Pleasure uncurled inside her even as she broke the quick kiss, surprised by what she'd done.

So was Ross, obviously. "What was that for?" he asked with one of his bone-melting smiles. His eyes were puzzled yet pleased.

"I just...felt like it," Amanda replied. She peered at him through the screen of her lashes. "Anything wrong with that?"

"Absolutely not." He slid his hand up and down her sleeve again. Slowly. The way he was looking at her made Amanda's stomach flutter, made her heart speed up. Made her feel as if they were the only two people in the world.

She might have kept staring up into those hypnotic, sexy blue eyes forever if she hadn't finally broken the spell to check on Jamie.

Now the clown was twisting balloons into animals, to the delight of his young audience.

Amanda leaned back against Ross's arm, almost—but not quite—snuggling against him. "There's something I've noticed that I've been meaning to mention to you," she said.

"Whatever it is, I promise I'll change it," he said quickly.

Amanda smiled. "It's nothing bad."

"In that case, I promise I'll keep doing it." He criss-crossed his heart with a finger.

She reached up to brush a lock of windblown hair out of his eyes. "I just wanted to tell you how much I admire the way you treat Jamie."

He caught her hand and clasped it in his. "What do you mean?"

Heat traveled up her arm and spread through her entire body. "I mean the way you don't spoil her, or give her any special privileges just because you can afford to."

"You mean the hard-hearted way I refused to buy that ship's model for her?"

"That, and other things, too." Amanda glanced down at their joined hands. "For instance, the way Jamie takes the bus to school instead of having someone drive her."

"Like a chauffeur in a limousine?"

"Exactly." She nodded, then realized Ross was teasing. She rolled her eyes and good-naturedly tried to yank her hand from his. "Go ahead and make fun if you want, but that's about what I expected."

Ross kept a firm grip on her fingers. "Did you figure she'd have her own personal maid to help her get dressed in the morning? A servant to push her on the swings at the playground? A butler to do her homework?"

"Cut it out," she said, laughing. "I bet lots of wealthy children have all that and more."

Amanda graciously let Ross win the tussle over her hand. His grin faded as he turned over her palm and began to trace lazy circles on it with his finger. "I guess it's always been pretty important to me that Jamie have a normal childhood like any other kid."

Amanda forced herself to pay attention and not get distracted by the delicious sensations his spiraling touch was arousing. "You mean, you don't want Jamie to feel different from other kids just because your family has lots of money."

Ross nodded. "Yeah. Especially when I look back at how Paige and I were raised."

"And how was that?"

His gaze focused somewhere off in the distance, though Amanda knew he wasn't seeing the crowded hills of San Francisco or the gulls swooping over the bay. "I guess I mentioned that our parents died when we were kids."

"When you were eleven, and Paige was three."

Ross glanced back at her briefly, as if surprised she remembered. "My grandfather raised us after that." Once again, he was looking at something far, far away. "Family is very important to Granddad, and I know he meant well, but the fact is, he would never have won any parent-of-the-year awards."

Amanda nearly groaned at the thought of two innocent orphans at the mercy of that ill-tempered, domineering tyrant. Wisely, she kept her mouth shut.

"He was too consumed with business. Too impatient to give us much attention. To make up for it, he gave us *things*."

"Material possessions, you mean?"

"Whatever we wanted. All we had to do was pester him long enough. It was undoubtedly easier for him to say yes than to keep refusing. Eventually, he didn't even bother refusing. Saved time, I guess."

"Sounds like every child's dream," Amanda murmured.

Ross snorted. "Yeah. Except I would gladly have given away every extravagant toy I owned if he'd spent one single afternoon playing catch with me."

Amanda squeezed Ross's hand. In his voice, she could plainly hear the sad echo of the lonely, neglected boy he'd once been. "What about Paige?" she asked gently.

His mouth tightened. "It was worse for Paige in a way," he said. "She was too young to remember our mom and dad. Granddad was the only parent she'd ever known. And he spoiled her rotten."

Amanda thought back to the two periods of contact she'd had with Paige Chandler. First, during Paige's pregnancy, while they were arranging the adoption and preparing for Jamie's birth. Then, years later, the custody battle. Of course, they'd had phalanxes of lawyers between them most of that time. Still, Paige's flamboyant personality wasn't the type to be eclipsed beneath layers of courtroom decorum or the conservative, judge-pleasing outfits that Amanda was certain she'd only worn under protest.

Spoiled rotten was an accurate way to describe her all right.

"She was stubborn and headstrong," Ross continued. "Yet I think, deep down inside, she was terribly insecure." He sighed. "She surrounded herself with people because she was afraid of being alone. And she behaved like a flighty, immature child because she was afraid of the responsibilities of adulthood.''

How *could* that dim-witted judge have awarded custody to someone so clearly unsuited to be a mother? Beneath the peaceful surface of Amanda's contented mood, resentment began to simmer. Resentment at Paige. At the judge. And at Ross, for refusing to stand up in court and say what he'd just said to her.

For Jamie's sake, Amanda did her best to clamp a lid on her simmering emotions. All that was history now. Paige was dead. The judge had gone on to other cases. Ross had kept silent for the sake of family loyalty.

What mattered now was that they were trying to build a *new* family. And dredging up past injustices would only make that tricky endeavor even more difficult.

But there was one more thing Amanda needed to know. A question that had tortured her in the past and still bewildered her. Might as well ask Ross right now, so she could bury it forever along with her other grudges.

"Something I've never understood..." she said hesitantly.

"Yes?" Ross's face was still clouded by that troubled, introspective gloom that seemed to drift over his rugged features whenever the subject of Paige came up. Amanda had assumed it was grief, but now she wondered whether there wasn't some guilt mixed in, as well.

Guilt about what, though? That he hadn't been able to guide his younger sister into responsible adulthood? That the wild, reckless behavior that had ultimately led to her death was somehow *his* fault?

Amanda gripped his hand tightly. "You were only a child yourself, Ross. You're not to blame for the way Paige turned out, for the way she chose to live."

A smile glimmered distantly on his lips before vanishing. "It's so hard to watch someone you love totally screw up her life. Like seeing a car wreck that you're helpless to prevent take place in slow motion right before your eyes.''

He grimaced at the unfortunate imagery. No doubt he'd replayed the accident that had killed Paige a thousand times in his head.

"She was drunk when she died," he mused softly, pain creasing his forehead. "Along with everyone else in the car."

"I'm so sorry," Amanda whispered.

"She was always taking crazy chances like that. She thought she would live forever, I guess. Or..." He frowned. "Maybe she was afraid she *would* die young, like our parents did, and that's why she seemed so desperate to grab as much fun and excitement as she could." He stared down at the ground and kneaded his forehead. When he looked back at Amanda, the lines of pain had faded. "Sorry," he said with a sympathetic smile. "I know the last person on earth you want to hear me ramble on about is Paige."

"It's all right." Amanda was touched that Ross had opened up to her, that he'd been willing to share his secret sorrow. She hoped that by listening, she'd eased his burden some. "What I wanted to ask you concerns Paige, in fact."

"Does it?" He lifted his brows.

"It's something that's baffled me ever since her lawyers informed me she was going to sue for custody of Jamie." Amanda closed her eyes, recalling the horror of that long-ago moment when all the dry legalese had sunk in.

She could lose her child.

And in the end, she did.

With a shudder, she reminded herself that she had Jamie back now. Nothing else mattered.

She opened her eyes. "I suppose you know the circumstances of Jamie's adoption, since everything came out in court," she said to Ross. "My hus—Paul and I had been trying to adopt a child for quite a while, but the waiting lists were so long. When we saw Paige's ad in the newspaper, it seemed like the answer to a prayer."

"So you met with her and arranged a private adoption."

"There was nothing illegal about it," Amanda said hastily. "We had a lawyer and so did she. Her lawyer was the one who'd placed the ad. We met with him first, actually. He told us Paige was only nineteen, that she was six months pregnant and that the father, well, he was out of the picture and wouldn't contest the adoption."

Ross dragged a hand over his face. "You don't need to sugarcoat it. I'm aware that Paige didn't even know who the father *was*." In disgust, he blew a stream of air out between his teeth. "Some ski bum she met while she was flitting around Europe the previous winter, no doubt."

"Um, maybe." Amanda cleared her throat. "Anyway, we agreed that Paul and I would pay all her medical expenses until after the birth." She pursed her mouth. "We didn't realize then that Paige was a far cry from destitute. Not that we wouldn't have gladly paid all her expenses anyway. But she certainly kept it secret that she was a member of the famous Chandler wine family."

"You weren't the only one she was keeping secrets from."

"You mean…you didn't know she was pregnant?"

Ross stirred as if the subject made him uncomfortable. "After Paige somehow squeaked through high school, Granddad sent her to Europe for a graduation present. He forced her to put in an appearance at home that first Christmas, but she was on the plane back to Paris about three hours after we finished unwrapping presents. She didn't come home again for nearly a year."

"And she never let you know she was going to have a baby?"

Ross shook his head, glancing automatically in Jamie's direction. "When we learned she was back in the States, in New York, I made a couple of attempts to see her while I was back east on business. Paige always had some excuse why we couldn't get together." He shrugged unhappily. "But that was par for the course. I never suspected she might be hiding something."

"When did you finally learn the truth? About Jamie?"

If Amanda hadn't been studying Ross so closely, she never would have seen the barrier that immediately shuttered his eyes. Like a drawbridge raised to protect the castle.

"I don't recall exactly," he said.

With a jolt, Amanda realized he was lying.

She clenched her fists. "What I don't understand," she said, unconsciously pounding her knee, "is what made Paige change her mind. What made her want to take Jamie back."

Ross's eyes grew even more guarded. "Lots of birth mothers have second thoughts once they actually see the baby, hold it in their arms—"

"No." Amanda thumped her knee so vehemently that pain shot up her leg. "That wasn't how it was with Paige." She jammed a hand through her breeze-blown hair. "Ross, I don't mean to be cruel, but Paige was no more interested in motherhood than she was in studying to become a brain surgeon."

Though Ross tried to maintain a neutral expression, Amanda saw the truth of her words flash across his face in acknowledgment.

"Believe me," she said through gritted teeth, "every time we met with Paige before Jamie was born, I watched her as if my life depended on it. Don't you think I knew what the risks were? If Paige had experienced the tiniest pinprick of doubt about the adoption, I would have detected it."

Ross bounded to his feet and propped his forearms on the railing. "She changed her mind *after* Jamie was born. It happens." His profile barely moved as he spoke, his jaw resembling a block of granite that refused to budge.

Amanda got up and joined him at the railing. "Ross, Jamie wasn't even a person to Paige. She never once referred to 'the baby' or 'him' or 'her' or even 'it.' She made it completely clear that her pregnancy was nothing but a problem that she was eager to make go away."

Ross appeared to be mesmerized by the murky bay waters undulating beneath their feet. His expression remained immovable.

"Paige's whole attitude conveyed absolutely no concern for anyone but herself." Amanda gripped the railing. The cold metal dug into her palms. She hated to keep bombarding Ross with these unflattering images of his sister, but she hoped that bit by bit she could chip away at that block of granite and eventually arrive at the truth.

"Every conversation we had," Amanda persisted, "Paige complained how the doctor had made her give up drinking and smoking for the duration of her pregnancy. Her big worry was how long it would take to get her figure back afterward." She grabbed Ross's arm and made him turn to look at her. "Does that sound like the kind of woman who would have a change of heart?"

The stony wall of his defenses seemed to crumble just a little. "Anything's possible." But he sounded resigned, as if he was on the verge of caving in.

"More than *three years* later?" Amanda pressed hard. "Paige had months to change her mind before the adoption was finalized. What would make her change her mind after all that time?" All the anger and fear and bitter frustration of the court battle came crashing down around Amanda like an avalanche. "Why did Paige lie on the witness stand and claim that Paul and I coerced her into giving Jamie up? That we tricked her and pressured her and took advantage of a confused, frightened young woman?"

Ross shifted his glance out over the bay again, as if he couldn't bear the glare of outraged injustice burning in Amanda's eyes. For just an instant, his shoulders slumped in defeat.

Then he hoisted himself upright, like a man determined to meet some unpleasant fate with dignity and pride. "You're right," he said quietly, the two words nearly snatched away on the wind. He turned back to face Amanda. The grim set of his features warned her that maybe she should have left well enough alone. "Paige didn't change her mind about giving Jamie up for adoption."

"Then...?"

"Someone changed it for her."

Amanda swallowed. "Who?"

Even as the strangled sound emerged from her throat, she glimpsed the answer. And suddenly wished she hadn't asked the question.

Ross fixed her with an unwavering gaze. Behind him, a gull swooped down to the greenish surface of the water and triumphantly plucked up his prey.

Ross said, "My grandfather forced Paige to sue for custody."

Chapter 8

"*Caleb?*"

During all the terrible hours Amanda had spent agonizing over what could have led to Paige's about-face on the adoption, this was one possibility she'd never even considered.

Heat flooded her face. Fury crept up inside her.

"Amanda, please." Ross laid his hand on her arm as if it might be necessary to restrain her from taking a swing at him.

But Ross wasn't the one she intended to vent her anger on. She yanked her arm away. "Why?" That single word fell between them like the stroke of a guillotine.

With a sigh, Ross turned back to the railing. Beyond him, Amanda could see a tour boat chugging out toward Alcatraz. Flags flying, cameras clicking, people waving. Ross, Jamie and she had been excited passengers on a similar boat just this morning. Only a few hours ago.

It felt like years.

"Tell me," she said, struggling to keep her voice on an even keel, "why Caleb forced Paige to get Jamie back."

Ross was careful not to touch her again. He didn't blame Amanda for being furious. In her present mood, he sensed that any physical contact would be the emotional equivalent of lighting a match to a powder keg.

He cast a searching glance over his shoulder, spotted Jamie. Still with the group of kids being entertained by the clown.

He looked back at Amanda. Her mouth was pinched into a white seam. Anger had painted dabs of scarlet on her high cheekbones. The salt-scented breeze whipped her brunette hair around her head.

There were a lot of aspects to the custody battle that he'd hoped she would never have to learn. This was one of them. But he couldn't deny that she *deserved* to know.

"None of us knew about Paige's pregnancy, about Jamie, about the adoption," he reiterated. "Not until Jamie was three years old."

"And then?" Amanda forced out the words through her teeth.

"Paige came home for a visit. She hated the estate, thought the Napa Valley was dull, but periodically she put in an appearance for fear that Granddad might cut off her allowance otherwise."

"Would he have?"

"That's what he threatened." Ross shrugged. "Granddad didn't put a lot of restrictions on Paige's behavior—by then I guess he'd learned it was pointless. But every so often, he insisted she come home. He loved her, in his own way." A rueful half smile tugged at Ross's mouth. "Though he spent most of their time together lecturing her."

"I can imagine," Amanda said dryly. "Tell me how he learned about Jamie."

"Paige never went anywhere without an entourage of friends." Something inside Ross's chest knotted like a fist. One of those so-called friends wound up getting her killed. "One afternoon, she was sitting around the pool with a girlfriend from New York. Apparently the woman she'd stayed with while she was pregnant."

Amanda pulled her sweater tighter and nodded for him to continue.

"Paige had sworn her friend to secrecy, but they both had a little too much to drink that afternoon and started talking too freely. Granddad overheard." Ross grimaced, recalling the ensuing explosion. "He sent all of Paige's friends packing and then had it out with her."

Amanda's stormy expression had remained bolted to her face during Ross's recitation. She had every right to be boiling mad, but maybe it would help if Ross could get her to understand his grandfather's side of things.

"Granddad...has a very strong sense of family. Despite his gruff manner." Ross smiled at Amanda, hoping she would return it.

She didn't.

"He was incensed that Paige had given away her own flesh and blood. That a member of the Chandler family was being raised by strangers." He winced, realizing how that would sound to Amanda. "Sorry."

"No doubt he would have been completely supportive if his unmarried, teenage granddaughter had come to him while she was pregnant." Sarcasm etched Amanda's voice like acid.

Ross sighed. "He would have hit the roof, naturally. But he would never have let Paige give the child up for adoption."

"Wasn't that *Paige's* decision?" Amanda's mouth pursed with bitterness.

"It should have been, of course. But I hardly need to

tell you that when Granddad gets worked up, he's like a steamroller.''

"Seems to me Paige could be pretty stubborn, too.'' Impatiently, Amanda shoved a swatch of blowing hair out of her eyes. "How did Caleb manage to bully her into bringing the custody suit if she didn't really want to?''

It would have been easier for Ross to answer if he'd glanced away from Amanda's injured, angry eyes. But he didn't.

"Granddad threatened to disinherit her. To cut her off without a dime of the Chandler fortune if she didn't get his great-granddaughter back.''

Amanda remained motionless, as if frozen to the ground. Then she broke the lock on their gazes to turn away and stare out over the water again. "It figures,'' she muttered.

Ross sensed her drifting away from him. Only minutes ago, he'd felt so close to her, close enough to tell her things he'd never spoken of with another human being. Something special had been growing between them, binding them together.

Whatever it was had been viciously uprooted now. Ross was desperate to catch hold of Amanda before she floated away for good. Before their precious, newfound intimacy was lost forever.

Her knuckles were a white ridge of bone where she grasped the railing. Ross covered her hand with his. Both her flesh and the metal were like ice.

"Amanda, I know how much his actions hurt you. But he didn't do what he did because he was evil. He did it because he wanted what he thought was best for Jamie.''

Amanda's eyes were bleak when she turned her head. Bleak and far away. With a sinking heart, Ross knew he'd lost her.

"You're wrong,'' she said steadily, looking straight

through him. "You have no idea how much his actions hurt me."

With that, she withdrew her hand and walked off across the pier. Toward Jamie. Her daughter. Whose childhood would always have a huge missing piece for Amanda.

Her first impulse had been to barge into the old man's room and wring his neck.

Fortunately, she'd managed to restrain herself. She could just hear Caleb chortling with glee from beyond the grave as she was hauled off to prison. Amanda refused to give him the satisfaction.

Besides, Jamie loved him.

So she gave herself a few days to cool off. To absorb the jarring blow Ross had dealt her when she'd made him admit the real reason Paige had insisted she wanted Jamie back.

Amanda could still barely wrap her mind around the concept that Caleb was the real villain behind the whole custody nightmare. Not only had he footed the bill for the anguish and unspeakable loss Amanda had suffered, but he'd been the instigator of it in the first place.

A scheming, diabolical puppeteer, manipulating the strings behind the scenes to serve his own selfish purposes, no matter who got hurt.

And Ross had been a party to it.

That was something else Amanda was having trouble absorbing.

She'd actually begun to think he might be different from the rest of the Chandlers. That he might be a man of honor and integrity. That he might be a man she could fall in love with.

If Amanda was being brutally honest with herself, she'd have to admit that she already *had* started to care for Ross. The physical attraction that kept proving harder and harder to resist had begun to deepen into something more. Until she'd found out that he was a true Chandler after all. Sneaky. Ruthless. Indifferent to any lives they destroyed in the process, as long as the family honor was upheld.

Family honor, be damned.

It shouldn't be too hard to harden her heart against him from now on.

And Amanda wasn't about to let Caleb off the hook, either. That wily old shark. Maybe she didn't have manslaughter in mind, but by God, she was certainly going to let him know what she thought of him. She wasn't some mindless little robot in the Chandler militia, ready to fall in line and obey orders whenever Caleb called the shots. Or yanked the purse strings.

So after their trip to San Francisco, Amanda waited until Wednesday morning, when Jamie was in school and Ross was at the winery and Nora was downstairs vacuuming. Then she marched in to confront the enemy.

He was propped up in bed, scowling over the *Wall Street Journal,* spectacles perched on his hawklike nose. As soon as he noticed Amanda in the doorway, he whipped off his glasses with surprising speed, invigorated by the tonic of vanity, she supposed. The quick, furtive motion reminded her of a snake.

"What are *you* doing here?" he demanded. "If you've come for the breakfast tray, there it is." He gave an imperious jerk of his gnarled hand. "Take it away."

The cat had been napping on a chair in a patch of sunlight. Suddenly, he streaked from the room as if sensing trouble.

"I'm not here to wait on you," Amanda told Caleb calmly. Not that she was exactly calm. But she hoped that's how she sounded. "I came here to inform you that I think you're despicable."

He squinted at her as if searching for some conversational turn he'd missed. Then he gave a bark of laughter. "Is that supposed to hurt my feelings?"

"*What* feelings?" she asked, edging into the room. "You haven't got any. You're a cold-blooded, merciless, self-centered, unconscionable..."

Caleb straightened up on his pillows, but if anything, he looked amused. "Please do go on," he said with another one of those haughty waves. "I assure you, my greatest concern in the world is your opinion of me."

Amanda's temper burst into low flame. "I won't bother appealing to your sense of shame or your guilty conscience, because you haven't got those, either." Caleb's patronizing smirk turned her temper up another notch. "But it's about time someone around here held you accountable for your actions instead of cowering in fear whenever you crack the whip."

Unfortunately, his mammoth ego seemed to feed on her indignation rather than wither in the face of it. His ancient eyes lit up and color restored a glow of health to his sunken cheeks. "Tell me, is this little exercise in character assassination to become a daily ritual? Or is this a special occasion?"

Amanda dug her nails into her palms. "I found out what you did." She had to force each word past the bile clogging her throat.

To her amazement, Caleb's smug demeanor cracked like a shoddy foundation. Within seconds, it had crumbled completely, taking all the color in his face with it. "What are you talking about?" he demanded in a hoarse voice.

Amanda didn't understand exactly what target she'd hit, but she certainly intended to keep aiming in the same direction. "The custody fight. Paige. Jamie. You were behind all of it."

"Lies!" The strain of rallying his defenses was scrawled

all over his haggard face. "I did nothing wrong! You'll never prove it!"

Why on earth was he getting so worked up about what Ross had told her? It hardly reflected well on Caleb, but he'd made it plain that he couldn't care less what people thought of him.

"I don't *need* to prove it." Amanda stepped closer. "It's enough that *I* know the truth."

Good heavens, was that actually fear lurking in his eyes?

"Bah! You don't know anything. You're just guessing." The cords in his neck pulled taut when he swallowed.

"I don't need to guess. Ross told me everything."

"Wha—*Ross?*" Agitation lifted him from his pillow. "Liar! He would never tell you. He swore he'd keep his fool mouth shut!"

Caleb's reaction continued to strike Amanda as way out of proportion to her accusation. Maybe the old bully *did* have a conscience after all.

"I'm not going to stand here arguing with you about what we both know happened," she said, folding her arms. "In the end, it doesn't matter, does it? Because despite your high-handed tactics, Jamie is still going to be my daughter again."

Scarlet flooded his face, but this time it was definitely not a healthy glow. "Over my dead body!" He shook his fist at Amanda. "And don't get any funny ideas, young woman. I'm a lot tougher than I look!"

"Ross and I are going to adopt Jamie." Amanda jerked up her chin, sounding a lot more confident than she felt.

"Never!" Caleb spat the word at her. "You can put that notion right out of your pretty little head this instant, because I'd give away every nickel of the Chandler fortune to panhandlers on the street before I'd let you get your hands on my great-granddaughter!"

Amanda felt a chill of fear in the pit of her stomach. Obviously, Ross hadn't yet convinced Caleb to go along with the adoption. If he'd even raised the matter at all.

"You thought you could worm your way back into Jamie's life by marrying my grandson, but it won't work!" Caleb bared his teeth in a snarl. "Jamie is *mine,* do you hear me? *Mine!*" He jabbed himself in his bony chest. "*I'm* her legal guardian, and they'll be growing grapes on Neptune before I agree to give her to *you* and that sentimental, mush-brained grandson of mine!"

Amanda's fear was rapidly approaching full-fledged panic. Caleb was right. Without his consent, Jamie would never be hers again.

"Jamie isn't one of your possessions! She's a little girl who needs a mother and father." Amanda fought to keep any note of pleading from her voice, sensing that any sign of weakness would only entrench Caleb more firmly on his course. Like a shark who smells blood.

"Jamie's a Chandler and she's going to stay one! Do you seriously believe I'd let you get your hooks into her so you can steal her away from her rightful home?"

"I've no intention of taking Jamie away." With a sinking heart, Amanda realized that reason was a useless weapon against someone who was completely unreasonable. "I know this is her home now. That she's happy here. But can't you see that she'd be even better off living in a normal family environment with a mother and father like other kids have?"

"Spare me the modern-day psychology." Caleb's thin lips curled into a sneer. "Jamie has everything she needs right now. You tricked poor Paige into giving her up once before, but you're not going to trick me into making the same mistake again!"

"You know perfectly well I never tricked Paige." On the roller coaster of her emotions, Amanda was climbing the hill of anger again. "Unlike you, I would never even *consider* uprooting Jamie from her home, tearing her away from the people she loves. Because my primary concern is what's best for Jamie, not what best serves my own selfish interests."

"*I* know what's best for Jamie, and don't you forget it!"

"If you cared about her, you'd—"

"Don't you dare accuse me of not caring about her! Why, if I hadn't—"

"If you hadn't interfered, she wouldn't have been wrenched from the arms of the only mother who ever truly wanted her!"

"You were never her mother! And you never will be! No matter how hoodwinked you've got my—"

"Truce! For God's sake, what's all the shouting about?"

Amanda whirled around to find Ross striding into the room.

"I want to talk to you, boy!" Caleb stabbed a crooked finger at him. "Did you tell this—this interloper that you and she were going to adopt Jamie?"

Ross was breathing heavily, as if he'd just raced up the stairs. He sent Amanda a look that conveyed both apology and apprehension. "Granddad, Amanda isn't an interloper." He moved beside her and placed his arm firmly around her waist. "She's my wife, and I'll thank you to treat her with respect."

"How touching." Caleb's mouth puckered as if he'd bit into something sour. "You're certainly two of a kind, I'll give you that. She sounds just like you do." Obviously, it wasn't meant as a compliment.

Ross lifted his brows. Amanda shrugged. She had no idea what Caleb was referring to.

"Trying to tell me what's best for my own great-grand-child," he muttered. "That I should have left Jamie with strangers, that I should have just *let* Paige give her away..."

Amanda's shoulders stiffened. What was he implying? That Ross had argued *against* suing for custody of Jamie four years ago?

"Granddad, we need to have a talk about Jamie. About what's best for her."

Caleb set his jaw at a stubborn angle. Amanda recognized the family resemblance. "Nothing to talk about. This adoption business is out of the question."

Ross gave Amanda a reassuring squeeze as he urged her gently toward the door. "I'll come back later. After we've all had a chance to cool off."

"Don't waste your time," Caleb hollered as Ross escorted Amanda from the room. "And who's running my winery while you're up here playing Sir Galahad, huh?"

His irritated voice trailed them down the hall. Mercifully, they couldn't hear him anymore by the time they reached the stairs.

"Amanda, I'm sorry." Ross bracketed his hands on her shoulders like a pair of bookends. "I know how difficult he can be. He's gotten much worse since he became bedridden." Affectionate sympathy filtered into his eyes. "I'm sure a lot of his behavior is because he can't stand feeling feeble and helpless."

"Feeble? Maybe. Helpless?" Amanda shook her head in frustration. "Hardly." A fistfight of conflicting questions was battering her brain, clamoring for her attention. "Ross, you still haven't talked to Caleb about our adopting Jamie, have you?"

His grip tightened. "I thought it would help to give him some more time to get used to the idea of our marriage."

"*Time?*" Amanda crimped her lips in disdain. "Jamie'll

be out of college and halfway through graduate school before he gets used to *that* idea.''

A ghost of a smile appeared on Ross's lips. "I'll talk to him this evening. I promise.''

"Ross, he said he'd never allow it! That we'll never be Jamie's legal parents!''

"Amanda.'' As he brought his face close to hers, she could see the steel glinting in his eyes. "I promised you we would adopt Jamie. And we will.'' His breath was warm against her skin. "Trust me.''

Trust him? Dear Lord, how she wanted to! She hated this breach that had opened up between them like a treacherous crevice in the ground. She missed the closeness they'd shared, the emotional attraction that had melted her initial suspicion and overcome the legacy of bitter pain that had once seemed an insurmountable barrier.

And she missed the comfort of his strong arms, too. The sensual warmth of his kiss. The exquisite sensations he aroused with his hands, his mouth, his tenderness. Standing this close to him now, Amanda had to fight the desire to move forward into his embrace. It would be so easy. Only a couple of small steps...

But there was so much Ross had hidden from her. Maybe even more he was still hiding?

Trust him. Well, what other choice did she have? She herself didn't have a chance in hell of convincing Caleb to see reason.

"Ross, your grandfather...he made it sound as if you spoke out against the idea of Paige's suing for custody.''

Amanda's eyes were questioning, hopeful. Ross saw now what a dreamer he'd been, believing they could sweep the whole ugly custody mess under a rug and leave it there. Clearly, Amanda had been haunted all this time by missing pieces of the tragic puzzle. If Ross could supply any of those missing pieces, he owed them to her. There was just one critical piece of information he could never, ever let her find out.

He dropped his hands from her shoulders. He couldn't concentrate when he was touching her. Because all he could think about was how much he wanted to run his hands over her soft curves. How much he wanted to feel her beautiful body responding eagerly to him. How much he wanted to make her his wife in the complete sense of the word.

Maybe that incredible union would actually take place someday. If Amanda could ever forgive him for being a Chandler.

"I did speak up against suing for custody." Ross's mouth formed a wry smile. "Not that anyone heard me too well, what with all the shouting going on around here."

"So you...you tried to talk Caleb out of pushing forward with the custody suit?"

Something in Amanda's face made her look so vulnerable, so fragile. But Ross knew she was neither. Otherwise she wouldn't have come through her heartbreaking loss intact.

"I knew Jamie would be better off with you than with Paige." Ross sighed. Even now, a finger of guilt prodded him for his disloyalty to his sister. "It wasn't fair to either you or Jamie to disrupt your lives, to tear apart the bond that had grown over three years."

Amanda's chin trembled. "I loved her the first moment I held her in my arms."

Ross wove his fingers gently through her hair. "I know," he said. "She's the greatest kid in the world. How could it not be love at first sight?"

"What about you?" She summoned a wobbly smile. "Did you love her at first sight, too?"

Ross's mind leaped back to his first glimpse of his niece.

It had been that awful day he'd witnessed the sobbing, terrified four-year-old torn from her mother's arms. Love? No. A fierce shaft of sympathy and remorse so sharp it threatened to cut him in two.

He let Amanda's soft hair spill through his fingers. "It was the first night she spent under this roof. The middle of the night, actually." Compassion roughened his voice as he remembered. "Paige had finally managed to get Jamie to go to sleep. Poor little kid. She was exhausted after the long plane ride, from all her crying for her mommy."

Amanda's eyes glittered with moisture.

"I was having trouble sleeping myself, so during the night I tiptoed into her bedroom to check on her. Sure enough, she was crying again. But softly this time, like she was just plain worn out."

Amanda pressed quivering fingertips to her lips.

"So I sat on the edge of her bed, stroking her hair and talking to her for a while. I don't remember what I said—probably just kept repeating that everything was going to be all right." He made a cynical noise. "How could everything be all right when she'd just lost her mother?"

Ross's throat tightened, but he forced himself to go on. "Anyway, by some magic, she finally drifted back to sleep again. And when I stood up to go, I realized she had her little fist curled around my finger."

He shook his head in wonder. "I'd never noticed before how tiny children's hands were. I just kept sitting there on the edge of her bed, staring down at those precious, perfect little fingers clinging to me as if I was some kind of lifeline." He swallowed. "This pressure built up in my chest till I thought it would burst right through my ribs. And that was when I realized I loved her."

"Oh, Ross." Amanda's face collapsed.

He drew her into his arms, grateful for the warmth and

sweetness of her body melded with his, for the feeling of rightness that settled over him when he held her.

He kissed her hair, treasuring the flutter of her heart as it beat against him like a dove's wing. He even cherished the tears that dampened his shirtfront.

When Amanda finally drew back, her eyelashes sparkled. "I seem to be doing a lot of this lately," she said with a wavery smile. "Crying on your shoulder, I mean."

"It's all right." He continued to stroke the region between the delicate arches of her shoulder blades.

She bit her lip. "It's just that I—I want so much for Jamie to belong to us! To you and me." She flicked a wisp of hair from her cheek. "Legally, I mean. Forever."

"Darling." He lowered his forehead to hers. "Jamie does belong to us. In every way that matters."

"No." Amanda retreated a step so that his arms wouldn't quite reach around her anymore. "You're only her uncle, and I'm just—well, I don't even know what I am to her." Her features arranged themselves to convey determination. "I want us to be Jamie's true, legal mother and father. So that Jamie knows it. So that the whole world knows it."

"I want that, too, Amanda." There was more Ross wanted. Much more. But until Jamie's future was settled, the future of his relationship with his wife would remain a question mark, as well. "I'll talk to Granddad tonight. I promise. And if I can't make him see reason, well...I'll use some other technique." He grimaced. "I've learned more from Granddad than just how to run a winery."

"But if he refuses..." Doubt shimmered in her eyes.

"Trust me, Amanda." The irony of his own words jabbed at Ross's conscience. Here he was, asking Amanda to trust him, yet at the same time he was more determined than ever to hide the truth from her.

But he had to keep what Caleb had done a secret. If

Amanda ever learned about the bribe, about the reason why Ross had married her, it would destroy forever any chance for them to be a family. Ultimately, it might even cost Ross the niece he'd come to love like his own child.

And for the first time, he had to admit that Jamie wasn't the only person he was afraid of losing.

Chapter 9

That night after Jamie and Caleb had concluded their reading session, Ross asked Amanda to put Jamie to bed, while he went in and spoke to his grandfather.

"And Pa went to town to trade in his furs and was gone for days and *days!*" Jamie was giving Amanda an enthusiastic recap of tonight's chapter. "When he finally came home, he brought Laura and Mary combs for their hair, and he brought crackers and pickles to eat, and you know what he brought Ma?"

"What?" Amanda asked, unfastening Jamie's ponytail.

"He brought her calico, to make a new dress!"

"I'll bet she liked that."

"Amanda?"

"Yes?"

"What's calico?"

Amanda smiled. "It's a type of material. Like cotton." With her fingers, she combed Jamie's beautiful blond hair down the back of her pajamas. "I used to love reading the *Little House on the Prairie* books when I was your age."

Jamie's brow pleated as she climbed into bed. "They had those books when *you* were a kid?"

Amanda laughed. "Way back then, yes." She drew the coverlet up over Jamie and sat down on the edge of the bed.

Funny. A week ago, she would have gloated at this chance to have her daughter all to herself. But tonight, she found herself wishing Ross were here, too. Sharing this special time of day with their child.

Amanda mentally crossed her fingers. Whether or not Jamie would actually become their legal daughter depended on how Ross's conversation with Caleb was going right now. She hadn't heard any yelling or breaking glass so far. Hopefully, that was a good sign.

Jamie's eyelids were half-closed. Amanda reached over to turn off the bedside lamp, leaving the room bathed in the pale glow from the night-light.

"Know what I wish?" Jamie murmured sleepily.

"What's that, sweetheart?" Amanda tenderly brushed her bangs off her forehead.

"I wish I had a Pa and Ma, just like Laura and Mary."

Amanda's breath caught in her throat. *Oh, Jamie, you don't know how much I wish that, too,* she thought. She blinked back tears. If only she could promise Jamie that her wish would come true. "Maybe someday," she whispered so her voice wouldn't break.

Jamie's lashes fluttered shut. Her breathing deepened. When Amanda covered her small hand with her own, Jamie didn't stir.

Without even thinking about it, Amanda began to sing softly. How many long-ago nights had she sent her little girl off to sleep with this same lullaby? After Jamie was taken away from her, Amanda hadn't been able to hear its familiar strains without bursting into tears.

Her voice felt a little rusty at first, but the words came

back easily. All at once, Jamie opened her eyes and looked up at Amanda with puzzled uncertainty. Self-conscious, Amanda stopped singing.

Jamie rubbed one eye. "You used to sing that to me," she said drowsily. "I remember."

"Oh, Jamie." A complicated mix of joy and sorrow rushed through Amanda. She scooped her daughter up in her arms and hugged her to her breast. Her little-girl hair smelled so sweet…the warm weight of her small body was so incredibly dear…. Jamie's arms crept cautiously around her. Amanda hugged her until she dared try to speak again. She lowered Jamie back to her pillow. "Yes, I used to sing you that lullaby," she said with a trembling smile. "Every night when I tucked you into bed."

Jamie's blue eyes were thoughtful, almost quizzical. "And…and Raffles?"

"Your teddy bear!" Amanda bit her lip. Jamie *did* remember! *Some* of their life together anyway. "I used to tuck both of you in bed next to each other, remember? You wouldn't go to sleep unless Raffles did, too."

Jamie cocked her head to one side. "I wouldn't?"

"Nope. One time, I thought we'd lost him, 'cause I looked *everywhere* and couldn't find him. You refused to go to sleep, and I was carrying you through the house, hoping you'd drift off, and you started to point and tug on my sleeve, and guess where he was?"

Jamie's eyes shone like stars. "Where?"

"You'd hidden him in the clothes dryer!"

Jamie giggled. "Tell me some other stories 'bout when you were my mommy." She drew up her knees beneath the covers.

"I'd love to, sweetie. But not tonight."

"Why not?" Her lower lip formed the start of a pout.

"Because it's past your bedtime, that's why." Amanda leaned over and kissed Jamie's forehead. Her heart rejoiced at this breakthrough they'd made. "But you know what? I have some pictures taken when you were a little girl. Would you like to see them tomorrow?"

"Yeah!" Jamie rolled onto her side and stacked her hands beneath her cheek. "Amanda?"

"Yes?"

"Would you please sing some more, so I can go to sleep?"

Tender warmth flooded her. "Of course I will, sweetheart."

"Nobody else ever sings to me," Jamie murmured.

Before Amanda could finish even one verse, her little girl was fast asleep.

"Granddad, we've got to talk about this."

Caleb rustled the newspaper screening his face. "Nothing to talk about."

"I understand that you're angry with me, but for Jamie's sake, would you please put down that paper so we can discuss her best interests?"

Caleb whipped the newspaper aside and let the pages drift to the floor. "Jamie's best interests are being served with things just the way they are."

"I disagree."

Caleb made a rude noise. "Tell me something new."

Ross eased himself into the chair next to the bed. He realized that speaking down at his grandfather put Caleb at a psychological disadvantage. One he was shrewd enough to recognize. And resent.

However they settled this matter tonight, they would settle it eye-to-eye.

"You can hardly argue that a child isn't better off with two parents instead of being raised as a sort of group project by an entire household."

Caleb still had all his own teeth. He clamped them together and forced his reply through them. "That Weston woman isn't getting her paws on Jamie, and that's final."

Ross sighed. "You're conveniently forgetting her name is Chandler now. She's part of our family."

"A mistake on your part I could easily correct if you weren't so pigheaded."

Ross swallowed his exasperation. Talk about the pot calling the kettle black! But his grandfather was right. Ross could be just as stubborn as he was, and tonight he intended to prove it.

"Granddad. Whether you approve or not, Amanda is my wife, and she's going to stay my wife from now on." Ross was surprised to discover how much he wanted that to be true. He and Amanda had never discussed what would happen to their marriage after Jamie was grown. He felt a twinge in his chest at the thought that she might someday leave him. Of course, that day would come sooner rather than later if she ever learned about the bribery. If she ever discovered how he'd deceived her.

Caleb crossed his arms and harrumphed. "You ask me, that woman's got you so flummoxed you can't tell up from down."

"I can still tell right from wrong. Amanda was done an enormous wrong, and I want to set things right to the extent I can."

Caleb's luxuriant white brows leaped together in anger. "That why you told her I bribed that judge?"

"What?" Alarm sped through Ross. "I never said a word. What makes you think she—"

"You and your lectures about how we have to do what's best for Jamie. Then you go and spill the beans to that woman! Will it be in Jamie's best interests to have the custody issue reopened? That's what your *wife* will do now, you know. Probably been running up my long-distance phone bill already, plotting with her lawyers back east.''

Ross lowered his voice. "Granddad, I swear to you, the last thing I would do is tell Amanda you paid off the judge." His heart took a steep dive. This was exactly the disaster he'd feared. "Why are you so sure Amanda knows about it?"

"Didn't she stand right here and accuse me?" Caleb speared a finger toward the floor. "'I found out what you did,'" he mimicked. "'Ross told me everything.'"

"Wait a minute." Ross ran his hand distractedly through his hair. "Did Amanda specifically refer to bribery? Did she actually mention the judge?"

"What else could she have been talking about?" Caleb snapped.

A tiny measure of relief crept tentatively around the edges of Ross's panic. "So she *didn't* specifically accuse you of bribery."

"What difference does it make? She—"

"Granddad, please. It's important. Try to remember."

Fidgeting as if there was itching powder between the bedsheets, Caleb pondered for a moment. "No," he said finally. "In all the accusations she was flinging around, I don't believe the words *bribery* or *judge* ever flew out of her mouth."

Ross backhanded a sheen of sweat from his brow. "Then she doesn't know about that part of it."

Behind his grandfather's irritable demeanor, Ross detected a flash of relief that mirrored his own. Then Caleb's scowl returned. "Exactly what part *does* she know?" he demanded suspiciously. "What lies have you been feeding her about me?"

"You know better than that."

"I don't know *what* you're liable to do these days. First you go behind my back and marry that woman, then you try to wheedle me into handing Jamie back into her clutches. For all I know, you—''

''I told her that you were the one who forced Paige to sue for custody. That's all.''

Indignation turned Caleb's withered folds of skin beet red. ''I convinced Paige to do what was right! If it had been up to you, we would never even have set eyes on Jamie. She'd still be a stranger to us. Is that what you want?''

Guilt and love played tug-of-war with Ross's conscience. Jamie was the joy of his life now. If he could go back in time and change things, would he have stopped the custody suit? Left Jamie with Amanda?

''The past is over and done with,'' he said wearily. ''We have to deal with the present. And the future.'' He scooted the chair closer to the bed. ''Granddad, there's no guarantee that Amanda won't ever find out about the bribe. Don't you see that if she does reopen the custody suit, it will strengthen our case if *I'm* Jamie's legal father?''

''I'm already her legal guardian.'' Caleb's jaw was wedged at that intransigent angle Ross recognized all too well.

He hated to hurt his grandfather, but maybe bluntness would be more effective than reason. ''Whom do you think a court will award custody to?'' he asked. ''An eighty-six-year-old man with a failing heart, or a young woman who raised Jamie the first four years of her life until she was illegally taken away from her?''

Caleb clenched his fists as if he yearned for the days when he still had the vigor to take a swing at someone. But he hadn't successfully run a flourishing business empire by ignoring reality. ''If I let the two of you adopt Jamie, that'll make *her* Jamie's legal mother. Are you forgetting that will also strengthen *her* case?''

''That's a chance we'll just have to take,'' Ross said

flatly. "We have to play with whatever cards we've been dealt." He didn't bother pointing out that Caleb himself had stacked this particular deck.

He sensed his grandfather weakening. No, that wasn't the right word. Caleb Chandler never weakened. He just retreated temporarily to reevaluate his strategy.

Ross moved in to take advantage of whatever territory he'd gained. "Look, if you're harboring some secret hope that Amanda is just going to fade out of the picture, you can forget it. I won't let you bully her into leaving."

Caleb's lip curled. "I think you underestimate your own wife, boy. You couldn't push that woman around with a bulldozer."

Ross stroked his jaw, trying to conceal a grin. "You're right about that, I suppose." He was proud of Amanda for standing up to his grandfather. "And the other thing I can guarantee is that she will never, *ever* give up Jamie again."

"Neither will I," Caleb growled.

"Fine. Then accept the fact that the best way we can ensure that Jamie continues to live here on the estate is to let Amanda and me adopt her."

Caleb moved his mouth as if chewing over his words. "It just gets my goat, the way that woman has us trapped between a rock and a hard place."

"You should have thought of that before you broke the law."

Ross had learned through experience that it was best not to back Caleb into a corner during a confrontation. He rose to his feet, intending to give his grandfather a chance to mull over the unpleasant truths Ross had laid out before him. That way, Caleb would have a chance to arrange his response so that it came out sounding like the adoption was *his* idea.

Ross was halfway out the door when his grandfather's

grudging words hooked him backward. "All right," he said.

Ross wheeled around and cautiously approached the bed. "You mean you'll agree to the adoption?"

"That's what I just said, isn't it?"

Ross took no satisfaction in his victory. He knew what this concession had cost his grandfather. But he couldn't help savoring his anticipation of Amanda's ecstatic reaction when he told her the news.

For the first time, it hit Ross that he was really going to be a father. That he and Amanda and Jamie were going to be a family. It was all he could do not to let out a whoop of delight and dance a jig around his grandfather's bed.

"You're doing the right thing," he said.

"Bah!" Caleb batted the air. "Didn't have much choice, did I?"

"It's what's best for Jamie."

"I suppose now *she'll* try to turn Jamie against me."

"Amanda's not like that. Besides, Jamie adores you. No one's going to turn her against you."

"Humph. We'll see. Now give me my paper, will you?"

Ross collected the pages strewn on the floor. His grandfather hadn't been wearing his reading glasses when Ross had come in, so he knew the newspaper was just a handy shield to ward off unwanted discussion.

"Here you are."

Caleb quickly hoisted the paper in front of his nose. But not before Ross glimpsed the unfamiliar pallor of defeat that dragged down his wrinkled features and made his grandfather seem even more ancient than he really was.

Amanda was too nervous to sit still while she waited for Ross to come and inform her of the results of his conversation with Caleb. After Jamie fell asleep, she paced the floor of her own room for a while, then wandered downstairs in search of a distraction. She felt as if her entire future was being determined this evening, along with Jamie's and Ross's.

Maybe a good book would help take her mind off that fact. If she could focus her mind on it long enough to absorb the words, that is. Well, picking one out would at least give her something to do besides worry. She wiped her damp palms on her thighs and walked into the library.

Amazing, she thought. *People really do have entire rooms in their homes filled with books.*

Amanda had been in the library before, of course, with its cozy arrangement of oak mission-style furniture. After more than a week in the Chandler mansion, she'd found the opportunity to explore the entire premises. But this was the first time she'd actually done a three-hundred-sixty-degree turn in the middle of the room and found herself surrounded on all four walls by books.

Three and a half walls, actually. Part of the fourth wall consisted of French doors that opened onto a secluded brick patio, where a couple of weathered Adirondack chairs practically invited you to sit in them and read.

It was dark outside now. Unless you shielded your eyes and pressed your face to the glass panes, it was impossible to make out the chairs or the potted plants arrayed along the edge of the patio. But Amanda could easily imagine herself curled up in one of those comfy chairs on a summer afternoon, absorbed in a book, absently sipping a glass of iced tea while the sun's rays warmed her skin.

Iced tea with a sprig of mint, perhaps.

She jostled herself impatiently from her pleasant fantasy. *Guess you aren't having any trouble after all, adjusting to your new lifestyle,* she thought with disgust. *You certainly seem to be losing your reluctance to avail yourself of all the advantages of the Chandler wealth.*

That damned Chandler fortune had been the bane of her

existence. It was the weapon Caleb had used to force Paige to sue for custody of Jamie. It was the bottomless fund he'd used to hire his mercenaries—high-priced lawyers capable of convincing a judge to send a terrified little girl back to a mother who didn't even want her.

Amanda twisted the wedding band on her finger. Till now, its symbolism had always seemed to mock her, to gloat over the fact that it joined her to the family and the vast wealth she'd once despised.

But perhaps she could turn the ring into her own personal talisman—a reminder of what it felt like to be at the mercy of someone else's money. So that she would never be able to forget the sense of powerlessness that imprisoned people who couldn't afford the price of justice.

But she still chafed under the feeling that somehow she'd been bought and paid for. She wasn't a real member of this family. Just someone else the Chandler wealth had purchased.

She glanced down at her ring again, surprised to discover that a teeny part of her actually *wanted* to belong to this family. If only—

"There you are."

Amanda swung her left hand behind her back as Ross entered the library.

"I've been looking all over for you."

Anxiety surged through her again, making her heart beat fast. "I, uh, came down here to find a book while you talked to Caleb."

She scanned Ross's face, searching for clues about how their conversation had gone. The room was illuminated by a single table lamp, which threw long shadows across Ross's prominent, chiseled features, making them hard to read.

His teeth gleamed in the subdued lighting. "Granddad said yes."

Amanda clapped her hands over her mouth. "Ross! Really?"

He nodded. Maybe it was just a trick of the light, but it seemed like some of the lines around his eyes had vanished, making him look younger, more boyish and carefree than Amanda had ever seen him.

"He's agreed to let us adopt Jamie." Ross's voice quivered slightly, as if with repressed emotion. "He'll sign the papers tomorrow."

Joy and relief swept through Amanda in an indescribable rush of exhilaration. Jamie was going to be hers again!

"Oh, Ross," she said breathlessly.

"Amanda, we're going to be parents!" All at once, Ross lunged for her, seizing her in his arms and whirling her around in circles.

Amanda laughed, giddy with happiness, dizzy with... well, affection. Call it that. Affection for her handsome, wonderful, persuasive husband. Only...could mere affection make you this dizzy?

Must be the way he was spinning her around.

He set her down at last, panting with excitement. He plunged his fingers through her hair, framing her face between his hands. "I can't believe Jamie's going to be our daughter! Our real, official, genuine, bona fide daughter!" He tipped back his head and yelled "Wow!" at the ceiling.

Amanda felt as if her smile would stretch past her ears and right off the edges of her face. Until this moment, she hadn't comprehended how much Ross wanted to adopt Jamie, too.

Her smile shrank a few degrees. "He—he won't change his mind, will he?"

"Who, Granddad?" Ross shook a tousled lock of hair off his forehead. "No. Believe me, once he's made up his mind, changing it requires a crate of dynamite." Ross's eyes burned like sapphires lit from within. "He's already changed his mind once today. You can bet he won't do it again for a good long while."

"I'll still feel a lot better once the papers are signed...." Even though she knew that adoption papers meant nothing to Caleb. But this time, she would have Ross on her side if Caleb decided to stir up more trouble.

"Amanda. Jamie's going to be ours. Forever." His fingers tightened in her hair. Then he tilted her face up to his and kissed her.

Amanda kissed him back eagerly. His lips moved over hers, sending a delicious tingling sensation clear down to the tips of her toes. Her heart nearly tripped over itself with happiness. With excitement. This was no cautious, restrained kiss but an exuberant, spontaneous rejoicing.

Ross's tongue playfully dueled with hers. Desire unfurled inside her. Desire and something else. As if her...affection for him had just expanded a notch.

They were both breathing hard when he finally broke the kiss. "Darling." He looped his arms around her waist and linked hands behind her back. "I promise we'll be happy together, Amanda. The three of us." Fierce determination glowed in his eyes. "Trust me."

It wasn't the first time Ross had asked her to do that. A few weeks ago, Amanda would have trusted a fox to guard a chicken coop before she would place her faith in anyone named Chandler. But Ross had delivered everything he'd promised, hadn't he? He'd made her his wife and given her back her daughter. And he'd actually fixed things with Caleb so they could be Jamie's legal parents forever.

Now he was promising the three of them would find happiness as a family. That both he and she were going to be real parents to Jamie from now on.

Real dad, real mom.

Maybe someday even...real husband, real wife?

Hope soared inside Amanda. All at once, the future seemed dazzlingly bright, filled with magical possibilities.

Trust me, Ross had asked her.

Amanda smiled up at him. "I do," she said.

He kissed her lightly on the lips as if to seal his promise. "Now," he said, donning a thoughtful expression, "there's just one more person whose permission we need to adopt Jamie."

For a second, Amanda's high-flying hopes faltered. "Who?"

Then she spotted the twinkle in Ross's eye. They both laughed as they bumped their foreheads together and spoke in unison. "Jamie!"

Ross winked at her. "Come on," he said. "I'll buy you a cup of hot chocolate to celebrate."

"Now there's an offer I can't refuse."

"Let's go."

Arms draped around each other's waist, they moved toward the door. Amanda savored the pressure of Ross's thigh against her hip, the feel of his strong ribs beneath her fingers. For once, she felt totally in sync with him.

"Tell me the truth," she said as they left the library. "Have you actually read all those books in there?"

"Every single one of them," he replied solemnly, making a crisscross motion over his heart.

"Liar."

"Well...every single novel about going off to sea."

"Melville? Conrad? Richard Henry Dana?"

Ross let out a whistle. "Wow, you really know your authors."

"I majored in literature for a while in college. Along with just about everything else."

"You, too, huh?" They reached the kitchen, where Ross momentarily disappeared into the pantry. He returned with a tin of cocoa and a canister of sugar. "It seemed like I

changed my major about once a semester,'' he said. "I'd
stumble onto some new field of interest, get all fired up
about it, then drop it when I discovered some other area
that fascinated me.''

Amanda propped her elbows on the counter and watched
while Ross expertly prepared the hot chocolate. She would
have figured he'd be helpless in the kitchen, having grown
up with a full-time cook at his beck and call.

Her husband was certainly full of surprises. "I would
have pegged you for a business major,'' she mused, "since
you must have known you'd be taking over the winery
someday.''

Ross made a face as he adjusted the heat beneath a pan
of milk. "Believe me, the last thing I intended to do at
that stage of my life was run the family business.'' His
mouth twitched into a rueful, boyish grin. "Guess you
could call it my rebellious period.''

"*You?* A rebel?'' Amanda smiled at the unlikely idea.
"Tell me more.'' And, over several delicious cups of
steaming hot chocolate, he did.

To Amanda's amazement, by the end of the evening,
that huge, gleaming, spotless kitchen actually felt cozy.

Chapter 10

Ross owned a practical sport-utility vehicle for everyday use, like tooling around the winery or driving into town.

Today, however, wasn't just any other day. It was the day he and Amanda were going to ask Jamie if she'd like to become their legally adopted daughter. So when he and Amanda coasted to the curb in front of Jamie's school that afternoon, they were riding in style in the charcoal gray European luxury sedan Ross had splurged on last year.

He ducked his head to peer past Amanda's shoulder toward the playground. "Any sign of her yet?"

"Not yet." She consulted her watch. "We're a few minutes early, though."

"Sure you want to go through with this?"

Amanda snapped her head around and fired off an indignant look. Then she realized he was teasing, and her lips curved into a smile that made something flip over inside his chest.

By God, Chandler, you sure picked yourself a pretty

wife, he congratulated himself. Even though he knew perfectly well that Amanda's beauty wasn't the reason he'd married her.

Or the reason he was falling for her, either.

Ross had had so many obstacles to overcome in the past several weeks. Convincing Amanda to marry him. Persuading Caleb to agree to the adoption. Trying to ease Amanda's transition into the Chandler household without neglecting Jamie or antagonizing his grandfather.

All those hurdles were in the past now. Yesterday, Caleb had phoned his attorneys, and within two hours, the firm's senior partner was at his bedside with the adoption papers ready for Caleb's signature. Assuming Jamie had no objections, Ross and Amanda could give the go-ahead for filing those papers today.

Now that all those roadblocks were behind him, Ross had had a chance to study the emotional terrain and figure out where he was heading. And discovered there was more to his feelings for Amanda than mere physical attraction.

Once the adoption issue had been resolved, it seemed as if the barrier of tension dividing Ross and Amanda had crumbled away. The past couple of nights, they'd sat up late together, just talking. Sharing all the personal history and intimate revelations that most couples exchange during courtship. Except that the two of them hadn't *had* a courtship.

Till now anyway. The idea of courting his own wife was exciting to Ross. Exciting…but terrifying. Because he was forced to admit that the desire he'd felt for Amanda all along was deepening into something serious. Something that scared the hell out of him when he considered how he could still lose her someday, if the truth ever came out.

From across the car, Amanda's dark brown eyes were watching him, sweet and tempting as chocolate kisses. Speaking of which…

Ross scooted over as far as his seat belt would allow and gave in to temptation. "Mmm." She tasted even better than he'd anticipated. When she dropped her hand to his thigh, a shaft of heat arrowed straight to his loins.

Across the playground, the school bell rang.

Amanda's eyes sparkled as she drew back to break off their kiss. "I hear bells."

"Me, too," Ross said with a grin, nuzzling the tip of his nose against hers. "And I thought that was only in movies."

She brought her hand to the side of his face and gave him a look that started his pulse racing again. "Guess we'd better keep an eye out for Jamie," she said softly, "instead of necking in the front seat like a couple of teenagers."

"Teenagers use the back seat." Ross's voice was muffled as he pressed his lips into her palm. "So I've heard, anyway."

Amanda rolled her lovely eyes. Then they both climbed out of the car.

Children spilled through the various doors of the elementary school, heading across the playground toward waiting buses or their parents' cars.

Amanda pointed. "There she is!"

They crossed the sidewalk and paused by the gate. Ross waved his arm. "James!" he called. "Over here!"

Jamie halted, glanced up in surprise and changed direction. She came flying across the playground, her backpack bouncing up and down.

"Uncle Ross! Amanda! What are *you* guys doing here?"

"We came to take you out for some ice cream," Ross said, rustling her pale corn-silk hair. His very own daughter. He couldn't believe it. "That okay with you?"

"Sure!" She waved over her shoulder at the two friends she'd been walking with. "Bye, Samantha! Bye, Jenna!"

She turned back around and said to Ross, "But you hafta tell the bus driver I won't be riding home today."

"Gotcha." He cocked his thumb at her. "Be back in a flash."

Amanda noticed a definite spring in Ross's step as he strode down the block toward the school buses. Ever since Caleb had agreed to it, Ross had seemed as excited about adopting Jamie as Amanda was. He was going to make a wonderful father, she thought wistfully. He adored Jamie.

Silly to hope that someday Ross might feel the same way about *her*. Theirs was a practical arrangement only, with no emotion involved other than their mutual love for Jamie.

But once in a while, like during that spontaneous, sensual kiss they'd just shared in the car, Amanda couldn't help wondering what it would be like to be Ross Chandler's wife in the true, full sense of the word. To share not only his name, his home and his child, but also his heart. And his bed.

During the past day or two, Amanda had felt closer to Ross than ever before. She couldn't believe how easy he was to talk to, how much they had in common despite their completely different backgrounds. Sometimes, while they were laughing over some childhood anecdote or commiserating about the angst of adolescence, Amanda almost forgot their marriage wasn't real.

She had to keep reminding herself of the reason she'd married Ross. Of the reason he'd married *her*. Which brought to mind a sudden, troubling thought. What if, after all this, Jamie didn't *want* them to adopt her?

Amanda donned a smile and held out her hand, reassured when Jamie grasped it. "Shall we go wait in the car for Ross?"

"Okay." Jamie skipped along beside her, regaling Amanda with the day's happenings at school.

Amanda's heart swelled with love and desperation. She was so close now to getting her little girl back for good....

Yesterday she'd shown Jamie pictures taken during the first four years of her life. Jamie had studied them closely, eyebrows knitted together in concentration. Maybe Amanda had only imagined it, but she could have sworn she'd seen a spark of recognition, a flash of memory in Jamie's inquisitive blue eyes.

Amanda knew she couldn't turn back the clock. She and Jamie could never return to those blissful, innocent days, or recover the years that had been lost. But they'd been granted a miraculous second chance to become a family again. A family that this time would include a father who wanted Jamie as much as Amanda did.

As she closed Jamie into the back seat of the car, Amanda looked up to see Ross coming toward them. His lean, muscular legs moved at a brisk stride that conveyed his eagerness to reach them. Sunlight burnished his hair, turning the strands to gleaming gold.

When his handsome, elegantly sculpted features melted into a smile, Amanda felt something dissolve inside her. Heat and a kind of helpless yearning spilled through her.

It was almost as if her boundless love for Jamie had spread outward to encompass Jamie's future father, too.

Ash and liquidambar trees shaded Main Street in the picturesque wine-country town of St. Helena. Licking ice-cream cones, Ross, Amanda and Jamie strolled past art galleries, upscale restaurants and trendy boutiques housed in vintage buildings of brick and terra-cotta and quarried stone.

Well, actually only Ross and Amanda were strolling. Jamie was alternately skipping circles around them and lagging behind to ooh and aah over various shop windows.

Mouthwatering aromas wafted through the doors as they

passed beneath the awning of a gourmet Italian grocery store. Though the town struck Amanda's east-coast eyes as pure California, the atmosphere had a definite Mediterranean influence she found quite pleasing.

As she savored her scoop of cappuccino ice cream, she had to admit she was actually starting to appreciate life in the Napa Valley. Someday soon, she was going to come back and check out some of these art galleries...maybe even drag her husband along for a romantic dinner at one of the chic restaurants....

Amanda blinked. For the first time, she'd thought of her relationship with Ross as something separate from her relationship with Jamie. Up till now, she'd pictured their marriage as sort of a delicately balanced triangle that would have collapsed without the presence of that critical third side.

But maybe their marriage was more like a circle, enclosing Jamie in their love for her, but also complete in itself. Complete except for one crucial aspect, of course. She and Ross weren't in love with each other. And Amanda had no intention of allowing the tender shoots of her feelings for him to blossom into anything more. Not when she knew Ross didn't feel the same way.

Oh, he was sexually attracted to her—she'd have to be completely blind to miss that. But even during their most intimate moments, Amanda sensed he was holding back. Keeping part of himself aloof from her.

She would have to be a fool not to do the same.

Still, sometimes it was awfully hard not to fantasize about what the future might hold. Especially at times like this, when he took hold of her hand and sent her one of his special, patented, heart-melting smiles.

"There's a park just up ahead," he told her. "I thought that would be a nice quiet place to talk to Jamie."

Amanda's heartbeat accelerated, and not just from

Ross's touch. What if Jamie turned out to be less than thrilled about the idea of adoption? After all, she'd already endured so many twists and turns during the course of her short life. She'd lost two mothers by the time she was five years old, for heaven's sake.

What if the idea of acquiring another new set of parents made Jamie feel *less* secure, not more? Amanda could hardly blame her for craving stability, for preferring that things remain exactly as they were. But she would be heartbroken nevertheless.

A wide expanse of green lawn opened off to their left. They veered onto one of the winding pathways curving through the park.

"Hey, James, how about sitting down here with us for a minute?" Ross motioned toward the first empty bench they came to. "Amanda and I have something we'd like to discuss with you."

"Uh-oh." Uncertainty clouded Jamie's sunny face. "Did my teacher call you? Is that how come you picked me up after school? Honest, I didn't mean to come in late from recess, but me and Samantha and Jenna didn't hear the bell ring!"

Ross struggled to keep a straight face as he pulled a handkerchief from his pocket. "Maybe we should take you to the doctor for a hearing test, huh?" He set to work on the chocolate perimeter of Jamie's mouth.

"Oh, no, I can hear perfect!"

"Except for school bells, I guess."

"Well...um..."

Ross made one last swipe to erase the chocolate, then tucked his handkerchief away. "Anyway, that's not what we wanted to talk to you about."

"It's not?" Immediately, she brightened.

"Nope." He gestured for Amanda to sit down, then

joined her. He patted the bench between them. "Come sit with us," he told Jamie.

She climbed up and swung her legs back and forth, swiveling her head expectantly between the two adults. Ross stretched his arm behind her to rest his hand on Amanda's shoulder. Whether to bolster his courage or hers, Amanda wasn't sure.

But all at once, she knew that *she* should be the one to bring up the subject of adoption. With a painful throb in her chest, she acknowledged that it would be easier for Jamie to reject *her* than to reject her beloved uncle. Jamie had to make this decision of her own free will, not because she didn't want to hurt their feelings.

Amanda clasped Jamie's hand in hers. "Jamie, your uncle Ross and I have come up with an idea, and we'd like to know what you think about it."

Jamie shrugged one shoulder. "Sure."

Amanda took a deep, quavering breath. But when she got the words out, her voice was steady. "Your uncle and I would like very much to adopt you, Jamie. But only if you want us to." Amanda was on alert for the slightest flicker of negative reaction. She allowed herself a tentative spurt of relief when she didn't detect any. "We'd like you to think about that idea," she went on, "and tell us how you truly feel about it."

Jamie's big blue eyes were somber. "Adopt me? Like you did when I was a baby?"

"Well...this time your uncle would adopt you, too. Both of us would be your parents."

Jamie spun her head toward Ross. "Does that mean you won't be my uncle anymore?" There was no mistaking the distress in her voice. Amanda's heart sank.

Ross stroked Jamie's hair. "Er, that's a tricky question, James." He sent Amanda a helpless glance. "I guess I could be both your uncle and your father at the same time. If that's okay with you, of course.''

Jamie tilted her head to the side. "Mmm...I guess that would be okay." She turned back to Amanda. "So you guys would be my mom and dad?"

"That's right, sweetheart." Amanda smiled at her. Once more the tide of hope was starting to rise inside her.

Jamie looked down at her swinging feet and mumbled something.

"What, honey?" Amanda gently coaxed up Jamie's chin.

"I said, will someone come and take me away someday?" Her voice was tiny and timid. "Like the last time I was adopted?"

Startled, Amanda glanced automatically at Ross. She fought hard, very hard, to keep any trace of reproach from her expression.

Guilt crashed through his eyes anyway. He cleared his throat. "That won't happen this time, Jamie. I promise."

Plainly, Jamie wasn't completely reassured. Amanda tiptoed cautiously through the minefield of the past, hunting for the correct words.

"Sweetie, I was very sad when you left me to go live with your other mom and Uncle Ross and your great-grandfather. I know you were sad, too, when it happened." She curved her arm around Jamie and drew her close to her side. "But nothing like that will ever happen again. You can count on it."

"I can?" Jamie's upturned face reflected the battle between uncertainty and her desire to believe.

"Your uncle Ross and I love you very much, sweetheart. We want to be your mom and dad." Amanda fingered Jamie's bangs off her forehead. "If you decide that you'd rather just keep things the way they are, though, that's okay." Pressure built inside Amanda's heart till it felt on the verge of shattering. "But I promise that no matter what you decide, Uncle Ross and I are going to make sure that no one ever, *ever* takes you away from us."

Her voice broke as she hugged Jamie tight, pressing her cheek to the top of her little girl's head. It seemed at that moment to Amanda as if everything that mattered in her life was contained within the unbreakable circle of her arms. And she knew with fierce certainty that no matter what unforeseen twists the future might take, she would never, ever give up her precious child again.

Maybe her unshakable resolution was transmitted to Jamie through the close contact of their bodies. When Amanda finally released her, Jamie gazed up at her with trust and reassurance shining in her eyes.

Amanda blinked back tears and gave both Jamie and Ross a shaky smile. Ross leaned over and kissed Jamie's forehead. "Take as long as you want to think about the adoption," he said with a wink. "We've got all the time in the world."

"Okay." Jamie angled her head to one side, pressed a fingertip to her chin and scrunched up her adorable face in concentration. "I'm done," she announced three seconds later. "I decided I want you to adopt me."

Amanda caught her breath. After an instant's startled numbness, joy spilled through her with a rush of euphoria. When she met Ross's eyes, she saw they were brimming with the same jubilant emotions. The broad grin on his face was as dazzling, as poignant as a glorious sunrise.

"We're awfully glad you feel that way," Amanda said as soon as she regained control of her vocal cords. She gave Jamie an exuberant hug.

Ross hugged her, too, then joined his fingers with Amanda's so all three of them were connected in a loose embrace. "Hmm. Now that that's settled, what shall we do to celebrate?" he asked.

"*I* know!" Jamie's eyes lit up. She peered first at Ross, then at Amanda. "How about...if I get to stay up till ten o'clock from now on?"

Both adults donned stern faces, then burst out laughing. It was the happiest sound Amanda had ever heard.

The muted knock on her bedroom door that evening made Amanda glance up from her book. Nora, perhaps, with a question related to some household matter? Except that Nora had continued to maintain her competent hand on the helm of the Chandler household without any course corrections from the new Mrs. Chandler, thank you very much.

Jamie, then. After a drink of water or one more story—anything to nudge her bedtime a little closer to her personal Holy Grail of ten o'clock.

Amanda bit back a smile as she cinched the sash of the Japanese kimono she used as a robe. She opened her door. "Is the sandman a little late on his rounds toni—oh!"

Ross stood in the dark hallway, amusement lighting his eyes. "I don't know about the sandman, but if it's too late for *me* to be bothering you..."

"Oh, no. No." Suddenly conscious that she was wearing only a short flimsy nightgown beneath her kimono, Amanda yanked the sash even tighter. As if cutting off her ability to breathe somehow made her appear more decent. "Please. Er, come in."

"Thanks." Ross stepped over the threshold.

It was the first time he'd set foot in her bedroom since she'd come to live here. Amanda wondered whether he was as acutely aware of that fact as she was.

He was dressed in the same white button-down shirt he'd worn at dinner, but with the sleeves rolled up to his elbows. The top two buttons were undone, revealing curly golden hairs at the V of his collarbone. Masculine energy seemed to radiate from him, setting up a low-key vibration in certain cells of Amanda's body.

She glanced toward the still-made bed, then hastily looked away.

Ross took in the sight of the open book on the chair beneath the stained-glass floor lamp and the half-empty cup of tea on the table next to it. "I'm sorry. I'm disturbing your reading."

"Actually, you're not." Careful to avoid brushing against him, Amanda stepped past and closed the book. "To tell you the truth, I was too excited about the adoption to concentrate anyway." Her lips slanted at a rueful angle. "I've already read the same sentence over and over about fifty times."

Ross grinned. "Yeah, I know what you mean. I talked to Granddad's lawyer this evening. He's going to file the papers first thing in the morning."

"How long until the adoption is finalized?" The first time with Jamie, there'd been a six-month waiting period. But that was in New York. Different circumstances. A lifetime ago.

"First, the Department of Social Services has to complete an evaluation. Then a judge has to schedule a hearing. It could take anywhere from two to six months."

Ross rummaged through the brown paper shopping bag Amanda had just noticed he was carrying. "Champagne," he announced, producing a bottle. "To celebrate."

For a disorienting moment, she flashed back to that other night when they'd drunk champagne together. Their wedding night. Only a couple short weeks ago, yet so many emotional changes had taken place since then, she felt like an entirely different person from the one in that luxurious Lake Tahoe hotel suite.

The champagne, however, was the same. Amanda recognized the exclusive label.

"I thought the three of us voted to celebrate with a hot-air balloon ride this Sunday," she said. She wasn't altogether sure how she felt about sipping champagne with a disturbingly attractive man in the intimate confines of her bedroom.

Even if he *was* her lawfully wedded husband.

"This particular celebration is for adults only." Ross hoisted his eyebrows as he drew two champagne flutes from the bag.

Whooo boy. Amanda's misgivings increased. But so did that low-level hum along her nerve endings.

Once more, she had to admire Ross's expertise with a champagne cork. And scold herself not to speculate about his expertise in certain other areas. She'd already learned that this husband of hers was a man of many talents.

The *pop* of the cork was like an exclamation point at the beginning of a sentence, followed by the seductive murmur of champagne flowing into their glasses.

"A toast to our new family," Ross proposed.

"To Jamie," Amanda responded. And was surprised to find she didn't mind sharing her with Ross at all.

The chime of crystal sang through the air as they tipped their glasses together. Gazes locked on each other over the rims, they sipped the delicious, exquisitely dry champagne.

Amanda crinkled her nose as the tiny bubbles tickled it. "Mmm. Yum."

"I couldn't agree more." But the slow, appreciative, head-to-toe survey Ross was giving her left no doubt that he wasn't talking about the champagne.

Amanda's bloodstream began to fizz.

"I like your robe," Ross said, tugging gently on the sash.

"What, *this* old thing?" Amanda chose to make light

of his admiration. "A friend brought it back from Japan for me. I thought it was too pretty to stick away in the closet, so I decided to put it to good use."

"Good idea." He fingered the flowing silk sleeve, then studied her with curiosity. "You don't talk much about your friends. And I never hear you making phone calls back east."

Amanda shrugged. "After I lost Jamie and then got divorced, I was determined to start all over. I don't have any other family, as you know. So I moved to Nantucket, got a new job and built a new life for myself."

The heat of his hand soaked through the fabric of her sleeve to envelop her arm. "A life without friends?" he asked.

"Not many," Amanda admitted. She took another sip of champagne. "I guess I didn't want to get close to anyone. I didn't want people asking personal questions about my past because I wanted to forget it."

"You didn't want to forget it entirely, it seems." Ross indicated the photographs of a younger Jamie that Amanda had propped on several pieces of furniture about the room. "Otherwise you would have thrown those pictures away."

One side of her mouth hitched upward in a sad smile. "I did hide them away in a drawer, though. Once in a while, I'd take them out to torture myself, but I didn't have them on display until just the other day." She reached for the nearest one and examined it wistfully. Jamie's second birthday party. "I brought them out for Jamie to look at. To see if they might…help her remember those early years a little better."

"Did they?" Ross took the picture from her hand and studied it with intense interest. Amanda had to remind herself that he, too, was missing a giant piece out of the childhood of the little girl he loved.

"Maybe some. I'm not sure." She sighed. "I guess I

have to resign myself to the fact that those years will probably remain pretty much of a blank for Jamie.''

Ross set down the photo. ''She was so young, Amanda.''

''I know.'' She swallowed some more champagne. ''But we shared such a powerful bond, Jamie and I. Mother and child. The most powerful bond on earth. It's hard to accept that nothing is left of that.''

''I think you're wrong. I think at some fundamental level, that bond is still there.'' Ross took the glass from her hand and carefully placed both their glasses on the table beneath the lamp. ''Just because Jamie was too young to retain clear memories of her life with you doesn't mean she's lost that connection.'' He grasped Amanda's shoulders. ''You were her mother during the most formative years of her life. You made her the child she is today.'' He gave her a slight shake for emphasis. ''So you see, that bond you forged with Jamie will always exist. Because your love and your influence on her is an integral part of Jamie herself.''

Ross lowered his head to peer more closely into Amanda's face. ''Hey, hey, what's this? Tears?'' Tenderly, he carried one away with his knuckle.

Amanda sniffed. ''What you just said means a lot to me, Ross.'' She produced a crooked smile. ''So don't blame me for going all mushy on you.''

He chuckled as he bundled her into his arms. ''You go as mushy on me as you want. I don't mind a bit.''

Amanda slid her arms around him and squeezed her eyes shut. She was so lucky to have a wonderful husband like Ross. He was the most caring, sensitive, thoughtful man she'd ever met. And that was just the beginning of a long list of his desirable qualities. She couldn't believe she'd once hated him.

His deep voice stirred wisps of hair at her temples. ''All

that matters now is the future, Amanda. *Our* future. With Jamie. She's going to be our daughter for the rest of our lives."

Amanda hugged him tighter. "I can't believe how lucky I am. To have this second chance."

Ross tunneled his fingers through her hair and lifted her head so they could look into each other's eyes. Amanda was vividly aware of the hard male contours of his body pressed against hers, of the seductive warmth that seeped through the thin barrier of their clothing.

Ross's rugged features were etched with a mixture of strong emotions Amanda couldn't begin to sort out. "*I'm* the lucky one, Amanda," he said hoarsely. "To have Jamie." As he brought his mouth close to hers, she could feel his breath on her lips. "To have you."

She couldn't have said which of them moved first. But all at once, Ross was kissing her, and she was kissing him back, and she didn't want it to stop. Ever.

Chapter 11

Ross was playing a dangerous game, and he knew it.

Coming into Amanda's bedroom. Plying her with champagne. Touching her. Kissing her. He was walking a high tightrope between some very strong feelings. His own. And Amanda's, too, judging by the way she was kissing him back.

God, but she felt good in his arms! Ross had assured himself the only reason he'd come to her room tonight was because he wanted to share with her the joy of knowing that Jamie would soon be really, truly their child.

But deep down inside, Ross's fundamental honesty forced him to concede that there had been another reason, as well. One he could hardly call noble.

Amanda's tongue curled around his, blotting out any logical reasoning and replacing it with blind need. Ross groaned, deepening their kiss. Desire kept driving him on and on, even though he knew he should stop before things went too far. He'd sworn he wasn't going to do this. But he couldn't keep his hands off her.

He managed to drag his mouth from hers. "So lovely," he muttered into the soft, sweet-smelling curve of her neck. "Amanda..." Her pulse throbbed rapidly beneath his lips. Wisps of her hair tickled his skin, teasing, arousing him.

The heat generated between them was incredible. Ross was swimming through it, barely able to breathe as he shaped his hands to the hourglass of her lush breasts, her narrow waist, the sexy swell of her hips.

He cupped his palms around the delicious curve of her bottom and pulled her against him. Muffling a groan, he let Amanda feel how much he wanted her. Her body was as soft and pliant as melting candle wax. She molded her luscious curves into him, turning up the heat, threatening to set him on fire.

"Do you have any idea what you do to me?" he asked, clamping his teeth together.

Amanda's lips were perilously close to his again. "I..." She trailed a row of kisses along his rigid jaw, like drops of liquid flame. "I've got..." Nuzzling, licking him with teasing little strokes of her tongue. "I've got a pretty good idea," she whispered breathlessly.

"Oh, yeah?" A sharp surge of satisfaction knocked Ross off balance. All at once, he couldn't hold himself back anymore and toppled off the high wire.

When he melded his lips with hers again, Amanda felt certain she would die of pleasure. There was a reckless urgency about him now, as if he'd broken free of that reserve she always sensed holding him back whenever they were together like this. Except they'd never been together like this before. The previous kisses they'd shared were like the steps of a genteel minuet in comparison to this wild, frenzied dance of desire.

They coupled their tongues with mounting hunger, tangling their bodies together so their breaths mingled in panting counterpoint and their hearts clamored against each other in frantic syncopation.

Ross loosened the sash of her robe with shaking fingers. Exquisite anticipation throbbed almost painfully at the core of Amanda's being when he slipped his hand inside and began to knead her breast through the thin film of her nightgown. A moan of primitive pleasure escaped her throat. The sensation was sheer ecstasy.

Ross peeled her arms from around his neck, one at a time, so he could slip off her robe. Amanda buried her fingers in his hair to draw his mouth even more snugly against hers. She felt the feathery silk pool around her bare feet when her robe dropped to the floor.

Ross's face was flushed when he broke their kiss. "Let me look at you." His voice was hoarse. He slipped his fingers beneath the narrow straps of lace holding up her nightgown.

A sudden knot of apprehension coiled inside Amanda. Then she straightened her shoulders and let it pass. Ross was her husband, for heaven's sake! He'd made it plain that he found her desirable, that he wanted her. As much as she wanted him.

He eased the straps off her shoulders, down the tingling flesh of her arms. With equal measures of feminine satisfaction and heightened desire, Amanda watched his eyes dilate like blue jets of flame as the lacy fabric fell away and he gazed for the first time at her naked breasts.

"Amanda." His Adam's apple bobbed up and down as he swallowed. His eyes jerked up to meet hers. "You're so beautiful. So incredibly beautiful."

She felt hothouse roses bloom in her cheeks. The warmth spread down to her breasts and beyond. She couldn't believe how much she ached to have Ross touch her, to fulfill the raging desire that begged for release inside her.

When he lowered his head and brought his mouth to her nipple, she thought she would explode. Her fingers convulsed in his hair. Wave after wave of pleasure and need coursed through her body. She arched against him, barely able to stand up as passion dissolved the strength from her limbs.

When Amanda's knees trembled and she swayed forward, Ross caught her in his arms and carried her swiftly to the bed. He wanted to fling her to the mattress, tear off her nightgown with his bare hands, make love to her until she screamed his name.

But even as he commanded his muscles to lay her gently on the bed, even through the thunder pounding in his ears, Ross heard that ominous, insistent warning signal from his conscience.

Better stop now, it warned. *Because in about two seconds, it's going to be too late. And then you'll really have something to feel guilty about.*

Through a crimson haze of passion, Ross looked down at his gorgeous wife. Her dark hair was a sensual, tangled swirl against the pillow. Her eyes were luminous with need, heavy lidded with longing. And her breasts…

Ross squeezed his eyes shut as he clamped down on the savage desire the sight and touch of her creamy, rose-tipped breasts had aroused. They were exquisite. Round and full and tempting as heavy, ripe peaches nestled perfectly in the palms of his hands…

Oh, man.

His mouth went dry. His self-control teetered on a very precarious perch. *Knock it off, Chandler! This has got to stop, right now, right here.…*

Amanda was everything he'd ever wanted in a woman. Caring, loyal, strong, courageous…not to mention sexy as hell. And Ross couldn't have her.

He could, of course, if he was willing to ignore the fact

that his warm, welcoming wife would coldly slap his face
and bitterly curse him if she found out why he'd married
her.

But he wasn't.

How could he make love to Amanda, knowing she
would kick him angrily out of her bed if she knew the
truth? It would be like seducing her under false pretenses.
Ross had already deceived her once. It would cost him his
honor and self-respect if he did it again.

Not to mention what it might cost Amanda someday.

Muscles quivering with exertion, he pushed himself off
the mattress and stood.

"Ross?" Her gentle voice was shy, bewildered.

When he turned reluctantly, he saw that she'd pushed
herself up on one elbow. He quickly averted his gaze from
her bare breasts.

"Ross, what is it? What's wrong?"

*Oh, nothing much. Just the fact that I've lied to you.
Manipulated you. Taken advantage of your deepest sorrow
to make sure I never have to suffer the same loss you did.*

"Nothing's wrong, honey." Even as he spoke the lie,
he saw something shift in Amanda's puzzled eyes. An
awareness that he was being evasive for some reason.

Think fast, Chandler. What halfway plausible explanation could he give her for dousing the fires of their passion
so abruptly?

Jamie might hear us. Not through these solid walls.

Early day at work tomorrow. Oh, that's right. He was
the boss.

Not tonight, I have a headache. As if *that* would have
stopped him.

*I didn't come prepared. I don't have any way to protect
you.*

With that last thought, it dawned on Ross that he didn't
even know if Amanda *could* become pregnant. The subject

of whether it was she or her ex-husband who couldn't have children had never come up. Somehow it just hadn't seemed relevant.

Till now.

He sat back down on the bed. The far end of the bed, where he couldn't touch her. He didn't have to worry about any more tantalizing glimpses of her breasts, though. While he'd been racking his brain for a decent excuse, Amanda had yanked her nightgown back into place.

She sat up now, shoulders hunched, arms wrapped around her middle. Watching him. Waiting.

"Amanda, can you have children?" he asked gently.

Surprise lifted her brows. "Is *that* what this is all about?"

"It just occurred to me that you and I have never even discussed the matter."

Her lip curled. "You sure picked a funny time to discuss it."

"I know. I..." He raked his fingers through his hair. He still owed her an explanation.

"Does that make the difference whether or not you want to sleep with me?" She hurled the words at him like a challenge.

"No! It doesn't matter! I mean, not that it doesn't matter, but that—"

"You don't want to plant any of the precious Chandler seed in barren soil, is that it?"

"For God's sake, Amanda, of *course* that's not it!"

She sprang off the bed and snatched her robe from the floor. "Then you're afraid that we *might* have a child? Is that it?" She stabbed her arms through the sleeves of the kimono.

"Amanda." He came off the bed and put his hands on her shoulders. She twisted away. Ross blew a stream of air through his teeth. This was getting even more complicated than he'd thought it was. "Look," he said, latching onto the subject he found easiest to deal with at the moment, "you and I are two responsible adults. And responsible adults discuss these things before they have sex."

Amanda tightened the sash of her robe with a sharp jerk that made Ross wince. Her mouth was basted in a taut seam. But she didn't contradict him.

"I know that most people have this conversation before they're actually married," he went on, offering her a rueful attempt at a smile, "but just because we're already married doesn't mean we can skip it."

Grudging acknowledgment flickered in her eyes. "All right." Her delicate jaw shifted forward a little. "I guess maybe we *should* have talked about this before. But under the terms of our marriage, it hardly seemed necessary."

"No, it didn't." Ross had so casually agreed to those terms. Anything to get Amanda to marry him. How could he not have foreseen that sharing the same roof with such an attractive, intelligent, compassionate woman was bound to turn into an ongoing battle between his libido and his self-control?

Of course, there was no law that said those terms couldn't be renegotiated. But there was still that pesky matter of his conscience.

Amanda picked up her discarded champagne glass. She swirled the contents around, studying them, then set the glass down as if she'd changed her mind about drinking.

She shoved a dark cloud of hair away from her face and looked straight at Ross. "*I* was the one who couldn't have children," she said.

Ross absorbed that news, analyzing his own reaction to it. It hardly came as a shock, but he'd be lying to himself if he didn't own up to a measure of disappointment. It didn't alter his feelings for Amanda in the slightest, however.

"I'm sorry," he said.

She shrugged one shoulder. "I thought it was the most crushing blow I'd ever have to cope with." Her eyes sought the nearest photograph of Jamie. "But it wasn't."

"I'm sorry for *that,* too."

"It wasn't your fault." She lifted her chin a notch. "Any of it. I know that now."

Ironically, the fact that she was absolving him of any blame for her past sorrows only made Ross feel guiltier.

Amanda noted the shadow that moved through his eyes like a forlorn figure passing behind a window shade. She struggled to submerge the hurt his rejection had caused her.

"If you're concerned about producing an heir," she said with a toss of her head, "it might not be a totally lost cause. You see, infertility treatment costs a lot of money, and it's not covered by insurance. Paul and I reached the point where we couldn't afford to keep trying."

Impatiently, she blinked back tears. "But now, of course, money is no object." She circled her arm through the air to indicate the house, the estate, the unlimited resources of the Chandler wealth. "Taking that into account along with recent medical advances, there's still a possibility that I could become pregnant someday." Her voice had climbed higher and higher while she spoke.

"Amanda." Ross captured both her hands in his and said quietly, "You and I already *have* a child."

She sniffled. "I know," she said in a squeaky voice that cracked.

Ross made a move to pull her toward him, to shelter her against that wide, strong chest where she'd taken comfort so often lately.

But Amanda knew there was no comfort to be found there tonight. She pushed him away, shaking her head. "I think we should say good-night, Ross."

He released her reluctantly, then stood there shifting his weight from one leg to another as if there was more he wanted to say.

But Amanda was emotionally exhausted. Ross had aroused every cell in her body to a fever pitch, then backed off. As the grand finale, he'd raised the question of her inability to bear children. Amanda had come to terms with that particular sorrow years ago, but it was hardly a subject that made her feel sexy and romantic.

Right now, her husband's arms were the *last* place she wanted to be. Besides, it was time she stopped depending on Ross to make everything all better for her.

"Please," she said wearily. "Just go."

Slowly, he began to tuck in his shirt, which Amanda's hands had coaxed out of his trousers during their earlier frenzied encounter. When he unbuckled his belt to make the task easier, an unwelcome spasm of desire clenched her insides. Heaven help her, she still wanted him so badly....

"Good night," he said quietly, leaning down to kiss her forehead before she had a chance to dodge his lips.

She pressed her eyelids tightly shut. When she opened them, he was gone.

An empty chamber of loss echoed inside her heart. What had gone wrong? What had kept Ross from making love to her as he'd certainly seemed intent on doing?

Amanda wrapped her arms around her ribs, but that hollow ache didn't lessen. Her glance fell on the champagne Ross had left behind.

Some celebration this had turned out to be.

She picked up the bottle and glasses and carried them into the bathroom. Staring back at her from the mirror was a woman whose hair was a mess, whose mouth was puffy from hard, hungry kisses, whose eyes were bleak with unfulfilled longing.

Quickly, Amanda looked away. With the mechanical movements of a zombie, she emptied each glass into the sink, then upended the bottle and watched the contents pour down the drain. Fizzling away. Just like her hopes for a real marriage.

She rinsed out the glasses and dumped the empty bottle in the wastebasket. Then she walked slowly back across the bedroom, scraping her hair off her face with both hands and pulling so hard that her scalp protested.

Was Ross's urgent need to know whether or not she could become pregnant the real reason he'd withdrawn from her with such abruptness? Amanda didn't think so. Because after he'd laid her on the bed, while he was hovering over her, panting, his body hard and eager with desire, she'd glimpsed some kind of inner conflict in his eyes.

She dropped her hands and left her hair to its own devices. The problem definitely wasn't that Ross lacked a physical attraction to her. Amanda had no inflated ideas about her own irresistibility to the opposite sex, but there were certain things a man couldn't fake.

What about things he *could* fake, though? She knew by now that honor and integrity were very important to Ross. Had he been afraid that if he made love to her, he might be expected to say words he didn't mean afterward? Words like…*I love you.*

Could that have been the conflict she'd sensed in him? Honor versus hormones. If so, it was further proof of what an exceptional man Ross was that honor had won.

Amanda found little consolation in that thought, however. Because the more she considered it, the more that seemed the only possible explanation for Ross's mystifying retreat. For the way he always held back whenever they were together.

She drew the draperies aside and stared unhappily into the darkness. Maybe Ross wanted to avoid any messy entanglements with a woman whose feelings he didn't return. Maybe he was afraid that if he made love to Amanda, she would inevitably fall in love with him.

Her lips crimped in derision. That theory would certainly jibe with the arrogant Chandler ego that was as much Ross's inheritance as this winery.

Her fingers crumpled the expensive weave of the drapery fabric. Only problem was, Ross might be right. If they made love, maybe Amanda *would* fall in love with him. She didn't have far to fall after all. Considering she was already halfway there.

Summer brought an unbroken spell of sunny days to the Napa Valley, along with lots of hot, dry air. They hadn't had rain since before Memorial Day, and already the lush emerald that carpeted the hillsides was changing to a light tawny color that would remain until rain returned in the fall.

The grapevines thrived in the heat and the fertile soil. Amanda's relationship with Jamie thrived, too.

Jamie was out of school now, but still plenty busy with all the activities Ross had lined up for her before he knew Jamie was going to have a mother to take care of her during the summer. Rather than bemoan all the hours those activities occupied, Amanda chose instead to participate whenever she could.

She drove Jamie to horseback riding and swimming lessons, then stayed to watch. Deciding it would be going overboard to hang around and watch Jamie at art class, Amanda spent those mornings at home reading on the library patio, enjoying the lazy drone of bees and the pungent perfume of roses as the warmth of the sun baked into her skin.

Once in a while, she went window-shopping in St. Helena before picking up Jamie. She still had a hard time grasping the fact that she could stroll into any of the chic boutiques and walk out with the most expensive item in the shop if the fancy struck her.

Wednesday mornings, she took Jamie to soccer practice. Jamie and her teammates were part of an organized girls' league that played games against each other on Saturdays.

Amanda and Ross usually stood on the sidelines with the other parents, cheering her on. Watching Jamie tear up the field, ponytail streaming behind her, face scrunched in fierce concentration, Amanda had a hard time reconciling her with the sweet, angelic, curly-haired four-year-old she remembered. The one who still sucked her thumb and hadn't quite shed the chubby clumsiness of toddlerhood when she was taken away from Amanda.

Sometimes, Amanda's vision would blur with wistful tears for all that she'd lost. But she was determined to appreciate the miraculous second chance she'd been granted. She and Jamie were together *now*. That was all that mattered.

Amanda was also determined to resign herself to her loveless marriage. Ross was a wonderful husband in many ways, and she realized she ought to consider herself lucky to have him. Wasn't she the envy of every other soccer mom? But she couldn't help secretly wishing for the one thing on earth he couldn't give her. His love.

Since that night several weeks ago when he'd nearly taken her to bed, he'd behaved like the perfect gentleman. Polite, considerate, friendly within certain limits. But he hadn't touched her. Not once. And if Ross missed the physical side of their relationship, he wasn't letting it show.

The two of them spent most evenings together, sipping brandy or iced tea after Jamie had gone to bed. Ross would tell Amanda about his day at work, while she kept him up-to-date on Jamie's and her own activities. Often they discussed some thought-provoking article from that day's newspaper or argued over current political events.

It was surprising the number of times they saw eye-to-eye on things, and even their arguments were good-natured, usually ending with an agreement to disagree. An eavesdropper would assume they had a perfect marriage, based on solid communication and shared values. Though an eavesdropper might also find it puzzling that, on the surface at least, this appeared to be a marriage without passion.

But night after night, Amanda thrashed between the sheets, overheated and sticky and unable to sleep, even in the air-conditioned coolness of her bedroom. She had the hots for her own husband. And there wasn't a damn thing she could do about it.

Sometimes at the soccer games, when Jamie's team scored, Amanda would glance over while clapping and cheering and jumping up and down with the rest of the parents. Ross would be whistling or whooping or punching a triumphant fist in the air. And once in a while, he would give Amanda such a dazzling, exuberant, handsome smile that it almost broke her heart.

She was trying so hard not to love him. But he made it nearly impossible.

One Saturday morning, Ross was tied up at the winery, dealing with a breakdown of the climate-control equipment in the storage rooms where the barrels of aging wine were kept. Amanda went by herself to watch Jamie's soccer game.

Though Jamie had assisted in making a number of goals this summer, she was one of the younger players and tended to be overshadowed by the older girls. She hadn't yet scored a goal of her own.

Today, however, while Amanda watched Jamie's team progress down the field, a funny prickle of excitement shimmied up her spine. She dug her nails into her palms. "Come on, Jamie, you can do it," she urged under her breath.

Back and forth the little girls kicked the ball, keeping it away from the opposing team. Slowly, they zigzagged their way down the field till they were within range of the goal.

Jamie's coach was crouched not far from Amanda, hollering instructions through cupped hands. The other parents shouted encouragement to their kids. Amanda stood frozen, never taking her eyes off Jamie.

Jamie took possession of the ball. She glanced quickly at the goal net.

"All right, sweetheart, you can do it...." Amanda's stomach was knotted as tight as her fists.

Jamie drew back her foot. Her eyes narrowed with intense concentration. She kicked. The ball flew toward the goal...

And straight into the net!

Amanda let out a shriek of joy. The other parents clapped and yelled and patted her on the back.

Amanda was ecstatic. She was so proud....

Then, through the chaotic commotion on the field, she saw Jamie flying toward her. She wore a jubilant smile that stretched from ear to ear. Her feet barely touched the ground as she raced toward Amanda, golden ponytail streaming behind her like a championship pennant.

"Mom! Mom! Did you see me? I scored a goal!"

Amanda caught her breath. She had to gulp down the lump of emotion clogging her throat before she could reply. "I saw you, sweetheart! You were great!" She pumped her fist in the air.

Mom. She called me Mom!

The girls weren't supposed to come over to their parents during the game, so hugs would have to wait till later.

Jamie halted a prudent distance away, bouncing on her toes while she flung her arms toward the sky and did a little victory dance. When her grinning coach motioned her back into the game, she gave Amanda one last enthusiastic wave before jogging back to her teammates.

Amanda watched her run off in her grass-stained shorts and sagging red kneesocks, her sturdy young limbs a blur of motion. She inhaled a deep breath and felt as if she was filling up with happiness.

Her own darling girl. Calling her Mom instead of Mommy now, but that was as it should be. For the first time since being reunited with Jamie, it seemed to Amanda that she truly had her daughter back. Not just in a physical sense, but in an emotional one, as well.

And it was all thanks to Ross.

Amanda knew she could never repay the debt she owed him. But the least she could do was accept the boundaries he'd drawn between them. She could still be a good wife to Ross even if he wouldn't accept everything she longed to offer him.

Even if it meant never letting her husband know the secret feelings she carried for him inside her heart.

Chapter 12

Fireworks blossomed over Lake Michigan. From his vantage point at the window of an air-conditioned skyscraper in downtown Chicago, Ross couldn't hear the explosions. The windows of the modern office building were permanently sealed, the walls soundproofed.

He *could* hear the argument continuing in the conference room behind him, though. His hotshot team of advertising executives, bickering over the new campaign to market Chandler wine.

There was a difference of opinion, it seemed, about the timing and direction of the upcoming campaign. Ross had arrived in Chicago three days ago expecting a slick, dynamic, finished presentation all ready for his approval. Instead, he'd found himself playing referee to a bunch of squabbling creative types.

Which was why he was working late into the evening on the Fourth of July, when he much would have preferred twirling sparklers and setting off firecrackers back home with Amanda and Jamie.

"Jamie'll be disappointed you won't be here to watch the big parade in town with us," Amanda had said when he'd phoned last night to let her know he wouldn't be home for several more days at least.

Had he just imagined it, or had Amanda sounded a little disappointed, too?

Her image shimmered in the glass pane in front of Ross's eyes, reflected against the darkness beyond. He was two thousand miles away from her, so it was safe to let his imagination linger on the vision of those full, sensual lips curving into a come-hither smile just for him.

Or those gorgeous brown eyes limpid with passion in that delicious instant just before he closed his mouth over hers.

Or her soft, warm, naked flesh straining beneath his hands...

Desire hurtled through him like a bottle rocket.

"Damn," he said.

Instantly, the arguing behind him ceased. He turned around to find every face in the room aimed in his direction.

Ken Abernathy, one of the firm's vice presidents and a longtime business associate of Ross's, distributed a warning look to his colleagues as he stood.

"Ross, I'm sorry." He spread his hands in a placating gesture. "I thought we'd settled this debate before you arrived, but..." He grimaced at the artwork and charts strewn around the conference table. "Look, we're all tired," Ken went on. "Why don't we head home for some shut-eye and start fresh in the morning?"

Home. Rolling hills, shady oak trees, fields of grapevines basking under clear blue skies. Amanda and Jamie.

His family.

All at once, Ross's eagerness to see them was so great it was like a sharp stab through his chest. He didn't *want* to go home to his impersonal hotel room. He wanted to be with the people he cared about. He wanted to eat breakfast with them and catch up with all the day-to-day news he'd missed out on this week. He wanted to hug his wife and tuck his little girl into bed.

Ross grabbed his suit jacket from the back of his chair. "Susan," he asked the note-taking secretary, who was stifling a yawn behind her hand, "would you mind calling the airline to see if you can get me on their last flight to San Francisco tonight?"

That woke her up. "Sure." Obviously happy for something productive to do, she bustled from the room. The remaining attendees eyed each other warily.

"Ross." Ken spoke up with a worried look of alarm. "I know this delay is inexcusable, but what if we can come up with two alternative approaches by noon tomorrow? You can decide which one you want to go with and still make it back to California in time for dinner."

Ross took a swallow of the cold dregs remaining in his coffee cup and made a face as he set it back down. He picked up his briefcase. "You make the decision," he told Ken. "I'm going home."

Ken dogged his footsteps across the plush conference-room carpet. "But I can't—you mean you don't want to—what are we supposed to—"

"Look." Ross paused in the doorway. "We've known each other a long time, Ken. By now, you've got a pretty good idea of what I like and don't like. I trust your judgment." He consulted his watch. "I'm leaving the direction of the ad campaign up to you. Call and let me know what you decide."

Ken combed nervous fingers through his thinning hair. "Well...sure. I mean, if *you're* sure."

Ross thought about the love and laughter awaiting him at home. About how he couldn't stand to wait even one more day to see the two people who meant most to him in the world.

"I'm sure," he said. Then he rushed for the elevator. He had a plane to catch.

Old houses creaked. And this house was nearly a hundred years old. Still, Ross had lived in it more than twenty years. By now, he had a fairly accurate map in his head about which floorboards to avoid.

He crept through the dark toward his bedroom, footsteps muffled on the hallway runner. With his briefcase in one hand and suitcase in the other, he couldn't check the luminous face of his watch, but he guessed it was close to three in the morning.

Jamie's door was ajar as he passed. Enough illumination from her night-light trickled into the hall so Ross could see where he was going without switching on a light that might disturb someone's sleep. Amanda's door was closed when he tiptoed by.

Just being this close to the two of them filled him with contentment and made the exhausting, late-night flight from Chicago well worth it. He grinned when he thought of how surprised they'd be to see him in the morning.

In his room, he set down his luggage and draped his suit jacket over the nearest chair. He'd worry about hanging it up tomorrow. Later today, rather. Right now, all he cared about was shucking off the rest of his clothes and falling into—

A light exploded into the room like sparks from a Roman candle as Ross was in the process of yanking off his second sock. He heard a startled exclamation. Momentarily blinded, he was still hopping up and down on one leg, fumbling with his sock, when his eyes readjusted.

Amanda stood wide-eyed in the doorway. Barefoot. One

hand clamped to her heart, the other clutching an antique vase over her head as if she meant to clobber him with it.

Ross straightened up, blinking. He commented, "That little knickknack you're holding is worth about ten thousand dollars."

"Huh?" she gasped. Her breasts rose and fell quickly beneath her filmy nightgown. Her face was drained of color. "What are you…" She glanced at the object in her hand. "This? It was the first weapon I—Ross, you're supposed to be in Chicago!"

"I decided to come home early." He edged toward her and gently extracted the vase from her hand. "This wasn't exactly the welcome I had in mind, though."

Amanda sagged against the door frame. "I thought you were a burglar! Or a kidnapper after Jamie, or—or—I don't know what. But I had to do *something*."

Her hands were trembling and cold as ice when Ross took them in his. "Honey, I'm sorry. I thought I could sneak in without waking anyone."

"Well, I—I happened to be awake. I heard a noise in the hall and all I could think about was Jamie, and I just—I just—oh, God, Ross, I was so scared!" Her chin quivered as her voice climbed to a high-pitched squeak.

"Amanda, I'm so sorry." Ross bundled her into his arms. What a woman! Charging out to defend her loved ones armed only with a fragile art object. Could a man possibly ask for a better wife? He stroked her hair, savoring its silky texture. "Haven't you ever heard of calling 911?" he teased gently.

"There wasn't time." Her voice was muffled against his shirtfront. "By the time help got here, the intruder could have…" She braced her hands against his ribs and lifted her head to regard him with suspicion. "Quit making fun of me!" She gave him a halfhearted slap on the chest.

"I'm not making fun of you," Ross said with a laugh,

coaxing her back into his embrace. He kissed the top of her head. "I think you were very brave." He kissed her temple. "I think you're wonderful." He tilted up her chin and kissed the tip of her nose. "I think you're..."

He swallowed. Amanda was staring straight up at him with those heartbreak eyes. Those deep, dark, irresistible eyes that lured a man toward them. Into them. Deeper and deeper, till he reached the point of no return.

"Beautiful." The word was like a sigh trapped in the diminishing space between their lips.

Stop! Don't do this! You'll regret it! his conscience warned.

But Ross couldn't stop. Not this time. He was too far gone.

Amanda's face filled his vision. The heat from her slender body enveloped him, drawing him closer. The delicious floral fragrance rising from her hair and from her skin enticed him like a bee toward nectar.

His fingers dented the soft, bare flesh of her upper arms, as if preparing to thrust her backward any second. But they didn't.

Her lips were as delicate as flower petals when Ross touched his tongue to them. That fleeting instant of contact was like setting a match to a stick of dynamite.

Desire exploded inside him. He crushed his mouth to hers. Amanda whipped her arms around his neck as if she, too, could no longer bear one more second of separation.

Instinctively, Ross succeeded in kicking the door shut. He groped for the lock, unwilling to break their kiss for even a moment.

He left the light on. The first time he made love to his own wife, no way was he going to do it in the dark.

He whisked Amanda up into his arms and made it across the room in three strides. Together they rolled onto the bed, limbs entangled, tongues entwined, straining against each other as if trying to fuse their bodies into one.

A flimsy nightgown, a cotton shirt were all that separated their thudding hearts. Easily remedied.

Ross raised himself up and fumbled with his shirt buttons. Amanda's mouth was sweet and hot and insistent as she kept her arms locked behind his neck to hold him close.

Somehow he couldn't quite convey the proper messages between brain and fingers to unfasten those damn buttons. A mounting sense of urgency drove him to desperate measures.

He dragged his mouth from Amanda's. Straddling her, he grabbed fistfuls of his shirt and yanked. Buttons flew everywhere. He whipped off his shirt and hurled it aside.

Eyes gleaming with admiration and hunger, Amanda trailed her fingers slowly down his chest. Ross balanced on his knees, barely able to restrain himself from falling on her and savagely taking her.

Her touch had the same incendiary effect as splashing kerosene on a raging fire. Inch by excruciating inch, she raked her hands down his torso. Collarbone...nipples...belly...finally his belt buckle.

The pressure building in that region was increasingly uncomfortable. Ross shifted his weight. "Turnabout is fair play," he said, reaching for the hem of her nightgown.

"Just try to leave it in one piece," she said breathlessly, her eyes twinkling. With Ross's help, she wriggled out of it in a flash.

"Amanda." Lying beside her, he skimmed his hand over her gently undulating curves. "You're so soft, so beautiful...." When he came to her panties, he slipped a finger inside the elastic. Moments later, she was completely nude.

"What was that remark about fair play?" She arched her eyebrows suggestively, tugging at his belt.

"Oh, well. If you insist." With a lazy grin, he climbed off the bed and stood before her. Deliberately, he unbuckled his belt, lowered his zipper. He slid off his trousers and underwear together. Amanda's eyes dilated with desire while she watched him. And Ross loved every lust-filled second of her scrutiny.

Heart pounding, Amanda recalled the moment she'd set eyes on Ross less than two months ago, when he'd arrived on her doorstep and asked her to marry him. That night, he'd reminded her of a well-dressed Greek god.

Tonight, *un*dressed, he brought the same comparison to mind. Amanda's mouth went dry as she studied him shamelessly. Broad chest covered with a sprinkling of golden hairs, tapering to a flat belly and narrow hips. Muscular, well-proportioned legs that looked capable of carrying him to victory in a marathon.

The proud, hard essence of his masculinity.

The glorious sculpture of his body turned Amanda's limbs to liquid. "Make love to me," she whispered.

She didn't need to ask twice. Even as a pinprick of doubt made her wonder if Ross would turn away from her this time, too, his blue eyes were glittering with shards of eagerness.

He sank onto the bed beside her. For a moment, he just looked at her, ravishing her with his eyes as if he couldn't believe she was real. "Amanda." His voice was husky as he laid his hand on her hip. "Darling, I want you...I want you so much...."

"Yes," she breathed, her throat filled with anticipation. She wove her fingers through the blond strands of his hair as he bent his head over her.

He began to worship her with his hands, his mouth, his entire body. Pleasure flooded through her. For a minute, she simply surrendered to the indescribable sensations, letting Ross mold her in his hands like a warm, pliant lump of clay. Wherever he touched her, tingling heat branded her skin and sent desire arrowing straight to her feminine core.

Then she remembered that making love required the efforts of *both* people.

Amanda reached for him. Ross let out a groan when her fingers closed around his rigid flesh. Slowly, she stroked him, reveling in her power to enslave him with her passion, just as he'd enslaved her with his.

His hot, moist breath fell faster and faster on her neck, her face, her shoulders. Her skin sizzled beneath his mouth.

"Whoa," he panted finally, covering her hand with his. "Honey, you keep that up and we're going to have our own private skyrocket show in a minute."

"Hurray for the red, white and blue." She gave him a sly, wicked smile.

Ross shook his head and chuckled. "You are something else, you know that?" He wiped his mouth with the back of his wrist. "All right, Miss Fourth of July. Two can play at that game."

He lowered his head to her breast.

Amanda moaned as he flicked his tongue across the hardened tip. Desire spiraled through her like a shock wave. Dear heaven, but she wanted him inside her! She'd waited forever, it seemed, to join her body with his, to become one flesh, to share with her husband the ultimate physical expression of their marriage vows.

She arched her back against his bed, dizzy with need, seeking the release only he could give her. His mouth closed around her nipple. Pure, white-hot rapture poured through her like molten steel. "Ross...darling..." she gasped. "Please..."

He lifted his head from her breast, eyes gleaming, mouth shiny with moisture. "Turnabout's fair play, remember?" He slid his hand lower, toward the writhing, urgent center of her need. When he parted the velvety, wet folds of flesh and located the tiny swollen bud, Amanda thought she would shatter into a million pieces.

"Ross!" she cried. "Stop or I'll—I'll—"

"Yes," he hissed through his teeth.

"Please…I want you…I need you to be…"

"Don't fight it, Amanda," he urged, strumming her with his fingertips, tickling her with his hot breath as he nuzzled her neck.

"Ross…"

"I'm right here with you." He brought his mouth to her breast again, teasing, sucking, kneading…

Desire clawed its way higher and higher inside her. Spots danced before her eyes. Her skin was on fire. Nothing had ever felt this good in her entire life. How could it feel like such torture at the same time?

She clutched at Ross, dimly aware of the rigid muscles beneath her hands, the delicious sandpaper rasp of his skin against hers and the erotic pressure that kept climbing inside her, higher and higher…

"Ross," she choked out. "Now…"

All at once, Amanda felt herself sailing off the edge of a cliff with a blazing burst of fireworks and a roar of sound rushing through her head.

Ross moved on top of her, his features taut with passion, his eyes wild with hunger. As he nudged against her, she opened herself to him and then he was inside her, filling her up, driving her over the brink of that cliff again and again.…

Ross held himself back as long as he could, but once he was sheathed inside his wife's sleek, sexy warmth, he knew his time was about up.

She was the most exciting, passionate, wonderful woman he'd ever known. He couldn't believe she was finally here in his bed, thrashing her head back and forth on his pillow, her beautiful face contorted with ecstasy.

He kissed her, plunging his tongue into her mouth while he thrust himself deep inside her, over and over, faster and faster. For so long, he'd fought to keep his desire for her at bay. All those weeks of frustration and pent-up longing now hammered at him, demanding escape.

His heart pounding, pumping...ragged breaths searing his throat...pleasure and passion mounting inside him with every stroke...

"Amanda," he gasped against her lips, "darling..."

And then he was soaring toward the sky, racing through a galaxy of pleasure that swirled around him, pinwheeling him head over heels, sucking the air from his lungs.

Dizzily, he floated back to earth. He opened his eyes to find Amanda curled next to him, giving him a dreamy, droopy-lidded smile.

"Fireworks," she murmured.

"Ka-*boom*," Ross agreed, miming a miniature explosion with his hands. Still trying to catch his breath, he slid his arm around her shoulders and cuddled her against him. "Honey, that was...incredible." He kissed the damp strands of hair clinging to her temples.

"Mmm." She twined her fingers through the wiry curls on his chest. "Makes me feel positively...patriotic."

Ross grinned. "Just call me Yankee Doodle."

Amanda laughed as she nipped him playfully on the shoulder. "What a way to celebrate the Fourth of July."

"Except now it's the fifth." Ross clenched back an enormous yawn. He couldn't believe it would soon be dawn.

He couldn't believe how utterly sensational making love

with his wife had turned out to be. More passionately rewarding than even his wildest fantasies.

In the back of his mind he heard guilt tap-tapping on his conscience. *You went and did it, Chandler,* it scolded. *Made love to Amanda even though she would hate you if she knew why you married her.*

Ross silenced his regrets for now. Somehow he would make it up to Amanda. Somehow they would work it out. After all, it wasn't as if he'd made love to her with ulterior motives, was it?

His desire for her had been genuine. Oh, *boy,* had it been genuine! And so was his desire to make their marriage work. Tonight had been a significant step in that direction.

So he hoped anyway.

"Honey?" He hugged her close.

"What is it?" she murmured sleepily. That dreamy smile was still attached to her lips.

Ross cleared his throat. "Will you...spend the night with me?"

She skimmed her knuckles lightly along his jaw. "What's left of it, you mean?"

"Yes." He kissed her hand.

"Hmm." She drummed her fingers thoughtfully on his ribs. "I will, on one condition."

Ross hoisted himself onto one elbow and looked down at her. "Oh, yeah? What's that?"

She licked her lips like a cat who'd just finished a bowl of cream. "That *I* don't have to be the one who gets up to turn off the light."

"Gosh, you drive a hard bargain." Ross scratched his head. "I guess I could get up and do it. If that's what it would take."

Amanda pressed a seductive necklace of butterfly kisses along his collarbone. "Hurry back to bed," she whispered.

Ross groaned. "Count on it." He rolled to his feet and staggered across the room, still feeling slightly punch-drunk with passion.

By the time he'd made his way back through the dark, Amanda had arranged the bedcovers over herself. Ross climbed in beside her. He couldn't believe how natural that simple action felt. As if the two of them had been made for each other.

Amanda snuggled against him, resting her head on his chest. Her breathing was a pleasing, warm rhythm against Ross's skin. Funny how protective he felt with his arm wrapped around her. As if a woman prepared to whack prowlers over the head needed any protection from *him*.

Ross grinned in the dark. He kissed Amanda's hair, inhaling the subtle floral scent of her shampoo. He was an awfully lucky man. And he intended to do everything in his power to make sure that this precious woman lying in his arms never had cause to regret marrying him.

He was hovering on the verge of sleep when her soft voice cajoled him back to wakefulness. "Ross?"

"What is it, honey?" He yawned, adjusting his position to maximize the amount of contact between their bodies.

"Why *did* you come back early from Chicago?" Amanda's question sounded far away, as if she, too, was teetering on the brink of sleep.

"Because I missed you," he replied truthfully.

"Mmm." With a tiny purr of contentment, Amanda burrowed her face into him and drifted off almost immediately. Ross could tell by the change in her breathing.

There was so much more he wanted to say besides *I missed you.*

But that would have to do for tonight.

Chapter 13

"And then we had a swimming race, just like in the 'Lympics, and guess who came in second?"

"Who?" Ross inquired on cue.

"Me!" Jamie poked herself in the chest, crossed her arms and gave her uncle a jumbo-size grin.

"You?" Ross put on a show of surprise. "That's terrific, James!" He reached across the breakfast table to tousle her hair. "Did you get a ribbon?"

"Yup, and it's red!" She happily attacked her scrambled eggs, watching Ross with adoring eyes.

Amanda knew just how she felt. She'd been sending her husband the same kind of looks ever since waking up next to him that morning.

A little thrill of pleasure skittered up her spine while she sipped her coffee. Even though she'd gotten a grand total of perhaps four hours' sleep last night, happiness raced through her bloodstream like a double dose of caffeine.

Now she and Ross were truly married at last.

Images of last night's passionate lovemaking danced through her memory again. Ross...so hot and hard and hungry, yet so tender and considerate at the same time. And her own wanton response, reaching for him greedily, unable to get enough of him, until that final glorious explosion...

"Sure is hot this morning, isn't it?" Ross's eyes twinkled suggestively at her.

Amanda's cheeks felt flushed. She felt warmth radiating from her skin. "Maybe we're having a heat wave," she said, giving him a playful kick beneath the table.

Ross hooked his foot around hers and nuzzled their knees together. The sexy, smoldering look he gave her melted her insides. Dear God, how was she going to make it through the day? Hours and hours threatened to drag ahead until she and Ross could be together in bed again....

"Do I hafta go to art class today?" Jamie asked, jarring the two adults from the meaningful, lingering glance they were exchanging.

"I thought you *loved* art class," Amanda said.

Jamie toyed with the rest of her eggs, which were no doubt cold by now. She'd been too busy talking to eat, filling Ross in on all the events that had taken place in their lives while he was out of town.

"But Uncle Ross is back now, and I'd rather stay home with *you* guys." Jamie's blue eyes were pleading.

Ross's chair scraped against the tile floor as he pushed away from the table. "I've got to go to work today anyway, James. Lots of catching up to do." He dropped a kiss on top of her head. "The three of us will spend a whole day together this weekend, all right?"

"Oh...all right." She clinked her fork against her plate, pouting a little with disappointment.

"You pick out someplace special for us to go." Ross

grazed one knuckle across her cheek. "How about walking me to the door, Amanda?"

When they reached the entrance hall, Ross whirled her around and hauled her into his arms. The kiss he gave her was hot, slow and deliberate, filled with passion and promise.

"You and I have lots of catching up to do, too," he told her in a low voice that sent vibrations tripping along her nerve endings.

"Mmm. I can hardly wait." Amanda brushed her lips against his, once…twice…three times.

Ross growled. "Keep that up and you won't have to wait for long." He circled his strong arms around her waist and gave her a hug that squeezed all the air from her lungs.

"Promises, promises," she teased breathlessly.

He pulled his handsome features into a stern expression. "Just you wait till tonight, Mrs. Chandler," he warned, wagging a finger in front of her nose.

Amanda caught his finger between her teeth and nibbled gently. "Don't you worry," she said seductively. "I'll be waiting."

Ross sucked in his breath, then let out a groan. "Good God, woman! How do you expect me to make it through the day when you look at me like that?" He dragged her against him again, running his hands all over her body while he buried his face in her neck and did magical things with his lips.

Laughing, Amanda finally pushed him away. "Cut that out! What if someone sees us?"

"So what? We're married, aren't we?"

She opened the front door and handed him his briefcase. "Have a nice day at the office, dear." She stretched up to plant a chaste kiss on his mouth, then demurely batted her eyelashes at him.

Ross grinned. "That's not exactly what I meant." He

kissed her once more, an impudent smack on the lips. "I'll show you tonight what I had in mind." The final look he gave her nearly scorched the soles off her feet. He jogged down the steps and sauntered off down the road to the winery, whistling.

After a few blissful moments of watching him, Amanda closed the door and leaned back against it. She shut her eyes and let a flood of exhilarating emotions pour through her.

Joy. Lust. Gratitude.

And most overwhelming of all, love.

Last night had proved to Amanda what she'd been trying to deny to herself for weeks now.

She was madly, completely, head-over-heels in love with her husband.

And one of the things she loved most about him was that he didn't have one deceitful bone in his entire gorgeous, sexy body. Amanda believed with soul-deep certainty that Ross hadn't been faking his feelings for her while they'd made love.

She released a long, shivery sigh of happiness. He hadn't *said* he loved her. Not in so many words. But he'd certainly *shown* her that he had strong feelings for her.

Maybe he wasn't ready to call it love yet. But in the depths of her heart, Amanda was convinced Ross and she were meant for each other. Now that they'd finally consummated their passion, surely it wouldn't be long before Ross realized it, too. Amanda's knees went weak when she recalled the sweet, eager ecstasy of their lovemaking.

How on earth was she going to make it till tonight?

A vaguely familiar car was parked in the driveway when Amanda arrived home after dropping Jamie at art class. An *expensive,* vaguely familiar car. Someone to see Ross?

Her pulse picked up its tempo at the prospect of this

unexpected chance to see her husband during work hours. But when she poked her head into the various rooms where Ross might be meeting with someone, she found no sign of him.

Nora was in the kitchen, banging pots and pans around and grumbling under her breath. Amanda inhaled the luscious cinnamon fragrance filling the air. "Is…something wrong?" she asked cautiously.

"Wrong?" Nora made a sour face. "Nothing much. Only the dishwasher is not working, and the repairman, he tells me he cannot come until this afternoon, so I have to wash all these by hand—" she waved with disgust at the stack of dishes in the sink "—and then Mr. Caleb's lawyer, he comes by without calling first, and Mr. Caleb tells me to bring them some coffee—*real* coffee, he says, not that decaffeinated kind, even though the doctor *told* him he is not supposed to—"

"Is there anything I can do to help?" Amanda asked hastily. Nora was steaming like a teakettle.

"*Ay!* My rolls!" She clapped her hands to her head, then snatched up a pair of pot holders. "Probably they are burned already," she muttered as she flung open the oven door and yanked out a metal sheet.

Amanda peered over her shoulder. "They look perfect to me," she assured Nora. "Mmm. And they smell wonderful."

With efficient swipes of her spatula, Nora loaded cinnamon rolls onto a plate. "Now I must take these up to Mr. Caleb." She transferred the plate to a tray containing a carafe of coffee and two cups.

"I'll take this up," Amanda told her.

Nora arched her brows at the surprising offer. It was no secret that Mr. Caleb's granddaughter-in-law preferred to give him a wide berth.

But Amanda was brimming over with goodwill this

morning. Now that her marriage was secure and Jamie's adoption had been set in motion, she saw no reason not to extend an olive branch toward her old nemesis. Or, in this case, a plate of his favorite cinnamon rolls.

After a brief tug-of-war, Nora relinquished the tray. "You are sure you do not mind taking this up?" she asked dubiously.

"You've got enough to do," Amanda told her, shifting the little containers of cream and sugar to balance the tray more evenly. "Don't worry. I'll leave before he starts throwing cinnamon rolls at me."

Nora giggled. She patted Amanda's shoulder, the first spontaneous display of affection Amanda had ever received from the older woman. "You just throw them right back, okay?"

"Good idea."

Happiness propelled Amanda upstairs so that her feet barely touched the steps. A new mood of harmony seemed to prevail in the Chandler household this morning. To Amanda's astonishment and delight, she realized that, for the first time, she truly felt like part of the family.

Like one of the Chandlers. Who would have thought it?

As she approached Caleb's bedroom, however, she detected signs that the new harmonious atmosphere hadn't yet infiltrated this wing of the mansion.

Caleb's angry words carried down the hall. "That's what I'm paying you for, isn't it? To make stuff like this go away."

A male voice replied, too low for Amanda to make out what he was saying. She recognized it, though, from the time when Caleb's lawyer had brought the adoption papers for signing.

She slowed down, reluctant to intrude on whatever private conversation Caleb was having with his attorney.

"I tell you, there's no way to prove it! It's my word against his."

Oh, dear. What past bit of skulduggery had finally caught up with Caleb?

Amanda was now close enough to decipher part of the attorney's reply. "...a serious matter. It would be best if you cooperated with the investigators when they arrive."

"Tell 'em I'm in a coma."

A frustrated sigh. "You know I can't do that. I'm an officer of the court. I can't lie to the authorities."

"Ha! You're a lawyer, aren't you?"

"Very amusing."

"What are they digging this up for now anyway? It happened a long time ago."

"Three years isn't a long time. According to what the D.A.'s office told me this morning, Judge Franklin came under suspicion several months ago in a different court case. Not unexpectedly, they've begun probing into other past cases, trying to find additional evidence against him."

Out in the hall, Amanda stood paralyzed, as if a bolt of lightning had struck her.

Judge Franklin?

Dear God, she would never forget that name. Never. The judge who'd taken Jamie away from her. Three years ago.

What had Caleb done three years ago?

Nausea churned in her stomach. She held her breath, listening.

"If those meddling legal beagles from New York think they're getting any help from me," Caleb warned, "they'd better think again."

"Look, the D.A.'s not after you," his lawyer said soothingly. "The smartest thing you can do is tell the truth, grit your teeth and take your medicine. They're not about to send an old man with a weak heart off to prison."

Caleb sputtered with indignation.

New York? Amanda thought wildly. There might be more than one Judge Franklin in New York. But not another one that Caleb Chandler had had dealings with three years ago.

Only…what kind of dealings could he have had that would result in the D.A.'s office wanting to question him now?

"You don't know what's at stake," Caleb insisted. And for the first time, Amanda detected a note of fear behind his ill-tempered bravado.

"I've already explained. The worst punishment you'd face would be some kind of fine. A slap on the wrist."

"That's not what I'm talking about," Caleb snapped. "I'm talking about *her*."

"Her? You mean Mrs. Chandler?"

"Who do you think I'm talking about—Queen Victoria?"

Irritation crept into the lawyer's patient tone. "Pardon me for being a little slow on the uptake, but I've had barely an hour to absorb the fact that my biggest client has allegedly committed bribery. I'm still a little stunned."

Bribery.

The tray Amanda was holding trembled so that dishes and silverware rattled faintly against each other.

"If that woman finds out I paid off the judge to make sure we got Jamie back, all hell's going to break loose."

A soft cry escaped Amanda's throat, a pathetic sound that was half moan, half whimper.

The lawyer made a shushing noise. "Did you hear something?"

The crash of china shattered the silence.

"Who's there?" Caleb yelled.

But Amanda was already stumbling down the hall, hand clamped to her mouth, running…running as if she would never stop.

"Word has it that Jared Whitney's going to be putting his place up for sale any day now."

"Oh, yeah?" Ross leaned back in his chair and regarded Ted Cardoza thoughtfully. "How come?"

Ted shrugged. "That winery was always more of a hobby to him than a serious business. Guess he decided to get a new hobby."

Ross tapped a pencil against his desk. "You think we ought to make him an offer?"

The operations manager grinned. "I was hoping you'd suggest that." He riffled through the stack of file folders he'd brought to their meeting and whipped one out with the same flourish as a magician producing a bouquet of fake flowers.

"I haven't suggested anything," Ross countered. "I'm asking *your* opinion."

"Okay. Here it is." Ted spread one of his beloved computer printouts across Ross's desk. Ross leaned forward to study it. "We're only talking about forty acres, of course, but that's prime growing land. Now, what I figure is—"

Just then, the door to the office flew open. Both men jerked up their heads as Amanda burst into the room. Ross was on his feet in less than a second. He could tell by her distraught expression she was struggling to conceal the fact that something was terribly wrong.

"What is it?" He came around his desk. "Has something happened to Jamie?"

"No! No, she's…fine." Amanda shoved her hair back with a shaky motion. "I—I need to talk to you."

Ted had risen slowly to his feet. "We can, uh, continue this later, Ross."

"Sure." Ross's gaze didn't budge from Amanda's face. She was as pale as parchment, her dark eyes enormous. Her skin had a pinched, taut quality that made her look haggard. Her lips were trembling.

God, what could be the matter?

Ted eased past her on his way out the door. "Nice to see you again, Mrs. Chandler."

She managed to acknowledge him with the barest flicker of a smile, obviously a purely social reflex.

After Ted shut the door behind him, Ross grasped Amanda's shoulders. "Darling, what's wrong?" Beneath his fingers, he felt her muscles quivering as though a high-voltage current were passing through her body.

She shrugged off his hands and pulled away. Vague, shapeless dread settled over Ross like an ominous fog. Only a couple of hours ago, Amanda had been warm and loving, sparkling with playful seduction. Now she couldn't bear his touch.

What could have happened since morning to cause such a complete change in her?

A distant voice drifted through that foreboding fog. *Maybe it's not something that* happened. *Maybe it's something she* learned....

Ross swallowed. "Amanda, whatever it is, just say it."

She paced the floor of his office, twisting her hands together, avoiding his eyes. He got the impression that if she was forced to stand still, she would fly into a million pieces.

But then she did stop, in front of the wall covered with framed awards Chandler wines had won over the years. "Caleb," she said, nearly choking on the two syllables. "He bribed the judge to take Jamie away from me."

Sinking feeling would hardly be adequate to describe the gaping chasm of apprehension that opened up inside Ross.

He edged closer to Amanda. "What are you talking about?" he asked, stalling for time. Time for what? To come up with another lie to explain his way out of this?

"The custody hearings." Her voice wobbled. Her eyes were wary and wild, like a frightened deer's. "That's why

Paige was awarded custody. Because *Caleb* paid off the judge.'' She practically spat out his name, and now Ross could detect the fury simmering beneath the surface of her agitation.

He chose his words carefully. ''How do you know this?'' he asked.

''Because the D.A.'s office in New York is investigating Judge Franklin for bribery and they want to talk to Caleb.'' Her upper lip curled with bitterness. ''I overheard him ordering his lawyer to buy his way out of *this* mess, too.''

''*What?* When?'' Alarm raised the hackles on the back of Ross's neck.

''Just now. At the house.'' She flailed an arm in the general direction of the mansion.

Ross's first instinct was to race home and find out what the hell was going on. But he realized he had a higher priority now than trying to save his grandfather's wily old hide.

He had to face his wife.

She jammed her fingers through her hair. ''That bastard.'' Icy anger was beginning to push its way to the forefront. ''He stole my child.''

''Amanda, Jamie's going to be our daughter, remember? Nothing's going to change that.'' Ross made an effort to soothe her, but it was like trying to douse a forest fire with a watering can.

She glanced at him sharply. Suspicion joined forces with the anger blazing in her eyes. ''You don't seem too surprised,'' she said slowly. ''I don't exactly hear you leaping to his defense and insisting he couldn't have done it.''

She was practically drawing Ross a map of his escape route. All he had to do was pretend to be as shocked and outraged as she was. His grandfather would back up his protestations of ignorance once Ross pointed out what the consequences would be otherwise.

But if he took the easy way out—the *deceitful* way out—he would never be able to look himself in the mirror again.

Amanda was studying him with a cold, intense scrutiny that sent a chill down his spine. "Why is that?" she mused as if posing a hypothetical question. "Why don't you seem the least bit astonished to find out Caleb's been accused of bribery?"

Ross squared his shoulders. Time to own up to the truth. The tangled strands of the deceptive tapestry he'd woven were finally coming unraveled. And there wasn't one single thing he could do to mend the damage.

He took a deep breath. "Because I already know what Granddad did."

Amanda flinched as if he'd slapped her. "You *knew?*" she asked, sounding as if the air had been driven out of her lungs. "You knew he'd bribed that damn judge, that he'd illegally stolen my child from me...and you went *along* with it?"

"I didn't know about it at the time," Ross said, scrambling for at least some small measure of redemption. "I only learned what he'd done after the fact. When it was too late."

"Too late to restore Jamie to her rightful mother?" Incredulity etched Amanda's tone like acid. "Too late to see justice done?"

Ross stood his ground. "This was Jamie's home by then. We loved her. She loved us." Even though what he said was true, guilt still nagged him. "Resurrecting the custody issue would only have traumautized her further. It seemed best to leave things as they were."

"Oh, I see." Amanda nodded in an exaggerated parody of enlightenment, tapping her chin. "And when exactly did this occur, Ross? Exactly how long ago did you find out what that rotten, ruthless child stealer had done?"

Don't ask me that! he wanted to warn her. Because he knew the answer might irreparably destroy their marriage. The marriage that, only this morning, had promised such bright, exciting possibilities for happiness.

Ross could take one of two roads. He could lie to Amanda, claim he'd learned of the bribery long ago, and probably smooth things over. Of course, that would doom forever any chance that he and Amanda could ever build a marriage based on honesty and trust.

Or he could take the decent, honorable road and confess the truth. For which Amanda might never forgive him.

Her gaze bored steadily into his. When it came right down to it, Ross discovered he really had no choice at all.

"I found out about the bribery just under two months ago," he said.

"Two months..." Her voice trailed off as she performed the rapid calculation in her head. Ross watched uncertainty, then dismay alter her expression. "Right before you showed up and asked me to marry you."

"Yes." No more lies, no more justifications.

Amanda's strained, pretty features, at once so vulnerable, so determined, turned hard. "That timing sure seems coincidental, doesn't it?"

Ross sighed. "It wasn't."

Even now, he detected in her eyes a reluctance to believe. A willingness to let him off the hook if only he would deny his guilt.

But he couldn't.

Amanda pressed her fingertips against her temples so hard that her nails turned white. "How did you find out?"

"I was in New York on business. I happened to spot an article in the *Times* reporting that Judge Franklin was under investigation." While Ross spoke, he helplessly watched the last vestiges of hope dissolve from Amanda's expression. "I flew home immediately and confronted Granddad. Eventually, he owned up to the bribe."

Pain filtered into her eyes. "And…and that's why you were so…desperate to marry me," she said haltingly, putting the pieces together. "You were afraid *I'd* find out about the bribe, too."

"Yes."

"And reopen the custody case."

"Yes."

"So that you might lose Jamie."

Ross dragged a hand over his face. "I would have done anything to keep her," he admitted.

Resentment twisted Amanda's lips. "So would I," she said, tossing her head with scorn. "Unfortunately, I didn't have the unlimited wealth and complete lack of scruples required to purchase the verdict I wanted."

Ross moved toward her. "Amanda, what Granddad did was wrong. It was unforgivable. Believe me, if I'd known about it at the time, I would have stopped it."

She backed away. "So your conscience is clean, is that it?"

"No."

"All *you* did was continue to cover up the truth. To lie to me. To trick me into marrying you." Amanda's voice wavered, but her outraged stare held steady.

"I told you that our marriage would benefit all three of us—you, me and Jamie. That much was true."

"I suppose you figure you deserve some kind of award for being at least partially honest, huh?" She flung her hand toward all the framed certificates hanging on the wall. "I guess for a Chandler that's quite an accomplishment. No wonder you're so proud of yourself."

"I'm not proud of myself, believe me."

"*Believe* you?" She gave a sarcastic laugh. "I'll never

believe you again, Ross. I was a deluded fool to believe even one word you've ever said to me.''

"Amanda, don't let this come between us. We could build a good life together, have a real marriage—"

"Based on what? *Lies?*" Her cheeks were stained with crimson. "Is that why you made love with me, Ross? To make sure our marriage would stand up in court if I ever claimed it was a fraud? To solidify your case if it ever came to another custody fight over Jamie?"

"No!" He seized her hands to keep her from retreating farther away from him. "For God's sake, Amanda, don't you know how much I care about you?"

"Please! Spare me the violin music, all right?" She struggled to wrest her hands from his. "You couldn't possibly have manipulated and deceived me this way if you cared the slightest bit about me. Now let me go!"

Though letting her go was the last thing Ross wanted to do, he released her. Amanda fell backward a step. The accusation radiating from every taut line in her body was like the lash of a whip.

She looked as beautiful, as merciless as an avenging goddess of justice.

"You Chandlers think you can trample all over other people without any regard for their feelings." She hoisted her chin. "Well, this time, you're not going to get away with it."

"Amanda, I never meant to hurt you." Ross stood as rigid as a stone statue while the ruins of his marriage came crumbling down around him.

"*That* much I can believe. It's obvious that your scheme never took my feelings into consideration at all."

"I did what I thought would be best for all of us."

"No. As usual, you did what you thought would be best for the *Chandlers.*" Her mouth crimped into a bitter line. "Here." With one abrupt twist, she wrenched her wedding ring off her finger and slammed it onto Ross's desk. "You can keep your precious Chandler heirloom. What it stands for makes me sick."

With that, she stormed past him.

"Amanda, wait."

She whipped open the door. "I'm late. I have to pick up my daughter at art class."

Before Ross could stop her, she slammed the door behind her and was gone.

The emotional dam inside him finally collapsed, flooding him with despair. Just when he'd finally found the one woman he wanted to spend the rest of his life with, his own selfish treachery had finally caught up with him.

Ross sank into his chair and buried his face in his hands. When he lifted his head a moment later, a glint of gold winked at him from across his desk. He reached for Amanda's ring and studied it unhappily.

How ironic. Now that he wanted Amanda to be his wife for all the *right* reasons, she had to go and discover the *wrong* reason he'd married her in the first place.

Would she carry out her implied threat and fight him for Jamie's custody? Ross's brain was still reeling from the devastating fact that he'd lost Amanda for good. The possibility that he could lose Jamie, as well, was a nightmare too horrible to contemplate.

He'd gambled that Amanda would never learn the truth about why he'd married her. Gambled, and lost.

Except now he realized the stakes had been much higher than he'd ever imagined.

Chapter 14

Part of the land behind the Chandler mansion remained in its natural state, untamed by the gardeners who'd weeded, mowed, replanted and pruned the rest of the grounds into submission.

Hiking across the uneven terrain, past brushy thickets of chaparral, beneath madrone trees with their smooth, brick red bark and sturdy oaks draped with moss, Amanda could envision what the rolling hills of the Napa Valley had looked like before the first settlers had arrived. She'd spent a lot of time roaming these woods during the past several days. It was an excellent way to avoid Ross.

Her heart constricted with a sharp throb at the thought of him. She leaned against the trunk of a tall buckeye tree to catch her breath, but the ache behind her breastbone wouldn't go away.

She'd loved him. God help her, maybe she still *did* love him. But she could never trust him again.

Across the valley, the setting sun painted the horizon in

neon streaks of peach and plum. Amanda's tears blurred them into a messy finger painting when she recalled how Ross had deceived her. For weeks, she'd thought they were building a real marriage, when all along it was nothing but a ploy to keep Jamie firmly in the Chandler clutches.

She should never have let down her guard. She should never have forgotten that Ross was a Chandler—that it was in his blood to lie, cheat, steal, *bribe* his way toward any goal he set his sights on.

Every time Amanda recalled how deeply she'd believed in him, how close she'd felt to him while he'd tenderly made love to her, something inside her shattered like spun glass.

Angrily, she dashed the tears from her eyes. And saw Ross climbing the hill toward her.

Her first instinct was to run. For three days, she'd successfully avoided being alone with him, or even speaking to him except for the occasional "Please pass the butter" she managed in front of Jamie. She didn't want to hear what Ross had to say. Because nothing he said could change the truth.

But she wasn't about to scamper off like a frightened rabbit. Ross had robbed her of her hopes and illusions, but he couldn't rob her of her self-respect.

Leaves and twigs crackled under his shoes as he approached. Amanda's heart beat faster. A bead of sweat trickled down her temple. The evening was still quite warm.

He didn't bother with a greeting. "It won't work, you know."

Amanda stiffened. "*What* won't?"

"Trying to hide from me." He braced a hand against the rough bark of the buckeye tree and crossed one foot over the other.

Amanda made a scornful sound. "Just because I prefer

to avoid your company doesn't mean I'm hiding from you."

"We're going to have to talk about this sooner or later."

"Later will do just fine." She stepped around him, but before she could blink, he'd moved his large, limber body between her and the house. Like a lion toying with his prey.

She noticed he was careful not to touch her.

"I want to get back to Jamie," she said, digging her nails into her palms.

"She's still reading with Granddad."

Amanda's nails dug deeper. She begrudged every second Jamie spent with the conniving old man who'd stolen her. But it would be wrong to keep Jamie away from someone she loved.

"Amanda, I need to know what your plans are." Ross loomed above her, blocking out the fading rays of the sun. Amanda hadn't stood this close to him in days. Now she observed the dark shadows puddled beneath his eyes, the weary lines bracketing his mouth. Even marred by these signs of stress, he was almost unbearably handsome.

She fought back the urge to cry. "My plans? Why should I have any plans? You Chandlers are the ones who call all the shots, remember?"

Ross moved slightly to one side as if trying to dodge her sarcasm. "Are you going to fight me for Jamie?" he asked quietly.

"Ah, that's the bottom-line question, isn't it?" Amanda tried to ignore the hurt splintering through her. "After all, that's what this whole charade of a marriage is all about. Who gets to keep Jamie."

A muscle flickered along his jaw. "Maybe that's what it was about in the beginning. But it's about a lot more than that now."

"Yes, now it's about lies. Deception. Betrayal."

"Amanda, I'm sorry I hurt you." He raked his fingers through his hair. "If I had it to do all over again, I— I'd..."

She saw the contradiction in what he was saying. "You'd do exactly what you did. Marry me under false pretenses. Admit it."

Ross dropped his hand helplessly to his side. "I love that little girl, Amanda." Powerful emotion appeared to clog his throat for a moment. "I'd do anything not to lose her."

"Yes, you've certainly proven *that*." She had to look away from him, to focus on something besides the unhappiness scrawled on his face. What right did *he* have to feel bad, when *she* was the one with the broken heart?

She wrestled once more with the dilemma that had tormented her for three days. But she could only come up with the same unpalatable solution again.

"I'm not going to fight you for Jamie," she told Ross.

A blend of wariness and relief immediately altered his expression. "You mean...?" Clearly, he wasn't sure *what* she meant.

"My only concern is what's best for Jamie," Amanda said. "Putting her through another custody battle would tear her apart. I refuse to do that." Even if there *was* a guarantee she would eventually win Jamie back. Which there wasn't.

Although this was the only decision Amanda felt she could make, it still chafed.

Ross kneaded the back of his neck. "What about...us?"

"There *is* no us," Amanda said, proud of how calm she sounded. "There's just a piece of paper that says we're married."

Ross looked as if he was about to argue the point, then thought of something more important. "The adoption..."

"The adoption will go through just as we planned. I'm

not about to throw away this chance to make Jamie my legal child again.''

Ross leveled his gaze at her. "She'll be *my* child, too."

"I'm well aware of that, believe me." What Amanda *didn't* know was how she was going to get through the next ten or twelve years, sharing her daughter with a man she couldn't trust. A man she would never forgive for making her fall in love with him. "We'll go on pretending to be husband and wife for Jamie's sake," she continued with more confidence than she felt. "But that's all it will be. A pretense." She gave him a shrug. "So it shouldn't be too hard for you to carry off."

Ross reached out and captured her wrist with his strong fingers. "I never pretended when it came to my feelings for you." His low voice vibrated along Amanda's nerve endings.

His touch made her vibrate, too, though for different reasons. Their glances collided...locked together. As if spellbound, Amanda stared into Ross's compelling eyes and felt an invisible force drawing her closer...closer....

For a brief moment, she saw in his face the Ross she'd thought was real, the man she'd believed in, the husband she'd fallen in love with.

Then she remembered what he'd done, and all she could see standing before her was the arrogant crown prince of the devious Chandler clan.

The man who'd betrayed her.

She summoned a disdainful look and stared pointedly at the hand grasping her wrist. Ross's fingers tightened for an instant, then released her.

Amanda's skin flamed where he'd touched her, like a bracelet of glowing embers. "I'm going back to the house now," she said. As Ross moved to go with her, she added, "By myself."

"All right."

The low angle of light cast long shadows across the planes of his face, throwing his aristocratic features into even sharper relief. The muted remains of sunset sprinkled his golden hair with coppery glints. His eyes were the same deep velvet blue as the eastern sky.

As she turned her back on him and started down the slope, a vise seemed to squeeze Amanda's heart till she thought she would cry out with pain. She couldn't believe she'd once slept naked with this man. Shared her innermost secrets with him. Made love with him.

All that, without even knowing who he really was.

She stumbled over a rock and nearly sprained her ankle. The sharp twinge that shot up her leg reminded her to pay closer attention to her surroundings.

The bold outlines of the Chandler mansion emerged through the gathering darkness. Regal in all its unabashed grandeur, the house seemed to perch above the valley like a medieval castle.

"Home sweet home," Amanda muttered under her breath. She hated the sight of the house and all it represented. This place would be her prison from now on. A luxurious prison that she herself would be mistress of, but a prison nonetheless.

She would willingly serve her sentence, though. As Amanda came out of the woods and spotted the light on in Jamie's bedroom, her heart lifted a little.

She picked up her pace and hurried across the neatly manicured lawn. Toward the only person on earth who mattered to her now.

It was good to come out here in the fields sometimes, to walk among the neatly planted rows, to spear his fingers into the dark, rich soil and inhale the vibrant, earthy fragrance of growing things.

The vines drooped now with their heavy, lush cargo of

ripening grapes. It was August. Harvest would be early this year, thanks to the unusually hot summer they were experiencing. In just a few weeks, it would be time to begin the ancient process that would turn fruit into wine. Ross could almost smell the yeasty aroma of crushed grapes.

Usually when the pressures of his job or the weight of family responsibilities got to be too much for him, he found a measure of peace and rejuvenation strolling out here among the vines. Something reassuring about the endless yearly cycle of budding, flowering, ripening, harvesting never failed to put his worries into perspective for him.

Until recently.

Ross had spent a lot of time aimlessly wandering these fields during the past several weeks, trying to figure out what to do about the terrible rift that had opened up between him and Amanda. But no amount of wandering could change the fact that Ross had shamefully manipulated her.

Every time he tried to talk to her about it, she refused to listen. And how could he blame her? What he'd done was unforgivable.

Guilt pressed down on his shoulders like the weight of the sun's broiling rays. He sniffed the faint tang of smoke in the air. As a result of this prolonged siege of hot, dry weather, wildfires had sprung up all over this part of the state. For days, an acrid haze of smoke had hovered over the valley. It seemed a constant, mocking reminder to Ross of the smoking ruins of his marriage.

He and Amanda had become like two actors forced to play roles for which they were completely miscast. They went through the motions of being married, but he doubted their wooden performances would fool anyone.

Only when Jamie was present were they able to inject any believability into their acting. Both were determined to create the illusion of a family for their daughter's sake so that she would grow up with the security of having two parents who loved her. Creating this illusion, of course, required that they speak to each other in front of Jamie. It was about the only time they did.

Ross heard a car door slam. When he turned, he saw his grandfather's lawyer hesitating by the gate in the fence. Ross couldn't help grinning while he watched the distinguished gray-haired attorney make his way gingerly between the rows of grapevines, walking with rather mincing steps as if afraid of getting dirt on his expensive Italian shoes.

But Ross's grin faded as he speculated about possible reasons for this visit. An assistant D.A. from New York had taken Caleb's deposition several weeks ago after an agreement had been worked out. According to its terms, Caleb wouldn't be prosecuted for bribery if he agreed to cooperate with the investigation of Judge Franklin.

Had there been some last-minute hitch in the agreement that might cause his grandfather more serious legal troubles?

"Hello, Walter," he greeted his visitor cautiously.

"Afternoon, Ross." The attorney pulled a monogrammed handkerchief out of his breast pocket and mopped his beet red brow with it. "Your secretary told me you'd be out here. You must be a glutton for heatstroke."

"Just out surveying my domain." Ross winked. "Don't tell Granddad I said that, though."

"Oh, I doubt it'll be much longer before Caleb sees the light and finally decides to turn it all over to you officially." The lawyer tucked his handkerchief back into the pocket of his elegantly tailored suit. "But that's not why I'm here today."

Ross's forehead creased. "Not more trouble with that bribery business, is there?"

"No, no, that's all been settled." Walter took off his glasses and dabbed at his eyes. "All this awful smoke in the air makes my eyes water." He settled his glasses back onto his nose. "I was going to be passing by here anyway, so I decided to stop by and deliver the news in person."

"What's that?" Tension shifted uneasily inside Ross. In his experience, lawyers were rarely the bearers of *good* news.

"I just got word from the judge's clerk down in Napa. The judge had a cancellation in his schedule, so as a favor to me he's agreed to hold Jamie's adoption hearing tomorrow."

"Really?" An enormous grin split Ross's face in two.

"That's if you don't mind having it on such short notice," Walter amended, his eyes twinkling.

"Mind? Are you kidding?" Ross punched his fists skyward in triumph. "This is the day we've been waiting for!"

"I didn't guess you'd object too much," Walter said.

Ross grabbed the attorney's hand and pumped it enthusiastically. "Thank you. Thanks a million for all you've done."

In the back of his mind, he was already picturing Amanda's delighted reaction when he told her. He could hardly wait to watch the joyful smile light up her face and turn her gorgeous eyes radiant with excitement. It would be the first time she'd smiled at him in weeks.

Ross could never make up for the hurt he'd caused her. But at least now he could bring her some happy news.

Jamie clutched both her parents by the hand as the three of them emerged through the courthouse doors. "Are you guys really, *really* my mom and dad now?" she asked when they paused at the top of the broad steps leading to the street.

"Really, *really*," Amanda assured her with a loving squeeze of her hand. She glanced at Ross over the top of Jamie's curly blond head. She knew Ross was as happy as she was right now, and their common joy somehow bridged the turbulent channel of pain and mistrust that had flowed between them for weeks.

Bridged it temporarily, anyway.

Ross sent her one of those devastating grins that had once melted her insides. "Here's the proof, kiddo." He produced a document from his inside suit pocket and waved it with a flourish in front of Jamie's eyes. "See? Right here." He pointed to the relevant section of legalese. "All official. You're stuck with us now."

Jamie's lips moved as she carefully studied the words. She handed the paper back to Ross. "Does this mean forever and ever?" She tipped her head to one side.

"Forever and *ever*." He folded the papers back into his pocket.

"Good!" Jamie beamed an enormous smile at her parents.

Ross dropped his arm around her shoulders and hugged her against him. Jamie was still holding Amanda's hand, and somehow the three of them wound up in the same embrace. For the first time in weeks, Amanda felt Ross's arm around her, felt his cheek pressed against hers, their lips only inches apart. She allowed herself to savor the familiar scent of his aftershave, the warmth of his skin. Dear God, but it felt like heaven to be close to him like this!

She had to choke back a sob as both joy and sorrow collected in her throat. Joy that Jamie was truly her child once more. Sorrow that she and Ross would never be a real husband and wife to each other.

How could she share her bed with a man who only wanted her so that he could keep their daughter? How could she give her heart to a man who'd used her, lied to her, betrayed her?

Amanda had so looked forward to sharing this wonderful day with Ross, to starting their life together as a real family. But she would have to let go of that dream. Because it would never come true.

She detached herself from Ross's embrace, pinning a bright smile to her lips as she looked down at Jamie. "Have you thought about where you'd like to go for dinner tonight, sweetheart? Your Uncle Ro—I mean, your father—" she flushed and sent Ross a quick glance "—your father promised to take us to the fanciest restaurant between here and San Francisco, remember?"

Jamie spun an excited pirouette on the toes of her polished white shoes. She looked like an enchanted princess, all dolled up in her ruffled blue dress. "I want pizza!" she announced.

Ross chuckled. "I might have guessed."

"With pepperoni and pineapple on top!"

Ross made a face while they descended the courthouse steps. "Ugh!" He and Amanda each captured one of Jamie's hands again.

"It's *good*," she protested.

Amanda rolled her eyes. "Maybe we'll order *two* pizzas."

"Excellent idea." Ross winked at her, an oddly intimate gesture that stirred up those wistful feelings inside her again.

She couldn't—*wouldn't*—allow him to keep affecting her this way.

They had nearly reached the car when an adorable cocker spaniel puppy bounded around the corner, straining on the end of its leash.

Jamie's eyes lit up. "Mom! Dad! Look at the puppy! Can I go pet it?"

Something expanded with a bump inside Ross's chest. No one had ever called him Dad before. To his amazement, he felt tears prickling his eyelids.

Amanda was smiling at him as if she knew exactly what he was feeling. If Ross wasn't mistaken, he detected a tear or two in her eyes, as well.

She called to the puppy's owner, "Is it okay if our daughter pets your dog?"

When the young woman nodded, Jamie took off like a rocket. Seconds later, she was scratching the puppy's belly and cooing endearments into its floppy ears.

Amanda peered at Ross. "Feels pretty good, doesn't it?"

"Yeah." Finally, his voice returned. "I can't believe she's really ours." He draped his arm around Amanda's shoulders and kissed her hair, an action as natural to him as breathing.

Amanda tensed. But she didn't pull away. A tiny thread of hope wove itself through Ross. Maybe this closeness they were sharing in these first moments of official parenthood could be the first step in mending the rift between them.

"Amanda, I shouldn't have tricked you into becoming my wife." He put his other arm around her so she was forced to face him. "But I'm not sorry I married you. Only for the way I did it."

Her luminous dark eyes searched his face. "Oh, Ross." Her lips trembled a little. "What kind of a marriage can we have when it was based on a lie from the very beginning?"

Ross brought his hand to her cheek. "I'm hoping we can have a *new* beginning. Start over. Today's our first day as Jamie's parents. Maybe it can be the first day of *our* new life together, as well.''

She dipped her head, shaking it slowly from side to side. "We can't build a life together without honesty and trust."

Ross tilted up her chin. "Amanda, you of all people should understand why I did what I did."

He glanced past her and saw the puppy busily planting paw prints all over the front of Jamie's best dress. A wave of love rose up inside him, so powerful it nearly knocked him off his feet.

"Jamie means everything in the world to me," he said hoarsely. *So do you*, he wanted to add. But he didn't have that right. Not now. "Wouldn't you have done exactly what I did if you'd been in my position? Wouldn't you have done *anything* to keep your child?"

She set her jaw in preparation for denial. Her eyes narrowed with indignation. But she couldn't quite bring herself to reply.

Ross pressed his case. "After all, the only reason *you* married *me* was to get Jamie back."

A hot breeze swirled around them. "I never made any secret of that." Amanda tucked a streamer of dark hair behind her ear.

"No. And I married you to *keep* Jamie." Beneath the lightweight fabric of her dress, Ross felt her muscles tighten with resistance. "Was what I did so much worse than what *you* did?"

"I didn't lie to you."

"You didn't have to. I did."

She held his gaze steadily. Maybe it was only his wishful imagination, but Ross thought he saw a glimmer of grudging concession in her eyes. He sensed she was searching for a reason to forgive him, for a way to close the gap of mistrust that still divided them.

"You're right," she said finally. Hope leaped inside his

heart. "Maybe I *would* have lied if it had been necessary to get Jamie back."

"I think we agree that we're both capable of desperate measures where Jamie is concerned." Ross drew Amanda closer, narrowing the distance between them. "Can't we agree to put the past behind us? To start our marriage over with a clean slate?"

The tug-of-war being waged by her feelings was plainly evident on her face. Ross held his breath, praying for his side to win.

"I—I just can't do that," she said finally, averting her eyes.

Ross's hopes sank.

Amanda wedged her hands between them and pushed herself away. Widening that gap between them. She turned to check on Jamie. When she looked back at Ross, he saw at once that he'd lost her.

Her face was pale yet composed. Resolute. "I can understand why you lied to me in the first place," she said. "Why you didn't tell me the real reason you wanted to marry me?"

Panic crept through him. "Amanda, things are different now. I didn't know—"

"I can forgive you for deceiving me initially." The unyielding lines of her posture warned Ross that touching her now would be a mistake. "What I can't forgive is that you kept on lying. That you didn't tell me the truth even after we started becoming...close." She swallowed, and a hint of the pain Ross had caused her shone briefly in her eyes. "Even after we made love."

It took every ounce of his self-control to keep his hands at his sides. "That's why I fought against our attraction so hard," he told her in a low voice. "I felt guilty enough as it was without making love to you under false pretenses." Even now, with their relationship in ruins, Ross's desire for her was like a physical ache, a sharp blade of need slashing through him. "But in the end, I couldn't fight what I felt for you," he said. "It was too strong, this passion between us."

Anguish flashed briefly over her delicate features. "A marriage can't just be based on passion, Ross. It has to be based on honesty. Mutual respect. Trust."

"Darling—"

"That's what hurts the most, Ross." Her mouth tightened into a bleak line as she struggled for control. "While I thought we were building a real marriage together, based on trust and honesty and...and *caring,* you were maintaining this monstrous lie between us."

"Amanda—"

"Our entire marriage has been nothing but a sham. All of it."

"No. Not all of—"

Amanda shushed him with a warning gesture. Jamie was coming toward them. It was amazing, the instinctive transformation that slipped over Amanda's face like a mask. "Did you have fun playing with the puppy?" With a smile, she caressed Jamie's hair.

"His name's Spencer and he's four months old." Jamie cast a longing look back over her shoulder. "Mom? Dad? Can I have a puppy?" She clasped her hands together in a beseeching pose. "Please?"

Amanda bit her lip. "I don't think Crackerjack would be too thrilled to have a dog around, do you?"

"I could teach them to be friends."

"Well...what if we talk about it later? Right now, I'm starved for some pizza. How about you?"

"With pepperoni and pineapple?" Jamie asked slyly.

Amanda laughed. "Anything your little taste buds desire."

"Yummy! Let's go."

As they all climbed into the car, Amanda carefully avoided meeting Ross's eyes. The aloof, implacable set of her features informed him that, while the subject of a puppy might still be open for discussion, any talk of a reconciliation was out of the question.

All at once, Ross didn't have much of an appetite.

Chapter 15

Amanda told herself the edgy, out-of-sorts mood she'd been in all day was due to the wind. After all, this was her first full day of being Jamie's legal mother again. She ought to have been walking on air, filled with relief and happiness and peace of mind.

But evening found her pacing in front of the windows, watching the huge eucalyptus trees sway in the wind while she wondered what was keeping Ross. Right after dinner he'd gone back to his office at the winery to pick up some papers and hadn't returned.

It was nearly Jamie's bedtime. Impossible to believe Ross had forgotten their evening ritual of tucking her in.

Amanda opened one of the living-room windows and stuck her head out. A gust of wind whipped her hair into her eyes. The air seemed even smokier tonight than it had in recent days. Another big forest fire had broken out yesterday in the neighboring county. No doubt the strong winds were carrying more smoke than usual.

Amanda propped her elbows on the windowsill. Maybe this itchy feeling of hers was due to the smoke. Maybe she was allergic to it.

"Knock it off," she scolded herself. "You know perfectly well what's got you so jumpy."

Ross.

The heartache Amanda had been fighting off all day finally grabbed hold of her and wouldn't let go. What she'd told Ross yesterday was true. She could accept the fact that he'd tricked her into marrying him. But what she couldn't accept was that he'd continued to maintain that fiction while Amanda had believed their marriage was for real.

Happily ever after. What a fairy tale.

Ross didn't love her. He *desired* her. He *needed* her to be a mother to Jamie. But in all his cajoling talk yesterday about new beginnings, there hadn't been one single word about love.

Passion, yes. But Amanda wasn't willing to settle for that anymore.

Now, if she could just get her foolish heart to see reason—

The phone rang in the other room. Amanda shut the window and was on her way to answer it when she heard Nora call, "I will get it."

Just then, Jamie's footsteps pattered down the stairs. "Mom? Mom, where are you?"

"Here, sweetheart." Amanda's spirits lifted as she crossed the tiled entrance hall. She would never, *ever* get tired of hearing Jamie call her Mom.

Jamie draped herself over the banister at the foot of the staircase. "Grampa and me finished reading *Charlotte's Web*. Now we need a *new* book."

"Grampa and *I*," Amanda gently corrected. "Tomorrow after swimming lessons, we can go pick out another one at the library, if you'd like.''

"Maybe someday *you* could come read with Grampa and I," Jamie suggested. "Dad does sometimes."

Amanda swallowed a smile. "Maybe I will." Though she doubted Caleb would appreciate her intruding on his special time with Jamie. Any more than Amanda would appreciate being cooped up in the same room with the crotchety tyrant who'd caused her so much grief.

"Remember that puppy we saw yesterday?" Jamie said with not-so-casual innocence. "I was wondering—"

At that moment, Nora hurried into the hall, hand pressed to her bosom, eyes brimming with alarm.

"Nora, what is it?" Amanda grasped her arm.

"That was Mr. Ross on the telephone." Nora was breathing as if she'd just run up a flight of stairs. "He says there is a fire."

"*Fire?* Where?" Instantly, Amanda's brain raced ahead, calculating which necessities she might have time to pack if they had to evacuate the house.

"On the next property. But coming toward the grapevines."

"Oh, dear." Amanda covered her mouth. The vines were Ross's pride and joy. Not to mention the source of the family wealth.

Nora calmed down a little. "Mr. Ross, he says not to worry, that the wind is blowing so that the fire will not come to the house. But he has to stay at the winery until they make sure the grapes do not burn up."

"What about the fire department? Are they on the way?" Amanda strained her ears for the sound of sirens, but all she heard was the wind howling through the trees.

Nora looked worried again. "Mr. Ross says they maybe cannot come for a while, that they are too busy with so many other fires."

The television news had shown footage of local fire-fighters being rushed off to other parts of the state, leaving only skeleton crews behind. Amanda's apprehension increased a notch.

Jamie's eyes were wide with fear. "Are we gonna burn up?" she asked in a quavery voice. "What about Grampa? He can't run away if the fire comes."

"Sweetie, you heard what your dad said. We don't have to worry about the house catching fire." *Unless the wind changes direction,* Amanda thought anxiously. She was determined to reassure her daughter, however. "Let's go upstairs. I'll read you a story after I tuck you into bed."

"But Dad's not here!"

"You'll have to make do with just me tonight. Dad will look in on you as soon as he comes home."

Jamie seemed to drag out her bedtime preparations even longer than usual this evening. Or maybe it just seemed longer to Amanda because she was so worried about Ross.

When she peeped through the curtains in Jamie's bedroom, she could see a narrow, ragged band of distant flames. Each time she checked, the fire appeared to have crept a little bit closer to the edge of the vineyards.

What would happen if it reached Chandler property? What if the firefighters hadn't arrived by then? Amanda knew Ross would be determined to save the grapes at all costs. What if he got hurt fighting the fire? Hurt...or worse?

A lump of fear clogged her throat. She couldn't stand not knowing what was happening out there. She couldn't bear the thought of Ross in danger.

Somehow she managed to get through the promised story without transmitting any of her fear to Jamie. Once Jamie had finally drifted off to sleep, Amanda hurried downstairs and back to the living-room window.

Through the screen of trees shielding the house, she

could see the glow of flames off in the distance. Though not as distant as the last time she'd looked. From up here on the hillside, the fire didn't appear all that menacing. But Amanda knew that down there in the path of the advancing blaze, it was a different story.

"Ross, Ross, please be careful," she prayed under her breath. But she knew her husband wouldn't stand idly by, watching his vineyards go up in smoke while he waited for the fire department to arrive.

Dear God, what was happening out there in the fields? Did he have enough people to help him?

Amanda was torn by a terrible conflict. It went against all her instincts to leave her child while a fire was raging in the vicinity, but Jamie was safe here for the time being. If the fire changed direction, Amanda could rush back and help Nora get Jamie and Caleb out of the house.

Ross might need her. Amanda didn't know how she could help him, but she was convinced with soul-deep certainty that her place was at her husband's side right now.

Call it a premonition. Call it a sixth sense.

Call it love.

She had to go to him. Now.

"Nora!" She dashed through the house, quickly explained where she was going.

Minutes later, she was driving like a maniac down the curving road to the winery, smoke stinging her eyes, fear filling her lungs.

Racing toward the man she still loved in spite of everything.

Smoke-laden air seared Ross's lungs with every excruciating breath he took. His chest felt as if a Mack truck were parked on top of it.

But he couldn't pause to rest, to catch his breath. Every

second of his efforts might make the difference between saving the grapes and losing them.

The advancing line of flame had made short work of the dry grass in the neighboring pasture. Ross was under no crazy delusion that he and his men could put out the fire themselves. It was too widespread, too fast-moving under these windy conditions. The best they could hope for was to keep the fire from spreading into the vineyards, to make a stand at the edge of Chandler property and hold that line of defense until help arrived.

If it ever did.

Too many fires. Too few firefighters spread too thinly all over the state.

Ross couldn't let himself think about that. All that mattered to him now was stopping *this* fire.

His eyes stung from a combination of smoke and sweat. A blizzard of white ash swirled through the air, creating the weird impression of a snowstorm even in the midst of this blistering heat.

Ross cupped his hand to the side of his mouth. "Dave!" he yelled to one of his workers. "Over there!"

The ferocious wind kept sending forth burning embers from the main body of the fire, like deadly scouts ahead of a rampaging army. Wherever they landed, spot fires erupted. Ross and the others were using the irrigation hoses that normally watered the vines to douse the flames as soon as they appeared.

Dave pounced on it immediately, and with a hiss of water and a last gasp of smoke, the small blaze was extinguished.

Two more immediately sprang up to take its place.

Once again, Ross was gripped by sinking despair, by the sense that they were fighting a losing battle. As soon as he'd glanced out his office window that evening and spotted the ominous cloud of smoke drifting this way, he'd snatched up the phone and summoned as many of the winery workers as he could reach.

Everyone he called had come. The problem was, they might not be enough.

Over the roar of flames and the crackle of burning vegetation, the rumble of an engine drew closer. Ted Cardoza was making another pass with the tractor, paralleling the fence line. If it wasn't for the wind, the fire probably wouldn't be able to cross the buffer zone of plowed-up field Ted had created by pulling the disk harrow back and forth behind him. But with bits of burning debris leapfrogging across the swath of churned earth with every powerful gust, holding back the main body of the fire wouldn't be enough.

"Ted!" Ross hollered, his voice hoarse from smoke. "That's enough! Come on back!" He waved his arms above his head.

Ted was driving the tractor awfully close to the approaching flames now, trying to widen the firebreak as much as possible. Ross shuddered at the vision of an airborne spark igniting the gas tank.

From the corner of his hazy, blurred vision, he saw another spot fire break out close to him. He grabbed up an irrigation hose and doused it. Then, as he was about to turn back and make sure Ted had gotten his signal, he caught sight of someone racing toward him between the rows of grapevines, from the direction of the winery.

As soon as the figure was close enough to recognize, Ross's blood ran cold. He sprinted forward to intercept her.

"Amanda!" He grabbed her roughly, halting her in her tracks with a jolt. "What the hell are you doing here?"

Her eyes were wide with fear, bright with smoke-induced tears. "I came to help." She doubled over with a fit of coughing as a particularly dense cloud of acrid smoke enveloped them.

Ross gave her shoulders an impatient shake as soon as the coughing eased. "The only way you can help is by going back to the house. Where's Jamie?"

"Sound asleep. Did you think I brought her with me?" Amanda pushed his hands aside. "What can I do to help?"

Ross gnashed his teeth. The one comforting thought he'd clung to during this losing battle against the fire was that at least his wife and daughter were safe at home.

"You'll only be in the way," he said, trying to turn her around and scoot her back in the other direction.

She refused to budge even as another spasm of coughing seized her. "You're wasting…precious time," she choked out between coughs. "I'm not…leaving."

Ross glanced quickly behind him. Several spot fires were blazing merrily away, dangerously close to the vines.

"All right. Come on." He knew all too well how stubborn Amanda could be. Realizing he didn't have time to sling her over his shoulder and haul her back to the safety of the mansion, he towed her along in his wake as he hustled back toward the battlefront. "Here." He thrust an irrigation hose into her hands. "Use this to put out any spot fires you see."

Without question or hesitation, she promptly doused the nearest one.

God, he loved her courage, her determination! Even her stubbornness.

"Go," she called, even as she went stumbling down the row of vines to extinguish another outbreak. "I can handle things here. I'll be fine."

Ross needed to get out there and drag Ted off that tractor before the damn thing exploded. But he spared a fleeting moment to imprint on his memory one final vision of Amanda's face—strained with physical effort, grim with concentration, alive with fear.

The golden reflection of flames leaped and danced

across her pale, taut cheekbones, shimmered in her huge dark eyes. Hers was the most beautiful face Ross had ever seen.

It hammered him like a fierce blow to his gut how much she meant to him. More than the grapevines. More than the winery. More than the entire family fortune. Far, far more.

But he'd already lost Amanda. He still had a chance, at least, to save the grapes.

Ross left her and ran back toward the fire.

Time lost all meaning to Amanda. There was nothing in the world but smoke and fire, sweat and dirt, heat and pain.

Her muscles screamed with exhaustion. But each time the wind launched another arrow of flame in her direction, somehow she forced her limbs to drag the hose over and put it out.

Her ears were filled with the roar of fire, the snap of burning brush, the shouts of the others working frantically around her. Tears and sweat streamed down her face. Her hair whirled into her eyes, blinding her, clinging to her sticky skin.

She kept going.

Every so often, she would catch a glimpse of Ross through the chaos, and her heart would constrict as if a fist had closed around it. These vines meant so much to him. Some of them were nearly a hundred years old, carefully cultivated and tended and passed down from one generation to the next. She knew Ross would rather fight to the death than watch his family's legacy go up in smoke.

His family. *Her* family, too, now. For the first time, Amanda felt a stirring of that same Chandler pride she'd always resented. It wasn't the wealth these vines represented that was so important, but the years and years of hard work and perseverance and vision that had gone into nurturing them.

The grapevines stood for struggle and sacrifice. For tradition. For excellence. They were a living symbol of the roots this family had planted in this valley more than a century ago.

Even though she was on the verge of collapsing from exhaustion, somewhere inside her Amanda found the extra reserve of strength she needed to go on.

She didn't even hear the sirens. The flashing red lights were camouflaged by the flickering flames, and the first she knew of the fire crew's arrival was when one of the firefighters, bulky in his bright yellow protective gear, took hold of her from behind and literally lifted her out of the way.

Suddenly, the vineyard was filled with yellow-clad figures, dragging heavy hoses, shouting instructions to one another. The fire trucks' headlights illuminated the scene with an eerie imitation of daylight. It looked like anarchy from where Amanda stood watching, gasping for breath, fighting to stay on her feet. But it wasn't long before she saw the tide of battle had shifted from pure defense to an aggressive offense against the flames.

Step by step, the firefighters closed the perimeter of the blaze. In all the commotion, Amanda lost sight of Ross. Then, when the fire had finally been contained to a few isolated patches, she saw him break free from a cluster of men and jog toward her between the vines.

Amanda staggered forward to meet him even as every muscle in her legs stiffened in protest. Ross's face was disguised by a mask of soot and sweat. But she would have recognized that dazzling, triumphant grin anywhere.

"We did it!" With a whoop of exultation, he threw his arms around her and spun her through the air. Amanda clutched his shoulders and hung on for dear life, laughing.

When Ross finally set her down with a bump, she could feel his heart galloping as if in a race against hers. "We saved the vines!" he crowed. "Hallelujah!"

Amanda flung her arms around his neck and allowed herself to sag against him, too worn out and weak with relief to speak. Ross smelled of sweat and smoke, and he felt absolutely wonderful.

He raked his hands through her hair and tilted her head back. "We couldn't have done it without you." His breath grazed her lips. His eyes were lit by a fire that this time came from inside him.

"I hardly did anything," she protested. All the sore muscles, the exhaustion and fear, the smoke-filled eyes and lungs had been worth it, she decided. Not only because they'd saved the grapevines. But for this heavenly reward of ending up in Ross's arms. Feeling close to him again.

If only there was some way to make this feeling last forever.

"You made all the difference." He brushed his lips tenderly against hers. "Things could have gone either way." He kissed her again, longer **this** time. "You tipped the balance so that we could hold off disaster."

"Just call me Wonder Woman," she murmured against his chin.

Ross chuckled softly. "Amanda." Then a ferocious intensity blotted all trace of amusement from his eyes. "God, I love you."

Even before his words could fully register on Amanda's stunned consciousness, he crushed his mouth to hers and kissed her for all he was worth.

And, being a Chandler, he was worth quite a lot.

Desire, confusion and hope swirled through Amanda in a maelstrom that made the wind whipping around them feel like a light breeze. Had she heard Ross correctly? And if she had, was it something he'd only said out of gratitude?

The way his mouth and hands were moving over her certainly created a skilled impression of love. But unhappy experience had taught Amanda that Ross was a master at hiding his true feelings, at creating whatever false impression would suit his purpose.

She'd believed in him once before, only to have that belief shattered along with her hopes and dreams for a real marriage. Did she dare take the risk of believing in him again?

Even as her heart held back, her body responded to him. The passion that had led her down the wrong path before surged through her bloodstream, making her light-headed. Reckless. Ready to take whatever foolish risk would satisfy this aching need inside her.

When Ross finally broke their kiss, Amanda was still hungry, greedy for more. She was *never* going to catch her breath at this rate.

He brought their faces so close together that the tips of their noses touched. "That's why I couldn't tell you the real reason I asked you to be my wife." His tone was regretful, yet somehow relieved as the words spilled out of him. "Even after it began to seem like we could have a real future together, I was afraid to confess why I'd married you.

"I knew that hiding the truth from you was wrong." He stroked her cheekbones with the pads of his thumbs. "But once I fell in love with you, it wasn't only Jamie I was terrified of losing. I couldn't face losing *you.*"

Amanda's eyes darted rapidly over his. Truth? Or more deception? Dear God, how she wanted to believe him....

"I knew you'd be furious if you ever found out how I'd tricked you." Ross's mouth tightened into a rueful line. "So I took the chance that you never would. I wanted so much for us to be happy together, I—I guess I convinced myself that a little evasion wouldn't matter.''

"But it did," she whispered.

Sorrow crossed his face like a shadow. "Yeah. It did."

"Mr. Chandler?" Ross let his arms slide to Amanda's waist as one of the firefighters approached. "Sorry to interrupt," he said, "but the chief needs to talk to you." He pointed across the field. A few glowing embers were still visible amid the smoldering remnants of the fire. "Normally, a couple of us would stick around till morning to make sure none of the hot spots flare up again, but because we're so shorthanded what with all the other fires..."

Ross nodded in understanding. "I'll ask some of my employees to stand watch."

"That'd be a good idea."

When Ross turned back to Amanda, she saw the creases of fatigue etched through the layers of grime coating his features. And she knew that Ross himself would be one of the men standing watch all night.

"You might as well go on back to the house," he said, smoothing her hair away from her face. "Get some rest." He pressed his lips against her forehead. "Kiss Jamie good-night for me. Looks like I won't have the chance."

"I already did." Amanda touched his cheek. "Be careful."

She made her way back to her car, stepping over hoses, dodging various members of the fire crew as they hurried to pack up. Her shoulders and feet dragged as if she were plodding through quicksand. Never before in her entire life had she felt so physically drained, so bone-deep exhausted.

But her mind was racing in overdrive, speeding around the same circle over and over again.

Ross had said he loved her.

Did he mean it?

Or was this just another trick...?

And if he did love her, did it actually change anything? Because unless Amanda could find the courage to trust him again, their marriage would remain a hollow shell.

She sank behind the steering wheel of her car with a weary moan. As desperately as her body craved sleep, she somehow suspected she wasn't going to get very much of it tonight.

Chapter 16

As Amanda had predicted, Ross didn't come home for the rest of the night. He stumbled into the house around noon, grabbed a shower, a brief nap and a sandwich, then headed right back to the winery.

"A few of the vines were damaged," he told her and Jamie. "Considering they all could have gone up in flames, though, we were incredibly lucky." He kissed the top of Jamie's head, then opened the front door. "I won't be home till late. There's still a lot of cleanup and repair to be done."

Amanda didn't bother suggesting that he didn't have to supervise it personally. In Ross's eyes, it would be a requirement.

As he left, he sent her one of those hooded, unreadable looks that used to baffle her during the early days of their marriage. What was going on behind those cool blue eyes of his? Did he regret last night's impulsive declaration of love? She spent the rest of the afternoon torturing herself with doubts.

Shortly before dinner, Jamie came downstairs and found Amanda on the library patio, staring into space.

"Grampa says can you come upstairs and see him?"

Amanda instantly gripped the arms of her chair, prepared to launch herself to her feet. "He's all right, isn't he?" Short of a medical emergency, she couldn't imagine any reason for Caleb to summon her.

"Uh-huh." Jamie nodded. "He says he just wants to talk to you, that's all." Obviously, she didn't find Caleb's request nearly as peculiar as Amanda did.

"Well…all right." For half a second, she considered asking Jamie to accompany her. Then she scolded herself. What kind of coward needed a seven-year-old bodyguard to protect her from a bedridden eighty-six-year-old?

The eighty-six-year-old in question was propped upright against his pillows, snarling at a stack of mail, when Amanda knocked cautiously on the open door of his room.

Caleb squinted over the top of his glasses. "Oh, it's you." He yanked off the glasses and beckoned impatiently. "Come in, come in. Don't just dawdle out there in the hallway."

Amanda gave the letter opener a wide berth as she edged around the side of his bed. Any pointed object could become a deadly missile.

"Jamie said you wanted to see me." She held her head high, refusing to convey the slightest subservient impression.

A sly smile cracked Caleb's face in two. "I figured if I asked *her* to deliver the message, you'd come." He nodded as if gloating over his own cleverness.

Amanda stiffened with antagonism. "What is it you wanted to see me about?"

"Hmm? Oh." He harrumphed loudly. "I, er, wanted to thank you."

Amanda blinked. "I beg your pardon?"

"You heard me." His clawed fingers plucked at the bedcovers. "Ross told me what you did. During the fire. You helped save the grapes." His mouth worked as if producing the next words required maximum effort. "Thank you."

"You're, uh, welcome." Amanda had been braced for a confrontation. Caleb's gratitude left her at a loss.

"I know we've had our differences, you and I." He fixed her with a hawklike stare. "Maybe it's time to let bygones be bygones, eh?"

Amanda's jaw dropped. *"Differences?"* she echoed. "Is *that* what you call them? How about lies? Bribery? Stealing my child?"

At least he had the good grace to appear uncomfortable. "That's all in the past." He gave a dismissive wave of his hand. "Besides, you got Jamie back anyhow, didn't you?"

"That hardly absolves you of your responsibility for the anguish I suffered." Amanda forced herself to unclench her fists. Anger wouldn't solve anything now.

Caleb poked his tongue into his cheek. "Maybe not."

"You can't expect me to pretend none of it ever happened."

He scratched his chin. "Guess that would be asking too much."

Amanda sensed the wily old warrior was setting a trap for her. He was agreeing *far* too easily. She began a prudent retreat toward the door. "Well...good. I'm glad you understand."

She'd nearly made her escape when Caleb's next words froze her in her tracks. "No doubt Ross has told you how his parents died."

Amanda felt an invisible trip wire reeling her back into the room.

"Yes. He told me."

Caleb winced as if his heart was acting up. "That was the worst time in my life, when my son and his wife died."

Amanda steeled herself against a twinge of sympathy. She would *not* let Caleb play her heartstrings like a violin virtuoso.

"Could be that's why I was so bound and determined to get Jamie back after I found out Paige had had a child." His eyes were clouded with thoughtfulness, as if he'd never analyzed his motives before.

For all Amanda knew, he hadn't.

"That doesn't excuse what you did. You had no right to take Jamie away from me after Paige had given her up for adoption."

Caleb sighed. "After losing my son and daughter-in-law, I just couldn't stand the idea that another member of my family was lost to me forever."

"But you didn't mind if *I* lost my daughter. Forever."

For the first time, Amanda detected genuine regret on his shrunken features. "I guess I convinced myself that Jamie couldn't mean as much to you as my own flesh and blood meant to me."

Amanda choked down a lump in her throat. "You were wrong."

"Yes," Caleb said. His jaw quivered. "I see that now."

Once again, she found herself at a loss for words. She could cope with Caleb's feisty self-righteousness. What she didn't know how to react to was his air of apology. Or this roundabout remorse that was as close to an apology as she was ever likely to get from him.

"One other reason I wanted my great-granddaughter back." Caleb's glance slid away from Amanda as if one more personal revelation was simply too much to confess eye-to-eye. "Jamie was going to be my second chance."

Amanda frowned. "Your second chance...to do what?"

"To do a decent job raising a child." The corner of

Caleb's mouth puckered in scorn, but Amanda realized he was disgusted with himself, not her. "Truth is, I failed miserably when it came to Paige. Ross I can't really take credit for. He was already half-grown when he came to live with me. Somehow he managed to turn out all right." Caleb's sunken chest seemed to expand a little with pride.

Then the light went out of his eyes. "But Paige was just a little slip of a girl. I didn't know what to do with her. So I just bought her whatever she asked for. Let her have her own way." He looked straight at Amanda again. "Unfortunately, I neglected to instill any sense of responsibility in her. Any sense of pride, or honor, or...what's that new-fangled term everyone whines about these days? Self-esteem."

Amazingly, Amanda found herself wanting to comfort the old man, to reassure him that he'd done the best he could. Except that he *hadn't* done his best. And that's what tormented him now.

"When I discovered Paige had had a little girl of her own, it felt like fate was handing me one last chance to do it right this time." His withered throat convulsed as he swallowed. "I knew it was too late to fix the damage I'd done to Paige by neglecting her. But by bringing Paige's little girl into this house, I'd have another chance to do it right." He curled his gnarled fingers into a fist and pounded the bed. His ancient eyes burned with emotion. "I *had* to do it."

He didn't *have* to do it, Amanda corrected silently. But for the first time, she understood why he had.

"Why are you telling me all this?" she asked softly.

Caleb got hold of himself. "Because I can't stand to see my grandson moping around like a lovesick baboon, that's why."

Amanda let out a startled laugh. "What are you talking about?"

"That's why you're giving him the cold-shoulder treatment, isn't it? Because you're mad at *me*." He jabbed himself in the chest. "Except I'm a pathetic old man who's too weak to fight back, so you have to take it out on *him*." He speared a crooked finger in the direction of the door.

Amanda propped her hands on her hips. "You're *not* a pathetic old man," she assured him. "But you're not much of a marriage counselor, either."

"Bah!" He gave an impatient flip of his hand. "Even a nearsighted old coot like me can see the two of you are gaga about each other. So why are you still sleeping in separate bedrooms, unless you're trying to punish him for what *I* did?"

Amanda gasped. "How do *you* know we're sleeping in—never mind." She should have known Caleb would find a way to keep a close eye on everything that went on under his roof.

Did that mean he knew what he was talking about when he implied Ross was crazy about her?

A strange feeling rose inside her. Sort of prickly, but pleasant. A good feeling, but one that would take some getting used to. The actual dawn of affection for this exasperating old man.

"I'll take what you've said under consideration," Amanda told him.

Caleb snorted. "You'll do exactly what you've made up your mind to do. Just like always."

"Just like *you*," she retorted. But she said it with a smile.

"Go on, get out of here. I've got business to take care of." He snatched up a fistful of correspondence from the bed.

Amanda was nearly out the door when she heard him mumble something. "What?" She cocked her head and came back in the room a few steps.

Caleb grabbed his glasses. "I *said,* if Paige had grown up to be more like you, I would have been a lot more proud of the job I did raising her." He jammed his glasses on his nose and bent back over his mail. "Now quit your chattering and leave me alone. I'm busy."

Amanda blinked rapidly to clear the mist from her vision. She paused in the doorway. "Maybe I'll stop by and listen while you and Jamie read this evening."

"Humph. Do as you please."

To Amanda, it was as good as an engraved invitation.

Ross covered a jaw-cracking yawn. Jeez, he was tired! He staggered along the upstairs hallway, where someone had thoughtfully left on a light even though everyone had gone to bed.

He flipped on the switch in his bedroom and closed the door behind him. At least tomorrow things would be back to normal. The damaged vines had been removed, the hoses restored, the fence mended. In the morning, it would be business as usual at Chandler Winery.

Maybe he would even find time to grab forty winks at his desk. Right now, he felt as if he would *never* catch up on his sleep.

He considered dumping his clothes onto a chair as a prelude to tumbling into bed, but habit was too strong a taskmaster. He opened his closet to hang them up properly.

And decided he must already be sound asleep and dreaming.

Someone had completely rearranged his closet, shoving *his* clothes all the way to one side and filling the other half with...

He inhaled a familiar floral scent. Amanda's clothes?

He whipped hangers from side to side, examining the garments like a factory inspector. What the heck were Amanda's clothes doing in his—

A faint knock at the door made him wheel around. This was one confusing dream.

Ross opened the door cautiously. Amanda stood in the hall, fully dressed, a tentative smile curving her mouth.

A suitcase in each hand.

"Better pinch me," he said. "I think I'm dreaming."

"I've got an even better idea." She angled her head to one side. "If you'll let me into our room, that is."

"Hmm? Oh, sure. Sorry." Ross stepped aside. Then he did a double take. "Did you say *our* room?"

"If that's okay with you." Amanda set down her suitcases with twin *thunks*. "There's just one matter I've got to verify first."

His tiredness had vanished. "What's that?"

She inched up her chin and looked Ross straight in the eye. "Did you mean it when you said you loved me?"

A big, goofy grin seemed to take possession of his face. He pushed the bedroom door shut. "Oh, yes," he said. "I meant it."

"Well. Good." She gave a curt nod of satisfaction. Then her calm, detached demeanor slipped away. She threw her arms around Ross's neck and brought her face close to his. "Because I love you, too, Ross Chandler."

"Amanda." Her name was like a song of joy on his lips, echoing the jubilation that filled his heart.

He kissed her tenderly, almost reverently at first. Then all that pent-up passion they'd both tried to contain for so long crashed through its barriers. They clung together as if trying to meld their bodies into one, deepening their kiss, weaving their hands through each other's hair.

The need for oxygen finally pried them apart. Amanda's eyes sparkled like diamonds. Her cheeks bloomed with happiness.

"What brought on this change of heart?" Ross asked,

lowering his forehead to hers. "Not that I'm complaining, mind you."

Amanda adjusted the position of her arms, tightening their circle around his waist. "Just a little talk I had with Caleb, that's all." A smile teased the corner of her mouth.

"Granddad?" Ross gaped at her. "You've got to be kidding."

"He said you were gaga about me."

"Well, he was certainly right about that."

"He said I was trying to punish you because I couldn't punish *him* for all the terrible things he did."

Ross's brow furrowed. "Was he right about *that?*"

"Not exactly." Amanda sighed. "I *was* furious with him, of course. But I was angry at you, too. Angry and hurt, because I'd fallen in love with you, only to discover our whole marriage was based on a lie."

"Darling." He tucked her head beneath his chin and held her close. "I'm so sorry. So very sorry."

"I know." She nuzzled her face against his chest. "I realized I would be punishing *both* of us if I didn't give us a chance to start over." She lifted her head. "Caleb told me he thought of Jamie as a kind of second chance to raise Paige all over again. Did you know that?"

Ross hoisted his brows in thoughtful surprise. "No, I didn't."

"So Caleb got his second chance. And I got a second chance to be Jamie's mother again." She hunched her shoulders and smiled. "It seems only fair that our marriage should have a second chance, too, doesn't it?"

In reply, Ross gently extricated himself from their embrace. He felt Amanda's puzzled gaze following him while he crossed the room to his dresser. *Their* dresser now.

He opened the top drawer and removed an object he'd hidden away for safekeeping with the heartfelt hope that someday he would have cause to take it out again. He walked back to Amanda and lifted her left hand. He heard her soft intake of breath as a glint of gold winked beneath the light.

"Let me see if I can do it right this time." Ross looked steadily into her eyes. "I love you, Amanda. Will you marry me?"

Her lovely face shone with serene radiance, with absolute certainty. "As many times as you want," she said.

Ross slipped her wedding ring on her finger.

*   *   *   *   *

DIANA PALMER
ANN MAJOR
SUSAN MALLERY

RETURN TO WHITEHORN

In **April 1998** get ready to catch the bouquet. Join in the excitement as these bestselling authors lead us down the aisle with three heartwarming tales of love and matrimony in Big Sky country.

A very engaged lady is having second thoughts about her intended; a pregnant librarian is wooed by the town bad boy; a cowgirl meets up with her first love. Which Maverick will be the next one to get hitched?

Available in **April 1998.**

Silhouette's beloved **MONTANA MAVERICKS** returns in Special Edition and Harlequin Historicals starting in February 1998, with brand-new stories from your favorite authors.

Round up these great new stories at your favorite retail outlet.

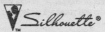

Take 4 bestselling love stories FREE

Plus get a FREE surprise gift!

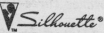

BESTSELLING AUTHORS
IN THE SPOTLIGHT

.WE'RE SHINING THE SPOTLIGHT ON SIX OF OUR STARS!

Harlequin and Silhouette have selected stories from several of their bestselling authors to give you six sensational reads. These star-powered romances are bound to please!

THERE'S A PRICE TO PAY FOR STARDOM... AND IT'S LOW

$1.99 U.S.
$2.50 CAN.
Special Offer

As a special offer, these six outstanding books are available from Harlequin and Silhouette for only $1.99 in the U.S. and $2.50 in Canada. Watch for these titles:

At the Midnight Hour—**Alicia Scott**
Joshua and the Cowgirl—**Sherryl Woods**
Another Whirlwind Courtship—**Barbara Boswell**
Madeleine's Cowboy—**Kristine Rolofson**
Her Sister's Baby—**Janice Kay Johnson**
One and One Makes Three—**Muriel Jensen**

Available in March 1998
at your favorite retail outlet.

PBAIS

ALICIA SCOTT

Continues the twelve-book series—36 Hours—in March 1998 with Book Nine

PARTNERS IN CRIME

The storm was over, and Detective Jack Stryker finally had a prime suspect in Grand Springs' high-profile murder case. But beautiful Josie Reynolds wasn't about to admit to the crime—nor did Jack want her to. He believed in her innocence, and he teamed up with the alluring suspect to prove it. But was he playing it by the book—or merely blinded by love?

For Jack and Josie and *all* the residents of Grand Springs, Colorado, the storm-induced blackout was just the beginning of 36 Hours that changed *everything!* You won't want to miss a single book.

Available at your favorite retail outlet.

Return to the Towers!

In March
New York Times bestselling author

NORA ROBERTS

brings us to the Calhouns' fabulous
Maine coast mansion and reveals the
tragic secrets hidden there for generations.

For all his degrees, Professor Max Quartermain has a
lot to learn about love—and luscious Lilah Calhoun is
just the woman to teach him. Ex-cop Holt Bradford is
as prickly as a thornbush—until Suzanna Calhoun's
special touch makes love blossom in his heart.
And all of them are caught in the race to solve
the generations-old mystery of a priceless
lost necklace…and a timeless love.

Lilah and Suzanna
THE
Calhoun Women

**A special 2-in-1 edition containing
FOR THE LOVE OF LILAH and
SUZANNA'S SURRENDER**

Available at your favorite retail outlet.

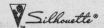